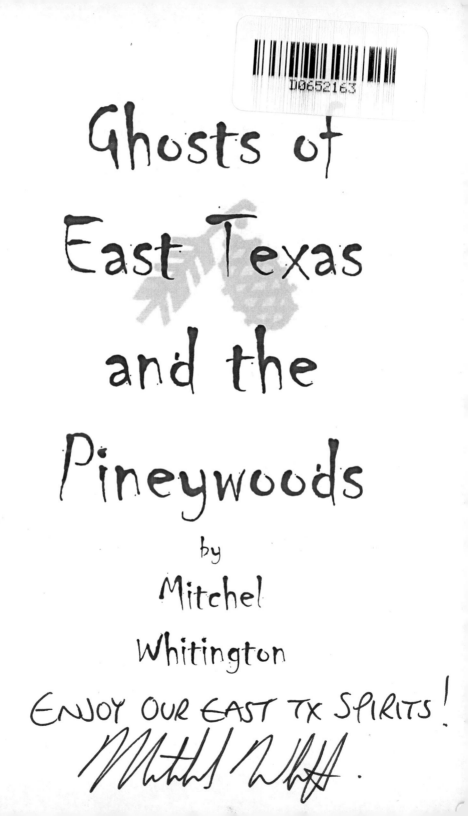

Ghosts of
East Texas
and the
Pineywoods

by

Mitchel

Whitington

ENJOY OUR EAST TX SPIRITS!

[signature]

ISBN
0-9706729-8-5 (10 digit)
978-0-9706729-8-8 (13 digit)

Third Edition

Printed in the United States of America
Published by 23 House Publishing
SAN 299-8084
www.23house.com

A Dedication...

As you will learn from this book, my wife and I own a historic old home known as The Grove in Jefferson, Texas.

We purchased it on March 8, 2002, and over the years the house has become an incredible part of our life. We have become obsessed with preserving the house and its history, and I can see us spending the rest of our lives at The Grove.

The thought of eventually passing the house on to another owner terrifies me... how could someone possibly love it as much as we do?

Not long ago, someone else with an equal love for the house faced that same problem: the former owner, Patrick Hopkins.

I'm sure that he was nervous about turning the place over to a couple that he didn't know, but he took that leap of faith. Patrick is responsible for saving the house back in 1991, and he has become a wonderful friend to Tami and me over the years as we assumed the role of caretakers to The Grove.

A hundred years from now when a future owner is giving a tour of the house, he or she will mention the name of Patrick Hopkins, along with our own names, in the list that includes Frank and Minerva Stilley, Daniel and Amanda Rock, Charles and Daphne Young, and Louise Young. I am honored to be a part of that list, and to have our names follow Patrick's. It is a genuine pleasure to know him.

Because of his love for The Grove, and his desire to preserve its history for future generations, I lovingly and respectfully dedicate this book to Mr. Patrick Hopkins.
God bless you, my friend.

Table of Contents

Welcome to the Pineywoods

A jail where inmates refuse to leave... even after their deaths. A mysterious network of underground tunnels that is rumored to lie beneath an East Texas town. The wailing voice of a young Indian maiden singing through the pine trees. A cemetery where a ghostly blue light chases away late-night intruders. These are all stories from the pineywoods of East Texas, one of the most notoriously haunted sections of the Lone Star State.

My name is Mitchel Whitington and I'll be your guide from Tyler to Texarkana, and Saratoga to Sulphur Springs. Of course, we're also going to spend a bit of time in one of the most historic old riverports in East Texas, the city of Jefferson.

I had a wonderful time on the road while I was writing this book, traveling to all of these locations and digging into their pasts – and of course, looking for the spirits at each of them. Not that I didn't run into a few difficulties. I found that the site of Fort Sherman is at the bottom of Lake Bob Sandlin, making it a little hard to reach. When I was looking for the Killough Monument, I got lost more than once on the winding little farm-to-market roads north of Jacksonville. I almost ran out of gas a few times when I didn't plan my trips well, and I drove around Kilgore for about an hour until I realized that I was looking at the map for a different city. Turns out that every place has a Main Street.

I felt sick to my stomach when I saw a statue in a cemetery

that I visited that had been vandalized, but I marveled at many of the historic old places that I had the chance to explore.

And the ghosts – yes, they were there, too. I encountered a woman from a bygone area who manifested herself as a cloud of pungent perfume strolling the hallway of an old hotel. In one particular graveyard, I couldn't leave fast enough, because I had the overwhelming feeling of panic and fear rushing through me. I interviewed people who live with spirits on a daily basis, and have included their personal stories in these pages just as they were told to me.

I'm glad to have you along for the ride, because we're going to take a look at many of these haunted places in this ghostly guide to the Pineywoods section of the Lone Star State. Turn on your lamp, pull the covers up tight, and let's get started on our journey!

The Perfumed Lady

of the Excelsior

House

Jefferson, Texas

I believe that my love affair with the City of Jefferson began on October 29th, 1995, while I was reading the *Dallas Morning News* and sipping the morning's second cup of coffee. One of my favorite columnists, Kent Biffle, had written a piece named *There Were Ghosts Among the Hotel Guests*, a title that immediately caught my attention. He painted a wonderful picture of mysterious Caddo Lake and a historic East Texas town named Jefferson. As I read about an encounter with a spirit of a lady in a black dress in the Jay Gould room of the Excelsior House, I knew that I simply had to pay the place a visit.

Of course, I wanted to do a little research in advance, and found several newspaper articles about the hotel. In the August 4th, 1974 edition of the *Marshall News Messenger*, reporter Mac Groves wrote that a specter of a man appears in the courtyard and wanders upstairs – some women have even awakened from a sound sleep to see him standing at the foot of their bed. Sissy McCambell, president of the Jessie Allen Wise

3

Garden Club at the time, was quoted in the article as saying, "Well, that could be Rothschild. He was known for his ways with the ladies." Abraham Rothschild was a visitor to town notorious for his suspected part in the murder of his traveling companion, Diamond Bessie.

No matter who the ghosts were thought to be, I was getting more excited about the visit. And so I prepared – with a quick phone call, my wife and I were booked in the room described in the newspaper. We headed out for a few days in Jefferson, anxious to experience all the charms of the old riverport city.

We arrived on a Sunday, and the town was bustling with visitors who'd been in town for the weekend. It wasn't hard to find the Excelsior House – it was on one of the main streets of the historic downtown district. One of the first things that struck me about the hotel was something as simple as the step on the front door. It had been worn down over the years by the shoes of countless visitors, including those of some of the hotel's more famous patrons: President Ulysses S. Grant, poet/playwright Oscar Wilde, Lady Bird Johnson, and the nineteenth President of the United States, Rutherford B. Hayes. Railroad baron Jay Gould is rumored to have stayed at the hotel, as is producer/director Steven Spielberg. All of those people, along with many, many others over the last hundred and fifty years, had stepped up off the sidewalk and into the lobby. I took a deep breath, and did the same. The Excelsior House is bathed in the class of a bygone era, and its lavish décor speaks to its rich history.

The hotel was originally built in the 1850s by Captain William Perry, the man who first opened navigation through Caddo Lake and brought the first steamship to Jefferson. After changing hands many times through the years, the Excelsior's salvation came in the form of the local garden club, who purchased it, restored it, and operate it to this day.

As I marveled at the beautiful lobby, I noticed a long glass case with memorabilia from the hotel's past, and took a few minutes to study its contents. Lying on top of the case, in a protective plastic sleeve, was Kent Biffle's newspaper column that had led me to the Excelsior House in the first place. I found it interesting that the people at the front desk didn't seem to know about any experiences in the Jay Gould room, even though the article was on display there in the lobby. I almost went back and pointed it out, but decided that instead I'd look for the place to sign up for the 2:00 afternoon hotel tour.

When you visit the Excelsior House, I highly recommend the guided tour of the hotel. It only costs a couple of dollars – free if you're a hotel guest – and the docent that we had was magnificent at weaving tales not only of the Excelsior, but of Jefferson as well – the two are so tightly coupled, that it is hard to talk about one without mentioning the other. As the docent led the group upstairs, she asked if anyone was staying at the hotel. We seemed to be the only ones, so I spoke up and told her that my wife and I were booked in the Jay Gould room. Her eyes got as big as buttermilk pancakes, and she said, "Have you heard any of the stories about that room?"

We just laughed, and told her that we'd welcome any details that she'd be willing to share. She promised a story or two when we got to that part of the tour, but in the mean time, the discussion had been opened up to the subject of ghosts. As the docent unlocked the shared outer door to the two presidential suites, she related a story of something that had happened to her there in the past. One of her duties was to check the rooms before the walking tour, and since the guests were reportedly out of the hotel at the time, she was just planning on sticking her head in to make sure that the rooms were in order. She opened the outer door, and as she put a key in one of the inner doors, a radio began to blare. Afraid that she'd been misinformed and there was actually a guest inside, she knocked on the door and waited – the only response was the loud music from inside the room. She put the key in the door and peeped inside, and saw that there was a simple transistor radio causing all of the noise. The radio was a very basic model, with no timer, so she had no idea how it turned on by itself. Thinking that the guests might have left it on for some reason, she pulled the door shut and turned the key in the lock. When she did, the radio stopped playing. The docent thought that was very strange, so she unlocked and opened the door again, and as soon as she did the radio started playing once again. She left quickly, and heard the radio shut off in the room behind her. After that, the docent was reluctant to go upstairs without someone with her.

When we arrived at the Jay Gould room, our guide pointed out a rocking chair and told us that one of the ladies who worked at the hotel had brought her child with her one day. She was in another room, when the little boy ran in and insisted that she come with him. The woman was led to the Jay Gould room, where the rocker was slowly moving back and forth. She thought that it must have been some sort of trick, so she examined it to make sure that there were no strings, wires, etc. – there were none. Hearing that, I was more than ready for our first night in the hotel,

After exploring the town a bit we enjoyed a delicious meal, then finished off the evening with a horse-drawn carriage ride around town. Exhausted from a wonderful first day, we finally retired to the Jay Gould room. I could see the famous rocker from my side of the bed, so I hoped that if it moved in the slightest bit I'd hear it creak and wake up.

Alas, the night passed uneventfully. No spectral forms, no knocking on the headboard, no rocking in the chair. It was a little disappointing, but I remember someone telling me once that spirits aren't here for our amusement – they have their own agendas and purposes, that may or may not coincide with the presence of a human.

We knew that we were going to have a great time in town whether we had any ghostly encounters or not, so we sat down to the legendary Excelsior House breakfast, complete with their Orange Blossom Muffins, and planned our agenda.

It was a full, enjoyable day before we finally settled back into our room. We'd explored antique shops, taken a boat trip down the Big Cypress Bayou where the steamships once traveled between Jefferson and New Orleans, and enjoyed a magnificent dinner – so much food, in fact, that we packaged up what remained for a midnight snack back in the room.

When it came time later in the evening to open up the doggie bag, I realized that it had been left in the car, so I volunteered to dash downstairs and retrieve it. The hotel was extremely quiet, since there was only one other couple staying there that evening. I walked the upstairs hall, descended the stairs, and as I passed through the downstairs hallway the smell of sweet, floral perfume overwhelmed me. It was as if a lady had over-sprayed herself with the scent right there in the hall.

In only a step, I was out of the perfume cloud, and kept going toward the lobby. I retrieved the doggie bag, thankful that the evening was cold and the food hadn't spoiled, then went back into the hotel. I stopped at the desk to ask a few questions about our itinerary for the next day, chatted with the lady for about five minutes, and finally headed back up to the room. I walked through the strong smell of perfume once again, and when I got to the stairs I stopped, realizing that the cloud of perfume should have dissipated while I was outside, but hadn't. Not only was it as strong as it had been ten minutes ago, but it had also moved! The more that I thought about it, the stranger it seemed. It was a Monday night, and there weren't many tourists in town, much less at the hotel. Only one other room was occupied, and we hadn't seen anyone but the night clerk that evening.

When I got back to the room I told my wife what had happened, and about fifteen minutes later we went downstairs to check it out again. As soon as my wife got to the bottom of the staircase, she found herself right in the middle of the perfume cloud. She agreed that it was very strong indeed, but had the smell of both perfume and make-up to it. I pointed out that it had moved to the staircase, and was no longer in the hallway. We walked all over the downstairs area to see if the smell was anywhere else, but its sole location was at the base of the stairs.

We went back upstairs to the room and enjoyed a late night snack from the doggie bag, and after fifteen to twenty minutes we went back down. The stairway was completely free of the smell, as was the hallway to the lobby. My wife took the downstairs hall in the other direction, which dead ended into a guestroom, and found the perfume cloud about halfway down the hall. At this point, it seemed to be that some unseen, perfume-doused person was wandering the downstairs area.

Once more, we returned upstairs and waited for about a quarter of an hour. We went back down to find that the perfume cloud had now moved between the stairs and the hallway's lobby entrance. Again, there was no trace of it in any of the other places that we'd found it. We stood there for several minutes, and the perfume cloud's position moved toward the foyer – the unseen person wearing the perfume was definitely wandering around. For the next half-hour, we stayed in the downstairs hall area, following the perfume as it paced up and down the hallway, and over to the bottom of the stairs. At one point, I just stood still and let the scented cloud move through me as it went past – a very exhilarating experience.

Had we found one of the ghosts of the Excelsior House? I have to believe so – there is no physical explanation for the cloud that we started calling "The Perfumed Lady". The hallway has doors on all sides, so there could be no breeze pushing the scents around. Even if someone had doused herself in perfume out in the hallway, it would have dissipated after a few moments, and there's certainly no way that the scent could roam the downstairs hall. I have no idea who this spirit-lady is, or why she was pacing the hallway, but she certainly gave us an evening in Jefferson that we'll never forget.

The Excelsior House
211 W. Austin
Jefferson, Texas 75657
903-665-2513
www.theexcelsiorhouse.com

The Spirits of The Grove

Jefferson, Texas

It wouldn't be possible to write about the ghosts of Jefferson without mentioning the historic old home known as The Grove. Construction on the house started in 1861, when a cotton broker named Washington Frank Stilley married Minerva Fox, whose father owned a cotton plantation in Marshall. Minerva's father financed the new house for the newlywed couple, and it had all the trappings of a fine house of the day, including a tongue-and-groove ceiling. The basic lines of the house were Greek Revival, although Frank was able to interject the Creole influences from Louisiana architecture, including a front and side gallery that were under the main roof of the house, no main connecting hallway, and an "L" shaped floor plan. One oddity about the house was that Mr. Fox put it and The Grove property in his daughter's name, not his new son-in-law's... something that was very strange for that time period.

The Stilleys lived in the house several years, and had two sons: John R. and Frank F. There is certainly more to the story that will never be known. As unusual as it was for a woman to hold property in the mid 1800s, it was even more unusual that her last will and testament left the property to her two sons and not her husband. Mrs. Stilley passed away in the early 1880s;

The Grove property was then sold by her husband Frank, acting as the guardian of their sons John and Frank, who were still both minors.

Over the years the house passed through several families, including that of Daniel Rock, an East Texas bridge-builder; Charles J. Young, a leader in the African-American community in Jefferson; Colonel Daniel Grove, a military chaplain; and Patrick Hopkins, a talented chef who opened the home as a restaurant. Mr. Hopkins reports that when he was purchasing the house, Mrs. Grove pulled him aside and said, "Before you sign your name, there's something that you should know about the house…" She went on to relate an experience that she'd had at the house one night, when she'd fallen asleep while reading in bed, and awoke to see a swirling black cloud above her. Mr. Hopkins has many ghost stories of his own, several of which have been chronicled in newspapers and books.

Looking back, historical records for the house indicate that on September 1, 1882, a man named T.C. Burks purchased The Grove for $175, and kept it for about six months before asking for his money back. There is no reason why listed in the deed records, but one could certainly speculate that there was something about the house that just didn't sit well with him.

Ms. Louis Young, who lived in the house for her entire life – except for her college days – always used to tell her friends about the ghosts that she shared the house with. Somewhere along the way, though, she became deathly afraid of the spirits, and spent the last years of her life living in only a few rooms in the house. The rest she kept tightly closed and locked.

For this book, I wanted to give some fresh, new stories about ghostly activity at The Grove, and I didn't have to look far to do that. You see, early in 2002, my wife and I purchased the property.

We literally fell in love with the house – its architecture, history, and gardens. The ghost stories were a bonus, and we soon found out that the tales were very true. While I could literally fill this book with things that have happened there, I'll try my best to keep it to a couple of the ones that I've found most interesting. There are many, many incidents such as the footsteps that we've heard in empty rooms, the times that we've seen the ghost of a man who wanders through the garden, or the many strange stories that we hear from visitors to the house. The ones that I find to be the most interesting are those in which the spirits of the house seem to be trying to tell us something.

One such incident happened on a Friday evening in August of 2002. We'd been away for a few days, and had just returned home. As soon as I opened the front door, the first thing that I noticed was the scent of something that smelled like paint. I knew that there hadn't been any painting inside of the house for several months, so it was a little odd, but I just dismissed the whole thing and went on.

I was carrying some groceries, so I didn't turn on any of the lights in the house – I just navigated my way through by the moonlight coming in through the windows. When I turned on the light back in the kitchen, I noticed that there was a single, round drop of a clear, yellowish liquid on the island. I thought that it was a little strange, since there were no other drops anywhere else, and the ceiling showed no evidence of anything dripping through. I pointed it out to my wife, and she touched it and rubbed the liquid between her index finger and thumb – it was very oily. I did the same, and when I smelled it, I realized that it had the same paint-like smell that I'd noticed when I first walked inside of the house. We didn't know what to make of it, so we went back out to the car to get another load.

We still hadn't turned the lights on in the front parlor, and as I went back inside, something caught my eye on the east side, in the south corner – it was a piece of furniture of some kind. I called for my wife to come take a look, and when I turned on the light, we saw that it was an antique sideboard for the dining room. It was a beautiful piece and made a wonderful addition to the room. I knew that my parents had been in town the day before, and figured that they'd run across it somewhere and picked it up for us. I soon noticed something very odd: directly in front of the piece was a puddle of liquid about two feet across.

I wondered if it had dripped from the sideboard – although it wasn't underneath the piece, the edge of the puddle was directly below the front edge of the sideboard. The sideboard itself was perfectly dry, so I was quite puzzled as to where the puddle had come from.

I then looked up and saw that something had leaked through the ceiling, and in fact was still dripping down a little. It was amazing that none of the liquid had fallen on the sideboard – I couldn't figure out how it had kept from getting on the piece of furniture. I realized that I smelled the paint-like odor again, so I reached down and touched the puddle of liquid. It was oily, and had the same scent as the drop in the kitchen.

Since it had obviously come from the upstairs attic, I grabbed a flashlight and headed up to take a look. When I got there, I saw that a piece of paneling had fallen over, and had knocked over a gallon jug of linseed oil. I'd never noticed it before, and assumed that the former owner had left it there. The jug was lying on its side in a puddle of the oil, which explained the liquid downstairs. I stood it up, then went back down to start the cleanup. As we were mopping up the oil with paper towels, I couldn't help but be amazed that the oil had come *so* close to the sideboard without even a splash getting on the furniture.

When we had the puddle cleaned up, I went back upstairs with more paper towels to take care of the mess up there. I was wiping off the gallon jug, and noticed something odd – the cap was one of those that had a plastic seal around the bottom, kind of like a milk jug. The seal hadn't been broken on the cap, and on closer examination, I couldn't find any holes in the jug at all. Now, if it had been some kind of varnish or something like that, as the liquid leaked out it would become thicker and eventually seal. Linseed oil doesn't do that, though. I could find no way that the oil got out of the jug.

I called my folks, and they said that they'd put the piece of furniture in the house the day before, so it had only been there for twenty-four hours, and the puddle of linseed oil wasn't there when they moved the sideboard in.

Now, I can almost buy the fact that the entire episode was a long string of coincidences: the new piece of furniture was put in the house, and the paneling upstairs somehow fell over right after that; the paneling knocked over a jug of linseed oil that happened to be near it; that somehow the plastic of the bottle and cap expanded/contracted due to the heat or something, and half of the oil leaked out and dripped downstairs, barely missing the new piece of furniture. With all of that, though, I can't explain how a single drop was placed on the kitchen island at the other end of the house. I don't know exactly what it means, but I've always interpreted it to be the spirits saying, "Just in case you thought the oil was a coincidence, it wasn't!"

I can't imagine what message they were trying to convey, however. While we were cleaning up the puddle downstairs, I stopped and turned around toward the center of the house. "You guys are going to have to be a lot more clear with your messages," I said to the empty room, "because I'm not smart enough to understand what this means!"

The other story about The Grove that I'd like to share is one where I really believe that the spirits of the house were protecting the place – from me! We were getting ready to go to a party one night in October. I was carrying several types of chicken wings for people to snack on: Soda Pop Cola Wings,

Uncle Bubba's Bourbon Wings, and Angelic Lemon wings. You might recognize those flavors from a humor-fiction book that I wrote several years ago: *Uncle Bubba's Chicken Wing Fling*. But enough shameless self-promotion and back to the story.

I'd put the wings in the sauces to marinade the night before, then popped them in the 'fridge. We were only a couple of hours away from the start of the party, so I turned on the old oven that was left over from The Grove's restaurant days. I opened the door about twenty minutes later, and found that the oven was ice-cold. Something was wrong, and the clock was ticking.

I tried the burners on the stove, and they lit right away, which made the mystery even stranger. It then occurred to me that we'd had gas heaters installed the weekend before, and that the gas had been cut off for a while in the process. I realized that there were probably two pilot lights on the appliance – one for the stovetop, and another for the oven. Knowing that I'd have to light the oven's pilot, I went to find a flashlight and a wand-type lighter.

Kneeling down in the space between the oven and the kitchen island, I opened the small chamber under the oven, and the odor of natural gas nearly overwhelmed me. I realized that there probably weren't any modern safety controls on the old stove, and so I'd basically been venting gas into the chamber for the last twenty minutes. I could see the jet for the pilot light with the flashlight, and knew in my gut that it was a bad idea to try to light it. I laid the lighter on the shelf and took one more look at the gas jet. Since we were running short on time, I couldn't help but think that perhaps if I got the lighter in there and back out again quick enough, the gas in the chamber wouldn't ignite. I remember thinking, "Man, I hope I don't blow up this house." With that I focused the flashlight beam on the gas jet, then reached back to grab the wand lighter. It wasn't there.

I looked around quickly, but it was nowhere to be found. The island was solid, so it couldn't have fallen underneath that, and besides, I *knew* that I'd laid it on the shelf on the island – it only has one. I was freaking out at this point. We didn't have another lighter in the house, and any hope of us making it to the party on time was rapidly fading. My wife was in the front part of the house, so I hollered at her to ask if she'd help me search for the lighter. I heard her say, "Just re-trace your steps and you'll find where you put it down."

I sat there for a second, then called back, "But I haven't taken any steps – I'm here on my hands and knees!"

She came in, and we turned the kitchen upside down. We moved the stove, cleared the shelf on the island, and looked everyplace possible for the lighter. Although I knew it was futile, we quickly scanned the rest of the house as well. Finally, my wife had the idea of lighting a taper candle on the stove burner, then using it to light the oven pilot light.

It was a great idea, and worked well. When I was doing that, I noticed that the smell of gas was no longer in the bottom chamber of the stove. Clearly, it dissipated in the twenty minutes or so that we were searching for the wand lighter. I was able to bake the wings and still get us to the party on time. I made a mental note to pick up another lighter the next time we were at the store.

A week or so later, we were having some friends over for dinner and my wife was opening an antique buffet where we keep dishes. In one of its cabinets, lying there on a bowl, was the wand lighter that I'd placed on the kitchen island shelf two weeks before. We rarely open that side of buffet, and in fact, probably hadn't opened that particular cabinet door for months. I can only imagine that after all these years of scaring people, the spirits finally got a scare themselves! They probably had a huge meeting with everyone who haunts The Grove there, and started off with, "We're in trouble – a real idiot has bought the house…"

There's no doubt that The Grove is haunted. We hear phantom footsteps in the front parlor or in the Blue Room, and occasionally glance up to see the figure of a man standing out on the Side Gallery. Stories like these go back through several previous owners and many visitors across the years. The spirits have always protected the house – I think that the one thing that has changed now is they have to protect the place from a crazy owner!

Strange occurrences continue to happen at The Grove, but we've never felt unwelcome or threatened. Some people have had those kinds of experiences there, though. One Sunday morning I was sitting out on the front porch sipping a fresh cup of coffee when a couple came walking up Moseley Street, staring over at the house. They stopped in front and asked if I owned the place, and when I told them that my wife and I did, they looked surprised. "I don't see how anyone could live here!" one of them said, and the couple proceeded to tell me their story. They'd visited Jefferson several years earlier when The Grove was empty and up for sale, so they decided to take a look around. All of the doors were locked, as were the windows, but they kept trying until they found a window that would raise just enough for them to squeeze through. It was summer, and the heat inside was stifling, but they began to explore The Grove. At some point they decided to take the stairs up to the attic, which is nothing more than rafters and cobwebs – there isn't any electricity or climate control up there. When they stepped inside, the attic was icy cold; the couple described it as stepping into a walk-in freezer. The temperature up there should have been even hotter than in the house itself, so they knew that something odd was happening to them. It scared them more than a little bit, so they rushed back down the stairs. When they got to the landing, they turned and saw that the front door was standing wide open, as was every window in the front parlor. They dashed out, never looking back.

Over the years we've heard many stories similar to that, where people came into the house and were suddenly frightened away. We sometimes wondered why we always feel welcomed, when others were driven out of the house.

Perhaps the answer to that question lies in something that happened in the 1990s. Chef Patrick Hopkins purchased the old home known as The Grove, performed a massive amount of restoration, and opened the building as a restaurant. Because of his love for the place, Mr. Hopkins didn't change any of the lines of the house, keeping it very true to its historic past. He had heard that there were ghost stories associated with the place, and wasn't surprised when supernatural occurrences began to happen there. The cuisine at the restaurant was regaled by both visitors and the press, and enjoyed a successful run. When it came time for him to move on, he prepared to turn The Grove over to new owners, hopefully ones that would love it as much as he did.

At that time, a psychic from Dallas was a guest at the restaurant and was walking through the house giving her impressions of the spirits there. When Patrick informed her that he would be putting the place up for sale, she paused for a moment, and finally said, "You're going to have a hard time selling this house." Patrick was a bit puzzled by her comment, and asked, "Why is that?" The woman just smiled knowingly, and said, "This house is going to pick its next owners."

And maybe it did. Whatever the case, we love the old house and are happy to be a part of its history.

The Grove
405 Moseley St.
Jefferson, TX 75657
www.thegrove-jefferson.com

The Gardens of The Grove

Jefferson, Texas

The 1861 house on The Grove property isn't the only place where spirits appear – the gardens of The Grove are quite active as well.

The property was originally part of the Stephen Smith Land Grant. In the late 1830s a man named Allen Urquhart, who had moved to Texas from North Carolina, purchased a parcel of land at the bend in the Big Cypress Bayou, anticipating a booming riverport there. In 1842 he laid out the streets of a city at an angle perpendicular to the river. About the same time, Daniel Alley purchased a 586-acre parcel adjacent to Urquhart's land and laid out another neighborhood on a north/south east/west basis that became known as Alley's Addition.

Because the orientation of the streets was different between the two halves of town, the two men drew a line between their properties and named it "Line Street". If you ever wondered why it is hard to give or follow directions from one side of town to the other, that's the reason!

While Mr. Urquhart set about setting up his business district, Daniel Alley proceeded to divide up his residential neighborhood.

One local legend tells the story of how Daniel Alley set up a table and chair out in front of his house one morning in 1847, and started selling off lots in his addition of Jefferson that he'd marked off.

The plots that would come to be known as The Grove were sold to an attorney named Amos Morrill. Mr. Morrill had his main residence in Clarksville, Texas, but set up two more homes for his convenience when he was traveling around East Texas practicing law. One of these was a log cabin built on the southwest corner of The Grove property. It was a classic dog-run style, with a breezeway between two rooms – a bedroom on one side, and an office on the other.

"The Mighty Morrill", as he was known because of his talent as a lawyer, owned The Grove for eight years. During that time, he made history by representing Harriet Potter in one of the first "Women's Lib" cases in East Texas. Much of the work that he did on that case laid the groundwork for the rights that women have in marriage today.

Amos was doing so well as an attorney, that he was invited to move to Austin to become a law partner of Andrew J. Hamilton. He sold The Grove in 1855, and by 1856 he had relocated to the State Capitol.

The new owners of The Grove were Caleb and Sarah Ragin. Caleb is listed on the census rolls as a merchant, but it is clear that he had many endeavors in the City of Jefferson. The couple bought and sold property all over town, and we like to tell visitors to The Grove that if you take any random property in the Historic District of town and trace back the title history, you're likely to see Caleb and Sarah's name somewhere there.

Caleb and Sarah kept The Grove for six years, selling it to Frank and Minerva Stilley in 1861. You'll read a little more about the Ragins in the Oakwood Cemetery chapter of this book.

One of the reasons that we find the pre-history of the current house so fascinating is that there are ghostly events that happen in the garden, where the old log cabin was located, that we don't experience in the house.

One of them is our "Garden Man", a gentleman who hangs out in The Grove's garden from time to time.

The first time that I saw him, my wife and I were walking out of the west side door, when I saw someone out of the corner of my eye. It was a person moving around, and when I looked to my right, I saw a man standing in our back yard, leaning over the fence and grinning at me. He stepped back out of sight, but I'll never forget that look on his face – it was if he was having a good laugh and saying, "Hey, I'm in your back yard! What are you going to do about it?"

I had the leash of our male basset hound, Murphy, so I quickly handed it to my wife and ran back into the house. "There's someone in back!" I called over my shoulder, and sprinted the five or six steps to the back door. I threw it open, and found that I was looking at an empty yard.

When I caught up with my wife, I was scratching my head. "I could swear that I saw someone back there," I said.

"Who do you think it was?" she asked, and I set about trying to remember the gentleman.

The more that I went on to describe him, the odder it became. While I don't remember much about his facial features, I know that he was grinning ear to ear. He was wearing an old-fashioned man's dress hat, with a black suit on. Certainly nothing conducive to that warm spring afternoon.

I was puzzled, so I called the former owner of The Grove, Patrick Hopkins. "Patrick," I said, "I just saw the strangest thing in the garden."

Without hesitation he said, "Well, if you saw it in the garden, then it was probably a man in a dark suit, and he was either laughing or grinning at you."

That was my first interaction with the "Garden Man", but it wouldn't be the last. I think that my favorite story about him comes from the time when The Grove was a restaurant. It had closed for the evening, and the staff was out on the front porch discussing some of the supernatural events that had been occurring over the past few weeks. One fellow scoffed, and as he was heading down the front walk said, "You people are crazy. I don't believe in all that ghost nonsense. They saw him get into his car, then suddenly fire it up and fishtail down Moseley Street.

When he came back to work the next day, the other folks on staff apologized for talking about ghosts and such, and promised not to do it again if it was going to upset him. The fellow just smiled hesitantly and said, "You don't understand. When I climbed into the front seat of my car, I saw a man in a black suit sitting on the passenger's side. He smiled, pointed straight ahead, then disappeared."

My last sighting of him happened at dusk, when the sun was just slipping down under the horizon. My wife and I were unloading the car, and carrying the items we'd purchased out to the little house in the garden. The small cottage was built in the 1990's by Patrick Hopkins so that he'd have a place to spend the night when he kept the restaurant open late. At one time it was like a small apartment, but during the period that the house sat empty waiting for us to buy it, termites grabbed a strong hold on the small structure, and damaged it to the point that it is no longer usable as anything more than a storage shed.

As we were carrying bags from the car to the cottage we were each moving at different paces, depending on the weight of the current load we were carrying, and at one point I saw someone to my left walking along with me just a few yards away. I assumed that it was my wife, until I heard her call to me from back at the car. As soon as that happened, I quickly looked to my left to see the man in the black suit, walking happily along. We were soon separated by one of the large bushes, and he never emerged from the other side.

Patrick, the previous owner of The Grove, had described his own sightings in much the same manner – a man in a dark suit strutting across the garden with a long, steady gait. As soon as Patrick started scrutinizing the intruder, the man would disappear.

Whoever this phantom is who appears in The Grove garden, he seems to be very interactive in our world today. After all, he was leaning on a fence that I'd just built a few weeks before, and at another time he was sitting in the front seat of a car.

We have no idea who this gentleman might be, but we've never seen him inside of the house.

But there are other stories from the garden as well – more random things, but just as unexplainable of our Garden Man.

The front steps of The Grove provide a never-ending source of work for us. Since they are directly under one of the huge Native Pecan Trees that gave the property its name, there is always something falling down on the steps. We have to scrape and repaint them several times a year, which is exactly what I was doing on an April Saturday in 2004. I saw someone out in the garden out of the corner of my eye, so I looked over toward the area where the log cabin had stood, then looked back down at my work. At first glance, I'd seen a woman in a white top, which I assumed was my wife – she'd been wearing a white tee shirt the last time that I saw her. I went back to scraping, but as my mind replayed what I'd seen, I realized that the women had also been wearing a long, black skirt. I turned my head back around, but no one was there. The woman had only been present for an instant, and I have no idea who she was.

Patrick, the previous owner, reports hearing a voice in the garden. When he was pruning back plants in the garden, he was about to cut one in particular, when he heard a voice saying, "Uh-uh!" He didn't cut it, and later found that it was a flower from the older part of the garden. To this day Patrick feels like it was the spirit of Ms. Daphne, who planted the original gardens, guiding him along.

Things continue to happen in our garden to this day, some that we're not even aware of. I received an email from a fellow who was standing out on Moseley Street, and wanted to come up into the garden to take a look at the flowers. He told me that there was an elderly African-American lady sitting out on the bench, and she seemed to be enjoying sitting there so much that he hated to disturb her. He left, then came back by, only to discover that she was still sitting out in the garden. He left without walking up onto the property, and once I received his email, I told him that no one had been present on the property that day.

The spirits that tend to show up in the garden don't seem to be connected to the house, because they won't cross that boundary. Are they tied to the log cabin, or only to the garden itself? Who knows – I only know that these spirits continue to show up there when we least expect them.

The Little Blond Girl of Sandtown

Jefferson, Texas

The poet John Donne once said, "Any man's death diminishes me." I kind of understand what he meant with those words, because nothing gives me more pause than seeing a funeral procession passing by.

Now, I'm one of those fellows that will pull over to the side of the road as the line of cars goes by out of respect for the family. If I happen to know the deceased, I'll even get out of my vehicle, take off my gimmie cap and hold it over my heart as the mourners pass along. There's just something about any death that brings a tear to my eye.

The thing that seems more difficult than any others, though is the death of a child. I can't even imagine how painful that must be. When friends of ours lost their young son, I cried at the funeral like I hadn't done at any other I can remember.

A family from the old days of Jefferson had a tragedy in that very same regard. F.A. and Ann Schluter purchased property and started construction on a home at the corner of Line and Taylor Streets in Jefferson back in 1850. Their palatial home wasn't completed for six years, but when it was finished it was a showplace of the community, with three stories and a basement. There was plenty of room for the family to grow. Once they were settled into their new home, life in Jefferson was good for the Schluters – then a terrible thing happened. One of their children took ill in 1859, and the others began to fall like delicate dominoes. The Schluters lost four children to disease over the period of four years, a fate that most people can't begin to comprehend. If you visit Oakwood Cemetery and travel to the very back, you'll see the Schluter plot, with its tiny little headstones for the children. You will never lay your eyes on a sadder sight.

Around Jefferson, the Schluter house is often associated with the legend of the doll in the uppermost window. The doll story begins with the very sad death of one of the youngest Schluter children, whose nursery was in the spacious attic of the house. When disease took the child, Mrs. Schluter couldn't bear to throw away a doll that she'd gotten for the child's bed, so she stood it up in the window, looking out across the park in front of the house. For years, passersby looked up to see the odd little figure in the window, and stories began to circulate about the house. As the tale goes, when one of the subsequent owners first walked up to the attic room and found the doll in the window, it literally crumbled in his hands when he touched it. The legend of the "doll in the window" died there, but there are still tales about the Schluter children that live on.

There's at least one ghost story related to one of the children, but it's not a terrible "spirit roaming the Earth" kind of tale. It instead celebrates the child's life, I think.

Long after the time of the Schluter family, a young blond girl has been seen throughout the area of Jefferson known as "Sandtown", and she is believed to be one of the Schluter children who returns periodically to play in the area of her old home – she runs in and out among the trees and homes there, smiling and giggling, and seemingly having a wonderful time. That story gives me hope for how delightful the afterlife must be.

In the previous chapter about The Grove, I couldn't begin to tell all of the stories associated with the place, but I'll add another one here that overlaps with the Schluter story. One of them concerns the same little blond girl, who's been seen playing out in The Grove's garden. It happened not long after the house – a restaurant at the time – had been put up for sale. A caretaker was living out in the garden cottage. His responsibility was to maintain the house, and show it when prospective buyers came by. On one sunny afternoon, he heard the laughing and giggling of a little girl out in the garden. Pulling aside the window of the garden cottage, the caretaker saw a little girl in a white Victorian dress running in and out between the flowerbeds.

He knew that such a well-dressed little girl could only mean that a family was probably over at The Grove taking a look at the place. He quickly changed clothes and went outside to greet the girl's parents and show them the house.

When he stepped outside, there was no car parked out front, and no family out walking the grounds. There was only the playful sound of the little girl, who ran through the garden one last time, and disappeared like the early morning mists of East Texas fog.

The little blond girl has been seen all over the neighborhood. In another famous story about her, a visitor to the town was driving along Line Street and threw on his breaks when a little girl ran in front of his car. When he didn't see her move past the front of the vehicle, he was sure that he'd struck her, even though there was no sound of impact. He threw the vehicle into park, then leapt out to try to render first aid to the unfortunate victim. There was no little girl to be seen. He searched the entire area, thinking that she must have sought refuge in a nearby home.

The man felt so bad that he went to the local police station and reported that he had accidentally hit a child in his car. Even though the local officers investigated the incident thoroughly, there was no indication that a girl had been present in the street at all. The man was sent on his way, puzzled at the day's events.

On another occasion, the little blond girl actually saved several lives. At one of the nearby bed and breakfasts, the guests had turned in for a relaxing evening in Jefferson. What they didn't know was that a terrible storm was headed for town. Even more than that, though, was the fact that a tornado was brewing inside it. In the dead of night, a little girl ran through the bed and breakfast waking the guests, knocking on doors, calling out a warning to dress and come downstairs. When the tornado passed over without any harm, the guests thanked the owner for her daughter's vigilance in waking them all up. The owner was puzzled, because she didn't have a daughter – the little blond girl of Sandtown had come to the rescue.

In this part of town, it might be easier to make a list of places where the spectral little girl hasn't been seen or heard. I doubt that the young Schluter girl is somehow doomed to haunt the neighborhood, though. I think that instead, she is simply returning occasionally to play in the area that belonged to her over a century ago. And who could blame her? It's a beautiful part of the city, with huge shade trees and many plush gardens. After I pass on, I'll definitely be tempted to come back to that beautiful part of Jefferson for a visit myself!

The Legend of Diamond Bessie

Jefferson, Texas

Jefferson's most famous ghost story may not be a ghost story at all. Still, it's hard to pick up any book or article about ghosts in Jefferson without the author invoking the legendary spirit of Diamond Bessie. On your visit to Jefferson, you will find it next to impossible to escape without hearing her name.

With that in mind, I'll spin the quick version of the story behind Jefferson's favorite daughter, and then talk for a moment about the ghost stories associated with her.

The tragic tale of Diamond Bessie is a story that is forever a part of Jefferson's colorful past. On Friday, January 19, 1877, a well-dressed couple arrived in town, signing in at a local boarding house as "A. Monroe and Wife". They were seen all around town for the next two days, flashing their expensive clothing and jewelry and acting like a happily married couple that didn't have a care in the world. The woman was introduced only as "Bessie". Because of her plentiful jewelry, it didn't take long for locals to pin the moniker "Diamond Bessie" on her.

That Sunday morning, "A. Monroe" purchased two picnic lunches from Henrique's Restaurant and the couple was seen walking together across the bridge over Big Cypress Bayou. It was the last time that anyone would see the woman alive.

A. Monroe was spotted walking back into town alone using another path, and he was noticed around town by himself for the next couple of days. When asked about his wife, the gentleman replied that she was visiting friends out in the surrounding countryside, and would return to town on Tuesday for their departure.

On Tuesday, the staff of their inn, The Brooks House, found Room 4 empty – A. Monroe had already fled the city of Jefferson. Some witnesses later reported that he left by himself on an earlier eastbound train with both sets of luggage.

It was a cold, stormy January in East Texas, and a snowstorm slowed the city down for the next week. When the snow began to melt, a local woman named Sarah King was out gathering firewood south of town and ran across the body of a well-dressed woman sitting up against the trunk of an oak tree. The remains of a picnic lunch were nearby.

The coroner ruled that the lady, who was the woman known in town as Diamond Bessie, had died by a gunshot wound to the head. All of her jewelry had been removed, presumably by her assailant. A warrant was immediately issued for the arrest of A. Monroe. Bessie had no family, no real identity, and no money left behind, so the citizens of Jefferson took up a collection to bury the poor woman.

When the local authorities began piecing the puzzle together, they learned that A. Monroe was actually Abraham Rothschild, the son of a wealthy Cincinnati jeweler named Meyer Rothschild, and a relative of the prominent European Rothschild banking family. As a traveling salesman, he was pitching his father's wares through the south when we met up with Bessie Moore at a brothel in Hot Springs, and she began to accompany him on his travels, before winding up in Jefferson on that fateful January day.

A new warrant was issued for Abraham Rothschild, who surfaced in Cincinnati. After an intense night of drinking there, he walked out into the street in front of the saloon and tried to take his own life because he thought that someone was after him. He only succeeded in blinding himself in the right eye, however. While in the hospital, he caught the attention of the local law enforcement officials who alerted the authorities in Jefferson.

Marion county officials traveled to Ohio, and although Rothschild's family put up a healthy fight, he was extradited back to Texas on March 19, 1877.

The trial became a media circus. Almost every prominent attorney in East Texas was somehow involved with the case, and those that weren't tried desperately to inject themselves into it. Those on the side of the state did so for the prestige, while the ones on the defense were hoping to get part of the Rothschild fortune that was put up for Abe's trial. Some of the talent that was involved with the case included Texas State Attorneys General, a future Governor of Texas and a United States Senator.

A trial ensued that took two and a half years to finish. When it was all said and done, Abe Rothschild had been found guilty of murder and was sentenced to be hanged by the neck until dead. One legend from the jury room says that the foreman, C.R. Weathersby drew a noose on the wall, signed it, and stated that it was the verdict as far as he was concerned.

The decision was appealed, of course, on the grounds that one juror had been selected even after he had stated that he had a preconceived opinion in the case, and that the court had been in error by ignoring one of the motions made by the defense. A mistrial was declared, and a new indictment was issued.

In the new trial, a witness was introduced who claimed to have seen Bessie in the company of a man other than Abe Rothschild. Although the testimony was shaky, enough doubt was placed in the mind of the jurors that they returned a verdict of not guilty on December 30, 1880.

The trial was over, but the legend of Diamond Bessie had just begun. Rumors and innuendos began to swirl around town:

that the jury had been bought by the Rothschild fortune; that the jurors had death threats issued against them, and some were carried out after the trial; that the verdict was not read until after the train whistle blew outside, so that no one could immediately leave town afterwards; and the most scandalous of all, that Bessie was pregnant when she was murdered.

One story is told for true, however, and is chronicled on the pages of *The University of Texas' Handbook of Texas Online*: "In the 1890s a handsome, elderly man wearing a patch over his right eye asked to be shown the grave of Bessie Moore. Upon seeing it, he laid roses on it, knelt in prayer, commented on the goodness of the citizens to provide a decent burial, and gave the caretaker money for the care of the grave. Folklore asserts that this was a repentant Rothschild visiting the grave. In the 1930s a headstone mysteriously appeared on the grave where none had been before, and in the 1960s the

Jessie Allen Wise Garden Club built an iron fence around the grave."

You may notice flowers on the grave – they are placed there by an unseen hand, keeping the mystery surrounding Diamond Bessie alive.

And what about the stories of her ghost? Well, I've never seen or heard anything definitive in that regard. Many, many places in Jefferson are haunted, and if someone happens upon a female spirit, it is certainly temping to declare her to be "Diamond Bessie". If the ghost of the celebrated young lady were to return to Jefferson for a visit from the other side, I suspect that it would be somewhere memorable to her – the woods where she picnicked with Abe, and where she spent the final moments of her life, or perhaps the area where the boarding house once stood where she and Abe slept while in town. I haven't heard any stories along those lines, so I'd be tempted to say that the last time anyone saw Diamond Bessie, it was on that terrible morning when her body was found. Who knows, though – Jefferson is a wonderful place, and is capable of tempting anyone back for a visit!

The Resident Ghosts of the Jefferson Hotel

Jefferson, Texas

Spend a day in the historic town of Jefferson, Texas, and you will find yourself surrounded by the style and beauty of the 1800s riverboat days. Spend a night in the stately old Jefferson Hotel, and you may also find yourself surrounded by ghostly visitors from that bygone past.

After the city's heyday as a riverport, the Jefferson Hotel spent decades changing hands and struggling to survive, until the town finally revived itself as a peaceful getaway for vacationers. Restored to its original beauty, the grand old hotel is alive again – and with it, a few unseen visitors that reside within its walls.

This was a fun chapter to write, because I've stayed at the Jefferson Hotel several times, and always came away with a new ghost story to tell. During my last stay, I had a chance to visit with the owner.

When I asked about the ghosts there, he smiled and said, "We have several non-paying guests." And he should know – many things happen there when he is working late and the hotel is quiet. "In the evening I'm often at the front desk, working at the computer and getting caught up. Once the traffic has stopped on the stairway, I'm used to the stairs 'un-creaking' from the day's activity. You know, a pop here, a snap there. But one night something different happened. I heard the distinct squeak of the stairs as someone walked down them. They were evenly paced steps, the kind of thing we hear all day long as guests go up and down. I thought that it was a little odd, since it was a weeknight and we didn't have anyone staying upstairs. They suddenly stopped after three or four steps, and when I glanced over, there was no one there. I was alone in the lobby – at least, I was the only physical person there."

It soon became that this was a common occurrence at the hotel. In fact, the stairway is one of the high-points of supernatural activity. A playful spirit once teased a hotel guest there who was attending a formal dance in town. She wanted to have her photograph made on the stairway to show off the back of her ball gown, so she spread out her gown and positioned herself halfway up the staircase. While a friend was getting ready to snap the picture, the guest suddenly screamed loudly and dashed down the stairs. "Someone grabbed my shoulder!" she squealed. When asked about the stairway, the hotel staff is quick to start relating their own experiences – there isn't a worker at the hotel that does not have a story about the old, creaking staircase.

A great deal of the activity takes place in the hotel rooms themselves. I had an interesting experience one evening while staying in notorious Room 19. We had turned in for the evening, when my wife woke up to see a strange, gray shape at the foot of the bed. She shook me awake, and I immediately grabbed our video camera from the nightstand, where I'd set it when we returned to the room earlier. It was equipped with night vision, so I hoped to capture whatever she was seeing on tape. While I couldn't see anything but the end of the bed and the far wall through the camera lens, I noticed something very strange happening. The camera has automatic focus, and it kept whirring as the lens moved in and out, trying to lock onto the area at the foot of the bed. When I pointed the camera toward anywhere else in the room, it snapped into focus right away. At the foot of our bed, however, there was something there that the camera couldn't grab. I finally moved the camera away from my eye, but since I'd been looking into the bright green of the night vision feature I couldn't see anything in the dark room – certainly not the form at the foot of our bed. When we played the tape back, it was obvious that the camera was having trouble focusing just on that one area, where my wife saw the gray form.

I'm not the only person who captured some unusual footage at the Jefferson Hotel, though. A couple that stayed in Room 21 had been taping the hotel, and had set a camera up in their room while they were at dinner just to see if anything ghostly would show up on film. When they returned and checked the tape, they found something startling. As the couple was preparing to head out for the evening, the tape showed bright orbs of light following each of them around the room. There were several different sizes. After the couple left, the orbs continued to float around the room in front of the camera, which was stationary.

Walking down the hallways and into one of the many rooms, a person might not suspect that the supernatural activity is so pronounced at the hotel. Room 5, for example, exudes warmth and welcome, with two four-post beds decorated with a country flair. A couple checked into Room 5 on a particularly cold evening, turned on the heat, and went to bed. The wife told a curious tale when they came downstairs the next morning. It seemed that she had awakened several times during the night, shivering in the cool air. It was cold enough that she didn't dare want to venture outside the covers, not even to turn up the heater. The woman suddenly sensed a warm, heavy blanket being placed on the bed, and it felt wonderful. She opened her eyes and was surprised to see that it wasn't her husband taking care of her. Instead, an elderly lady dressed in a white, flowing dress with her hair in a bun was standing beside the bed. The old woman reached out and touched her hand softly. The wife never felt threatened, and in fact was very calm. She stretched over to wake her husband, and as she did the elderly woman faded away – but an extra blanket was indeed on the bed.

Other experiences are less dramatic, but still send goosebumps up the spine of hotel guests: cold spots in the rooms and halls, knockings on the walls and headboards of the beds, mysterious whispers in the hallway. As the guest journal testifies, it is hard to spend a night in the Jefferson Hotel without something to report when the sun rises. Each room seems to have its own particular curiosities. Room 1, with its wrought iron beds and Victorian decor, is a place where shadowy figures are frequently seen moving around the beds and in the bathroom. Odd noises are heard throughout the night, and people who have slept in this room have often reported very strange dreams.

A visitor to the hotel will find something very unusual in Room 17, where several guests have witnessed the closet door opening by itself, even though it had been securely closed. After one such occurrence, a pillow flew out of the closet and into the room. What significance could this simple act have? "Our ghosts love to play tricks on the guests," The hotel manager told me during my visit. "None of them are harmful at all – they're very playful, in fact." When asked to pinpoint the paranormal activity, she just laughed. "It's everywhere: all the rooms, the hallways, the restaurant, even the lobby. I was visiting with one of our guests at the front desk when we both heard a gun discharge right there beside us, just a few feet away from the desk. The shot wasn't outside, or in another room, it was right there! We were both startled, especially since we were alone in the lobby at the time. There's just always something happening."

That may well be true, since the stories cover the width and breadth of the hotel. In Room 7, a maid heard mischievous laughter as she was cleaning the room after the previous night's guests left. The maid had been expecting her grandchildren to stop by, and assumed it was them. When she turned around, though, there was no one else in the room. She looked for them out in the hallway, only to discover that she was completely alone upstairs. Starting to feel a little eerie, she ran downstairs to find the desk clerk, and together they went back into Room 7. There wasn't a child to be seen, but in the light coming through the window they noticed two small sets of handprints on the bottom panes of glass. The maid later learned that several weeks prior, a family had stayed in the hotel with children that repeatedly got in trouble for romping and playing in the hallways The youngsters explained that it was the "other" kids that were making all the noise, even though there were no other children present in the hotel at the time.

As I mentioned before, dark, foreboding Room 19 is the center for much of the activity in the hotel. The former owners reported that some occupants have asked to change rooms in the middle of the night, and others have flat refused to sleep in Room 19 after spending a few minutes inside. A woman and her daughter once left in the middle of the night, leaving a check at the front desk with a scribbled note explaining that they simply could not stay another minute in the room.

So who are these spirits, these specters that seem intent on remaining at the Jefferson Hotel? No one really knows. The owners once hired a psychic to examine the building, and after thoroughly exploring the hotel, she announced that seven different entities were involved in the haunting. During our visit, the manager summed it up with the explanation, "It's really no surprise that the hotel is haunted. Jefferson was like a mini New Orleans in the 1800s. Along with the proper society folks, the town also had riverboat gamblers, robbers, thieves, money and a little bit of everything else."

Some people who know the history of the hotel believe that a woman named Schluter, one of the proprietors during the 1890s, may be one of the phantoms. There is also a legend of a bride who hanged herself in one of the rooms at the turn of the century when her groom sent a messenger with the word that he had changed his mind about marrying her. True or not, there are definite, individual spirits that frequently make their presence known in the hotel.

A guest in Room 25 came out of the bathroom one evening to find a young girl standing in the room with shoulder-length brown hair, dressed in a pink floral dress with 1920's flair, who turned to the guest and actually spoke. "I'm waiting on a young man," the ghostly girl said, "and we're going to dance the night away!" As the guest approached, the girl's image faded without another word.

A couple that was a repeat customer at the hotel described another example of a particular apparition. On each of their visits, they asked to stay in Room 12, which is decorated in traditional Victorian motif with a king-sized, antique bed. They finally confided in a hotel clerk that their insistence on Room 12 wasn't because of the beauty of the room, but was instead due to an entity that they had encountered there on previous stays. On past visits, the wispy image of a thin, blond woman had appeared at the foot of their bed during the night. She stayed for some time, and exuded a feeling of total peace and unconditional love. It was such a spiritual experience for them that they sought it on repeat visits. The previous owners of the hotel moved the bed from Room 12 to Room 14, and to the couple's disappointment, the spectral lady stopped appearing.

A masculine spirit in the hotel seems to be that of a man in a long, dark coat wearing high boots. He has been seen roaming the first floor hall, and ducking into the alcove between rooms 20 and 21. Steps are often heard in empty hallways, and may belong to this mysterious gentleman. To punctuate the dark man's presence, a couple walked into the lobby one morning and reported that their child woke them during the night, complaining that he couldn't go to sleep because, "The man with the tall boots wouldn't go away."

Is the Jefferson Hotel haunted? Skeptics might try to explain away the nocturnal knockings, subtle pinches, and spectral sightings that occur weekly in the rooms and hallways of the regal building. Look into the eyes of the staff, or any visitor that descends the stairway in the bright light of morning, however, and you will know the truth. As Mr. Lakey says with his playful smile, "We have some very interesting things going on here at the Jefferson Hotel."

The Jefferson Hotel
124 W. Austin Street
Jefferson, Texas 75657
903-665-2631
www.historicjeffersonhotel.com

Ghosts & Good Food

– Lamache's

Restaurant

Jefferson, Texas

At the foot of the stairs in the lobby of the Jefferson Hotel is the entrance to Lamache's Italian Restaurant. Not only can you get wonderful meal there, but you might also just have a brush with the supernatural.

Ghosts or not, this is one of my favorite Italian restaurants in the world. Since I love spicy foods, their Chicken Diavolo is the perfect dish for me. It has tender chunks of chicken over a plate of pasta, with a red sauce that can be custom-prepared to your desired level of heat. I always order it, "as spicy as the chef can make it!"

Be warned, though – the place is extremely popular. On Friday and Saturday evenings, you'll probably have a short wait to be seated. The dining experience is well worth it, though.

Long before the restaurant moved in, back when the Jefferson Hotel first opened, the place that is now Lamache's was a dance hall named the Crystal Palace. Home to many galas and formal events, the Palace also had a reputation for being a meeting place for lonely men traveling the river and the city's "tainted angels", the ladies of the evening that worked the waterfront.

No one knows whether the spirits of those women are the ones who haunt the award-winning Italian eatery, but when the lights are turned off and the doors are locked, there are reports of mysterious activity that takes place inside.

"Guests who spend the night in rooms above or adjoining the kitchen sometimes have stories for us in the morning," the hotel owner told me. "They hear pots and pans banging loudly, dishes crashing on the floor, and all sorts of noise in there. When we open the doors to the restaurant every morning, though, nothing is disturbed. We even had to take two elderly ladies inside one day to reassure them. Their sleep had been disturbed all night long by a commotion in the kitchen, and they were convinced that someone had been tearing up the place."

Other guests have reported hearing music wafting from the restaurant in the early morning hours long after the door have been locked and the lights turned out. Perhaps it is a ghostly, audible remnant of the dancehall days. While the rest of the hotel sleeps, there may still be a room full of phantom couples, waltzing to the tunes from long ago.

Lamache's Italian Restaurant
124 W. Austin Street
Jefferson, Texas 75657
903-665-6177

Etchings of the Past: Falling Leaves B & B

Jefferson, Texas

It's not often that a spirit actually leaves her name behind for future generations to contemplate, but that may very well be the case concerning a young lady named Eloise at Falling Leaves Bed and Breakfast.

Just who was Eloise? Well, if you look out of the western window of the Magnolia room, you'll see her name etched into the glass of a windowpane.

Mike and Lisa Barry – the innkeepers – know a bit about this lady. She was the daughter of the third family to own the house, and as the story goes, scratched her name into the glass of the western window of her room in 1867 with her diamond engagement ring. We'll never know whether that was a tradition of the past, or if she simply wanted to see if her betrothed had given her a genuine diamond – after all, only the real stone will cut glass. Eloise lived in the house until after World War I, but according to Mike and Lisa, and many visitors to Falling Leaves, she may reside there to this very day.

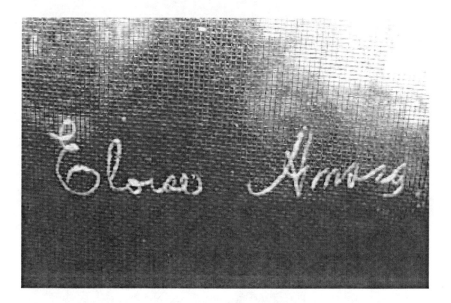

The house has a long and interesting history. Falling Leaves was constructed for John and Victoria Sabine, members of the same family for which the Sabine River was named. The house was actually built by John's brother Sid Sabine – short for Consider Sabine – as a wedding gift.

The Sabine's were in the mercantile business in Jefferson, and worked to make their home a showplace. They named it "Magnolia Hill", and planted a Magnolia tree in the front yard the first year they moved in. After all these years, the tree still stands, and is a wonderful place to curl up with a book on a lazy afternoon.

For now, though, back to the past for a little bit longer. Magnolia Hill passed to a new owner or two, and remained one of the more stately homes in the Historic District of Jefferson. Its antebellum Greek Revival architecture and beautiful grounds made it a wonderful part of Jefferson Street.

Over the years, its name was lost to history. "Magnolia Hill" wasn't used as much, so when Balthezar and Doris Koontz purchased the house in 1961 they re-named it "Falling

Leaves", a moniker that has remained with the house for almost half a century. The Koontzes were philanthropists and were respected members of the Jefferson community: they supported the Jefferson Historical Museum, bought additional land for Oakwood Cemetery, and acquired the Alley-Carlson home for the museum. They passed away in the 1990's, and Falling Leaves was put up for sale.

In 1993, the house was purchased by a couple named Bell, and was opened as a Bed & Breakfast. Visitors to Jefferson were soon able to enjoy the hospitality of the old home once again.

It wasn't long before strange happenings were observed at Falling Leaves. Joe Bell used to tell the story of standing in the dining room with several guests when one of them posed the question, "Is the B&B haunted?"

Bell gave a definite, "No!" At that exact moment, the door

leading to the guest rooms in the front of the inn swung closed with a slam, while the doors on the buffet on the opposite side of the dining room opened up. There was no breeze, no movement, nothing else in the room – only the apparent dissatisfaction of a resident spirit with Joe's answer.

The current owners experienced strange happenings from the day that they purchased the B&B. Lisa has walked through the house when no one else was there, and heard the rustling of old-fashioned skirts in the hall. She looked around, but could find no explanation for the sound.

On another night, Lisa was lying in bed and heard a minor disturbance in the master bath. Originally the toilet facilities were located outside in the form of an outhouse, but there was a "bathing room" off of the main bedroom. Presumably one would be able to walk in and find an old tub that could be drawn with a bath, whose water was freshly heated on the kitchen stove.

The bathroom is modern now, with all of today's conveniences including a ceiling fan. The noise that had awakened Lisa was the sound of the fan's chain being pulled, so strongly that the bobble on the end bounced around like a ping-pong ball. Their cat Spanky was sleeping in bed, and she noticed that Spanky was taking notice of the noise as well. What she didn't know was that her husband was also awake, listening to the whole thing. He finally broke the silence by asking if she'd heard all the noise from the ceiling fan. To this day, they're not sure what was happening – it was one of those rare evenings when there was no one else at the inn.

The spirits of Falling Leaves seem to be friendly and innocent, never really bothering the guests, just showing up every now and then for a visit. On two different occasions, guests came to breakfast with tales of a mysterious fiddle player out in the central hallway in the wee hours of the morning. Both times, after the revelation that there was no one there, Lisa asked them what they thought about the music. The guests replied that it was old-fashioned, melodical, and actually quite pleasant. She asked them if they'd ventured outside the room to see who might be responsible for the late-night concert, but neither had dared. They simply tucked further under the covers, and let the music continue.

During Jefferson's Historic Pilgrimage of 2002, a lady was staying in the Magnolia Room – the one with Eloise's signature in the window. She woke up about 2:30 in the morning to find a woman standing between her bed and the doorway. The lady was about five foot four inches tall, with a very slender waist, and was apparently just watching her sleep. She wasn't scared, but had an intense feeling that she needed to let the woman know that she meant no harm – that she was merely a guest there. When she vocalized these feelings, the woman nodded, then slowly faded away. Could it have been Eloise, come to see who might be sleeping in her room? Perhaps – at least, the innkeepers are inclined to attribute any happenings in the Magnolia Room to her. After all, she did sign her name there for future generations to see.

The spirits of Falling Leaves certainly don't just confine themselves to Eloise's activity in the Magnolia Room. A couple had just checked in and carried their bags to the Pine Room, where they were getting settled for their weekend in Jefferson. They raised the shades to let some light into the room, and distinctly remembered that they'd been a little careless, and the shades were raised to different heights – the uneven appearance stood out in a room that was otherwise symmetrical and tidy. Thinking that they'd adjust them later, the couple went on about their business of unpacking, and suddenly made a startling discovery – while they were just a few feet away, some unseen hand had adjusted the shades so that they were perfectly level. They weren't frightened, but instead a little amused that the ghost of their room paid such attention to detail and service.

Good service – even by the spirits there – is a recurring theme at Falling Leaves. A woman staying in the Dogwood Room came to the breakfast table with a tale from the previous night's sleep. Sometime in the night she woke up a little warm, so she kicked the covers off – she distinctly remembered doing this because it was a little difficult to do, since they were tucked in around the mattress. When she woke up that morning, not only was she covered back up, but the covers were once again tucked firmly around the bed. While some places have ghost stories about specters that scare people, the unseen residents of Falling Leaves seem to be trying to keep the guests happy.

Occasionally the spirits get curious about the guests, though. One woman who was staying in the Magnolia Room left a bottle of perfume – *Aromatics* by Clinique – sitting on the dresser when she left for the day. When she unlocked the door, the room smelled strongly of the perfume, and the bottle was sitting where she left it with the cap off. She closed the bottle and went on about her business, but the pattern continued to repeat itself during her stay. Several times she'd come back to the room to find the fragrance filling the air, and the cap off of the bottle. The innkeepers assured her that no one had been in the room, and when Lisa followed her up front to investigate, the smell of Aromatics was even permeating the hallway. Apparently Eloise was very taken with the woman's choice of perfume.

The spirits of Falling Leaves also manifest themselves in sounds that echo through the house when everything is still and quiet. The sound of children laughing has been reported by guests; many children were raised in the house over the years, so they may simply be visiting an old, familiar place.

When you stay at Falling Leaves, you might not encounter Eloise or one of its other spirit inhabitants, but you will certainly be pampered by the resident humans. Innkeepers Mike and Lisa Barry have a beautiful home with first class accommodations. Each room is filled with antiques, and you will sleep on one of the most comfortable king-size beds that you're likely to find.

The music room features a 1875 rosewood Steinway Square Grand piano, and visitors to the inn have enjoyed some of the most beautiful impromptu concerts when one of the guests sits down to play. You may also want to spend some time enjoying Lisa's Madame Alexander doll collection, on display in the doll room of the house.

One of the most delightful things about a visit to Falling Leaves, however, is waking up in the morning to the smell of fresh coffee and a delicious breakfast. All of the inn's guests gather in the formal dining room that features beautiful furniture circa pre-1850, each piece older than the house itself.

A typical breakfast starts with specially blended coffee and fresh fruit with orange poppy seed dressing. Guests are then treated to one of the inn's many specialties, such as baked orange pecan French toast, Cajun eggs, and smoked ham or sausage. It is the perfect way to start your day in Jefferson. Since Falling Leaves is on the Historic Walking Tour of Jefferson, you can take to the sidewalk to explore the city. A few blocks away is a plush, picturesque park lined with stately old churches and featuring a gazebo and arbor. Downtown Jefferson is only a short walk further, where you can enjoy the many charms of the city.

Returning to the inn for the evening, don't forget to stroll the grounds of the bed and breakfast. You'll enjoy the finely sculptured plants, including a Magnolia Tree planted by the original owners in 1855 and a Crepe Myrtle planted in 1875 next to the old well house, which is still standing today. The screened back porch is the perfect place to relax at the end of the day, and the innkeepers provide complementary soft drinks and wine for the guests to enjoy.

Falling Leaves is a delightful home; it is listed on the National Register of Historic Places, and is a recorded Texas Historical Landmark. Perhaps the best testament to its charm, however, comes from the fact that the innkeepers used to stay at Falling Leaves years ago when they came to Jefferson as visitors. After repeated weekend trips there, they were so in love with the place that they purchased the property, moved in, and continue to operate it as a bed and breakfast to the delight of their many guests – and from all indications, Eloise is a little fond of them as well.

Falling Leaves Bed & Breakfast
304 Jefferson St.
Jefferson, TX 75657
903-665-8803
www.fallingleavesinn.com

Mysterious Murder Alley

Jefferson, Texas

Okay, it's definitely time to dispel a few myths about this place known as "Murder Alley". I first heard of it while gathering information about a trip to Jefferson many years ago – a website had posted stories by local high school students about ghostly places in town, and one of those mentioned was "Murder Alley". Sounds ominous, doesn't it?

Well, when we got to town I asked our innkeeper to point out the location of Murder Alley on a map – we simply had to visit. She took a pen and drew a dot on the southeastern side of the town's historic district near the river, and we went there the next day. There was nothing remarkable about it at all, just an overgrown alley where it looked like there would be more snakes than spirits.

On our next trip to Jefferson, I asked someone else about Murder Alley since I no longer had the original map, and they pointed to a different location with just as much confidence. We went there to take a few photos – it was near the river as well.

This process continued until I had pictures from at least half a dozen different "Murder Alleys". After moving to Jefferson, I realized the one truth about the location: ask a dozen different people where Murder Alley is, and you'll get a dozen different answers.

But what is this elusive, notorious place? Simply put, it was a back street in the seedy part of town where it was rumored that the Sheriff would reportedly find at least one dead body every morning. Over the years, its reputation grew along with its wicked moniker. I'm afraid that the exact location is probably lost forever, if in fact it actually described a single, tangible location and not just an area of town.

The one thing that is certain is that during its heyday, Jefferson definitely had a seedier side. If you take a river tour or train ride in today's Jefferson, you'll see the ruins of all sorts of manufacturing plants, warehouses, and other businesses along the Big Cypress Bayou. Closer to town, the businesses lining the river began to meld into a more carnal nature: bawdy houses, saloons, dance halls, and gambling establishments. The river rats – those roughnecks who worked the docks and steamships – frequented these type places and there was often foul play by the time the morning sun rose.

So where is Murder Alley? If there was such a specific place, its identity has been lost to the annals of time. It has instead been replaced with the tales of long ago – of roughnecks, robbers, river workers and lawmen.

Pick a place near the river, and close your eyes for a moment. Chances are, you're standing near a notorious hotspot at one time in Jefferson's past... perhaps even Murder Alley itself.

Aunt Pearl and the McKay House

Jefferson, Texas

One of the most endearing ghost stories in Jefferson comes from a fictitious little lady named Aunt Pearl, a spirit who makes her home at the beautiful, old McKay House Bed and Breakfast.

That sounds like a contradiction, I know: a fictitious being haunting an inn. At the McKay House, though, the hauntings are very real, and are lovingly attributed to a woman called Aunt Pearl who was created by the collective consciousness of a group of English teachers who stayed there one weekend.

The McKay House Bed and Breakfast, otherwise known as the "Alley-McKay House", was constructed in 1851 by one of the co-founders of Jefferson, Daniel Alley.

If you've driven the streets of Jefferson, you may have noticed that the town's layout is a bit confusing. That's only until you examine the motives of the two town fathers, Allen Urquhart and Daniel Alley. Both men had purchased parcels of the Stephen Smith Land Grant, and envisioned a city located on the Big Cypress Bayou. The only problem was, the pair couldn't agree on a plan for the city. Urquhart wanted a street layout for his business district that was perpendicular to the river for a business district. Alley, on the other hand, had a genteel residential district laid out on a north-south grid. Since the two could not agree, they drew a line between their two land parcels and dubbed it Line Street. To the west of Line, Alley's addition had streets running N/S and E/W. On Urquhart's side, the streets run NW/SE and NE/SW.

Alley built the structure now known as the McKay House in the heart of his addition there in town. Like most homes of the day, the kitchen was built as a separate structure in back of the main house. Since fires usually blazed in the kitchen's fireplace from dawn to dusk, the risk of it getting out of control was a very real concern. If the unthinkable did happen, though, only the kitchen would burn down, not the rest of the house.

The main house was done in a classic Greek Revival style. Common traits of this include a large central hallway with rooms on either side. One side of a Greek Revival house would mirror the other – in fact, if you drew an imaginary line down the center hallway and could fold the house over, the rooms should overlay each other fairly well.

Cypress wood from the area was used in many houses in Jefferson, and the McKay House is no exception. You can see the cypress floors in the original four rooms today. Each room also features a fireplace that burned coal during Daniel Alley's time, but have since been converted to natural gas. By the same token, the central hallway light fixtures once burned gas, but now use electricity, even though all of the original gas fixtures are still there.

Mr. Alley sold the house, and it rolled through a few more owners. One necessary modification that was made to the property was at the back of the garden: the slave quarters. After the Civil War, the slaves were freed and the old quarters were renovated and turned into a "Sunday House" – a place where visitors who came to Jefferson on the weekends to shop and attend church could stay.

The house was purchased by Captain Hector McKay in 1884. The McKay family left their mark on the place, since it was kept in their family for the next century. During that time, the breezeway from the main house back to the kitchen was enclosed to make a porch.

In the 1950s, the Sunday House was torn down and replaced with a slightly larger structure from the same time period. It was also originally a slave's quarters, and was moved to the property from a farm near Naples, Texas.

A full restoration was done on the McKay House during the 1980s. A Victorian-style addition was completed in the 1990s, changing the breezeway/porch into a full dining room, and adding a second story. To keep the historic architecture of the house intact, the addition was done with materials that were rescued from other Victorian-era homes in the area that were being demolished. The gables are from a historic home in Waco, Texas named the "Old Prescription House".

In 2002, the McKay House was purchased by innkeeper Hugh Lewis, who continued the process of careful restoration of the home and gardens. Today the inn is decorated with furniture from many different periods of his history, from a four-poster canopy bed that belonged to the McKay family, to a half-tester bed that was purchased on Canal Street in New Orleans in 1880 and shipped to Jefferson by steamship.

The Bed and Breakfast has played host to many dignitaries and celebrities, including former First Lady, Lady Bird Johnson; author Alex Haley, most famous for his book "Roots"; director Martin Jurow with credits such as "Breakfast at Tiffany's" and "The Pink Panther"; supermodel and actor Fabio; and former president George Bush's staff.

There are some occasional inhabitants in the house who have become almost as famous – at least among the innkeeper and guests. These inhabitants don't need a room, aren't issued a key, and certainly don't mean any harm. They're the spirits of the McKay House, the supernatural beings who show up from time to time to check on their old home, and sometimes choose to make their presence known.

Innkeeper Hugh Lewis believes that one of the spirits is that of Bess McKay. Her activity seems to be most prominent in the original part of the house. But why does Hugh believe that Bess is paying an occasional visit? One of the reasons is that a photograph of her in the Lady Bird Johnson Room seems to move around on its own. Normally it sits on a top shelf that is accessible only by ladder. Should someone move the picture, whether by accident while dusting, or in an attempt to rearrange the items on the shelf, the photograph will eventually make its way back up to the top shelf – by its own accord. When Hugh loaned the photo to the local Garden Club to be copied, there was a constant disturbance in that part of the house until it was finally returned.

Another of Bess' favorite tricks is to ring the front doorbell. It is a pushbutton type, so either it's pushed in to ring, or it's not… except when Bess is playing one of her tricks, that is. Hugh has often heard the bell ringing oddly, as if someone had pushed it halfway in and managed to stick it in the ringing cycle, which through his experimentation has turned out to be impossible. Still, the front bell will ring in that peculiar manner, but no one can be found outside.

Lamps also turn on and off by themselves on the odd occasion. The key-style lamp in the Lady Bird Johnson Room, for example, has been known to turn on in the middle of the night with an audible "click".

Other things happen at the inn as well. A guest was staying in that same room one evening, and happened to be looking at the ship's cabin hook that is used as a lock on the inside of the door. As the guest watched, the hook swung open by itself, as if some unseen hand reached out and flipped it open.

Bess also plays tricks with the telephone. She has been known to ring an internal-only line, when no one was around to make the calls. Because the internal phone was ringing so much by itself, the owner unplugged the offending phone because it was becoming such a nuisance. After he left the room, it rang three more times.

Hugh was installing hardwood floors in the inn soon after he purchased it, and while he was working, the block and hammer tools kept moving around. He would lay them down in one particular place, then return to find them somewhere completely different. If it only happened once or twice, it could be written off to forgetfulness. It was such a common occurrence, though, that it was obviously Bess at work.

During the second floor expansion, heart-of-pine paneling from the historic "Old Prescription House" was being used in the Grand Gable room upstairs. In the process a couple of old photographs were found in a wall – since they went with the old house, they were framed and hung in the upstairs room. Someone seems to have accompanied the photos when they were placed in the room, though. Guests there have sometimes reported waking up to see a woman sitting on the settee. When they speak to her to inquire who she is and how she got into their room, she looks away and slowly vanishes. She's never frightening or threatening; instead, the lady seems to just be resting in the room that used to be her home.

Other odd things happen at the McKay House. Hugh has heard noises such as walking, moving around, etc, when no one is in the house, and sometimes walks into cold spots – small pockets of air where the temperature drops drastically.

And then there's Aunt Pearl; her tale is not the typical ghost story. It all started one weekend when the bed and breakfast was completely booked by a group of English teachers who rendezvoused there for a relaxing weekend. As they sat around one of the rooms laughing and talking, they began swapping stories about their friends and relatives, and before too long an amalgam had been created. They fashioned Aunt Pearl in their minds as a little old woman who looks at people knowingly, as if she was privy to their personal secrets, but always has a smile and a nod for them. Each of the teachers wrote a short story about Aunt Pearl that weekend, giving her a life and personality. The owner liked the stories so much that he named one of the rooms in the Sunday House, "Aunt Pearl's Room". The collected works about her must have impressed one of the spirits at the McKay House as well, because from that time on, she took the persona of old Aunt Pearl.

The activity seems to be triggered when her name is mentioned in the room, and after that, objects tend to move around. Guests will place something on a chair or the bed, only to later find it in across the room. Aunt Pearl also likes to play with the thermostat in the room; one couple staying there found that every time they returned, the temperature had been adjusted to the extreme – either all the way up, or all the way down. Lights have turned on or off by themselves, and one couple even woke up in the night to see a woman at their bedside trying to serve them pie. When they jumped out of bed and turned on the light, the lady was gone.

With all of the supernatural activity that goes on there, the spirits of the McKay House aren't constant residents. They merely seem to come back for visits occasionally, and sometimes interact with the owner and his guests.

Your stay at McKay House may not include a glimpse of a ghost, but there are many things that are guaranteed: a warm welcome, a good night's sleep, and a delicious breakfast. Victorian nightshirts and gowns are provided in every room, and many people wear them to the sit-down breakfast in the dining room. A typical breakfast that you might enjoy at the McKay House would be orange flavored French toast, bacon or ham, apple dumplings or cinnamon sugar fried apples, homemade biscuits with local Blackburn syrups, shired eggs, baked avarte cheese creams and seasonings, or any number of other seasonal favorites.

There are many different rooms for you to enjoy, from the classic, historic original bedrooms to the Garden Gable room featuring two toe-to-toe antique clawfoot tubs – a favorite for couples. You can enjoy Aunt Pearl's room out in the Sunday House, or book the Rustic Keeping Room that is true to the original look of the 1800s structure, where the bathroom is even camouflaged as an outhouse.

McKay House also specializes in weddings, anniversaries, and retreats, along with just a romantic weekend for two. During your visit, you may even want to add your own personal Aunt Pearl story to the house collection. Who knows – maybe Aunt Pearl herself will show up to thank you!

McKay House Bed & Breakfast Inn
306 East Delta Street
Jefferson, Texas 75657
903-665-7322
www.mckayhouse.com

The Specters & Spa

of

the Claiborne House

Jefferson, Texas

Visitors to the Claiborne House are treated to a night in a historic old inn, a delicious breakfast in the morning, the opportunity to enjoy a trip to their wonderful spa... and if they're lucky, perhaps a visit from a spirit or two.

The bed and breakfast is noted not only for its hospitality, but also for the *Touch of Class Day Spa* located in part of the inn complex. There you can enjoy any number of therapeutic treatments designed to rejuvenate your mind, body and soul.

In the elegant surroundings of the bed and breakfast, though, it's easy to forget that this house is as rich in history as the city of Jefferson itself. Like most of the properties on this side of town, it was originally part of the Stephen Smith land grant in 1842, and was sold to Daniel Alley who demarked it as part of his family neighborhood in the western half of Jefferson.

Alley sold the property to T.B. Goynes and his wife Caroline, and they in turn sold it to J.B. Cole and Sarah Self for $500 in 1862. With their different last names, it is assumed that they weren't married. At that time, of course, it would be unthinkable for an unwed couple to be living together, so it is assumed that J.B. and Sarah were brother and sister.

The house changed hands several times over the years that followed. In 1869, a merchant named Littleberry A. Ellis purchased the home for $1000. One of Ellis' interesting claims to fame was that in the Rothschild Trial in 1877 – the famous "Diamond Bessie" trial – he was the foreman of the grand jury that indicted Abe Rotshchild.

The economy must have picked up after that, because V.H. Claiborne, the current namesake of the house, purchased the property from Littleberry Ellis in 1871 for the sum of $1800. Claiborne hailed from Virginia; he had been a prospector in California during the "gold rush" days, then returned to his home state during the Civil War where he was given a captain's commission. Claiborne had been engaged in many battles in Mississippi and Arkansas, before being ordered to

Jefferson, Texas, where he was to orchestrate an effort to supply the Confederate Army with food.

This was all before he purchased the property, though. In fact, during that time Captain Claiborne erected a large packing establishment in Jefferson to send beef, bacon, and other meats to the Confederate troops. After the war, he purchased the house and property that is now named for him and married Miss Lucy Perry, daughter of William Perry, who founded the Excelsior House hotel and other businesses in Jefferson.

The house saw several different owners come and go, until the current owners Steve and Elaine Holden fell in love with the Claiborne House and turned it into the beautiful showplace that it is today.

It didn't take long for them to start noticing that they were not alone in their inn, however. One of the things that they insist upon is attention to detail – when you stay at Claiborne

House, everything is orchestrated toward your comfort. When Elaine began to observe that the bedspread in Browning's Room was often rumpled, she spoke to the housekeeper about it and insisted that the bed be perfectly made. Try as they did, the bed would still be found with the spread wrinkled as if someone had been sitting on it – even if no one had been in the room. A clue to what might be happening was finally captured by Elaine on film, when she was snapping photos of the different rooms. A picture that she took of Browning's Room showed a form sitting on the side of the bed in the exact location that they always found tussled.

On another occasion, Steve and Elaine were out of town, and left a housekeeper to mind the inn for them, since they had guests booked for the weekend. The visitors had been out late in Jefferson, and when they got back to Claiborne House the place was dark and quiet. They drove around to the side, parked their car, then got out to the sudden surprise that every light in the house was blazing – upstairs and down. When they got inside, the housekeeper was still in bed, and not another soul was in the house.

A few of the spirited encounters are even more interesting, though. One particular guest was sleeping upstairs in Browning's Room when she was awakened by the sound of someone talking outside of the door. It was a woman's voice, and when it didn't stop, she opened the door into a very small crack so that she could look out into the upstairs hallway. As she peeked out of her door to see what was going on, she saw that out in the sitting area was a woman in an old-fashioned dress, rambling on as if she was talking to someone. A young boy walked up, and said something to her about taking a bath, and the woman sent him on his way. The guest shut the door and went back to sleep, thinking that it was a family who had arrived at the inn late. The next morning on the way down to breakfast, she noticed that none of the other upstairs rooms had been slept in, and in fact, there was no such woman and son checked in.

These types of occurrences certainly don't happen all the time, but Steve and Elaine do strive to make a visit to their inn a memorable one. The Touch of Class Day Spa is one way to make sure that the stay won't soon be forgotten.

The spa offers both therapeutic massages and body treatments to pamper you during your stay in Jefferson: a Swedish massage to relax your muscles, a Shiatsu deep tissue massage to enhance energy pathways, or a Myofascial Kinetics massage to help joint and body movement. Couples can enjoy simultaneous messages – each person will have their own massage therapist and table, and will be treated to a combination of all three massage techniques: Swedish, Shiatsu, and Myofascial Kinetics.

You can also enjoy a body treatment like a salt or sugar scrub designed to exfoliate the skin, a revitalizing chocolate nutty scrub, a detoxifying mud wrap, or reflexology to massage the pressure points of the feet.

The Spa has many more relaxing, therapeutic treatments that will melt your stress away. A visit there is the perfect way to enhance your stay in Jefferson at the historic Claiborne House!

Claiborne House
And
A Touch of Class Day Spa
312 S. Alley St.
Jefferson, TX 75657
903-665-8800
www.claibornehousebnb.com

A Stroll Through Oakwood Cemetery

Jefferson, Texas

Just about every time that I talk to a new visitor to town I get a question about Oakwood Cemetery. I always say the same thing: definitely go there for a visit, but I wouldn't expect to find any ghosts among the graves.

There are certainly some cemeteries that are haunted, especially those located on battlefields or other historic grounds. When it comes to spirits, though, Jefferson's Oakwood is simply a plot of land set aside as a final resting place for those who have passed on.

Not to minimize the historical significance of the place; it is a tribute to some of the most fascinating people that you're likely to find. There are veterans from almost every war that America has waged, including a section that contains the remains of Union soldiers stationed here after the Civil War who died in Jefferson.

You'll find a marker for the legendary scoundrel Cullen Baker lying next to the Confederate Army Colonel Crump. There's a fenced grave for the mysterious Diamond Bessie, erected by townspeople when they discovered that she didn't have a cent to be buried – and to this day, flowers are placed on her grave by an unseen hand.

On the north part of the cemetery you'll find the Mt. Sinai

section, a Jewish burial ground, while the Catholic portion is on the southern part of Oakwood.

Some graves are unmarked, their headstones having deteriorated over the years and the people forgotten. Others are well worth stopping by, however, but they're simply too many to name.

One that you may want to visit is that of a legend in East Texas and beyond: Cullen Baker. As you enter the cemetery, go straight up Webster Street until you cross Line Street. On the left just after that you'll find his grave. The outlaw Cullen Baker was both a hero and a villain in his life, depending on whom you ask. It is recorded that he killed at least two men before joining Confederate Company G, Morgan's Regimental Cavalry, on November 4, 1861, at Jefferson, Texas. He was later discharged due to illness, and there are many stories and speculation about his activities through the end of the Civil

War. The most notorious tale concerns a band of outlaws led by Baker that preyed on civilians and soldiers from both sides of the conflict. When the war was over, Baker's reportedly outlaws turned their attentions to carpetbaggers and freedmen in the East Texas area, harassing and killing even black women and children. The U.S. Army was searching for Baker and his gang, but could never capture them. In December of 1868, Baker's outlaws disbanded and went their separate ways, with Baker himself settling in Cass County. Shortly thereafter, a group of neighbors poured the poison strychnine into his whiskey jug – when Baker drank from it and was dying, they sent for the law so that they could collect on the dead-or-alive bounty on Baker's head. Some people see the outlaw as a vicious killer, while others temper that image with that of an overzealous Rebel who refused to accept the outcome of the Civil War. Louis L'Amour immortalized Baker in the western novel *The First Fast Draw*, and there have been several non-fiction books about the life of Cullen Baker. No matter what stories you hear, there is no doubt that Baker will go down as an occupant of Oakwood Cemetery with one of the most colorful pasts.

After Baker's grave, keep going up Webster Street, and just as it takes a bend to the right there are four graves in a row together just before a large tree. This is the Ragin family, who were owners of the log cabin on The Grove property from 1855 to 1861. On March 17, 1855, Caleb Ragin and his wife, Sarah Wilson Ragin, bought The Grove property from Amos Morrill. At that time, Caleb had already established himself as a prominent citizen of Jefferson. According to the Cass County Genealogical Society's history of Jefferson in their publication *The Jefferson, Texas Cemeteries*, Caleb served as postmaster for the city from December 31, 1849 to August 4, 1851. A 1965 edition of the "Jefferson Jimplecute" on file in the Lucile Blackburn Bullard Collection of the County Historical Museum documents the founding of the Jefferson Masonic

Lodge #38 A.F. & A. M. on June 23, 1847 (although it was not officially charted until January 24, 1850). The Junior Warden for the lodge at that time was Caleb Ragin.

On the 1850 census, Caleb was listed as a white male, a grocery merchant who was born in South Carolina. His wife Sarah was recorded as being a white female born in Arkansas.

While the exact details of Caleb's business aren't clear, on December 18th of 1851 "Ragin and Company" purchased the east corner, Lot 3, Block 74 on Marshall Street in Jefferson from William Brooks and Brothers. The exact text of the sale reads:

"It being on the alley running parallel with Marshall Street and the 1st alley below said Marshall Street next to the steamboat landing and that portion of Lot 5, Block 4 on the alley...parallel with Lake Street and upon the border of which the blacksmith shop now stands which is occupied by Irvin and Jones at this time." (Cass County Records Book F, Page 601)

Caleb Ragin and his associate Hiram Tomlin also purchased land in Jefferson between Austin and Dallas streets from P. Moseley for $600 (Cass County Records Book H, Page 254). It appears that in addition to his business as a grocery merchant, Caleb traded in Jefferson real estate quiet a bit. Records indicate that he sold property to a William H. Nichols, Chester A. Buckley, and to Richard Waterhouse, who was later a Brigadier General in the Confederate Army during the Civil War.

Caleb and Sarah were married on December 11, 1849 according to Cass County marriage records. Miss Sara Wilson was the daughter of Colonel John Wilson, and officiating at the ceremony was Rev. B.B. Dyes.

The interesting story about Sarah Wilson Ragin comes from her father. Back in Arkansas, Colonel John Wilson was the Judge Advocate of the Militia, President of the first

Arkansas constitutional Convention, President of the Real Estate Bank (the first bank in Arkansas), and speaker of the House of Representatives of the first General Assembly of the State of Arkansas. The following account of Col. Wilson comes from the archives of the Old State House in Arkansas, and the 12/16/1937 edition of "The Charlotte News," which published the account of a hundred years before.

Back in 1837, during the very first legislative assembly, a bill was introduced on the floor to offer bounty fees for the pelts of timber wolves. Major J.J. Anthony, the Randolph County representative, seemed to be opposed to the bill because he mused that if such a law was enacted, the pelts would become tradable commodities much like currency. He went on to add a sarcastic remark that perhaps a local magistrate shouldn't pay the bounty for the wolves, but instead the President of the Real Estate Bank should handle the task personally, signing the pelts to make them legal tender. Colonel Wilson took offense to this, and asked from the podium whether or not Major Anthony meant the remark as an insult. Anthony replied, "I believe there should be more dignity attached to the office of one who receives oaths in the state of Arkansas."

Colonel Wilson was incensed at the remark, and leapt from the podium to challenge Major Anthony physically. Wilson drew his nine-inch Bowie knife, and Anthony pulled out his own, a twelve-incher. A fight ensued, and after Major Anthony slashed Col. Wilson on the forearm, Wilson buried his knife in Anthony's chest – the man died on the floor of the House of Representatives.

Wilson was tried and cleared on the account of "excusable homicide", after which he invited the entire courtroom to drink with him at a local bar. He won the day, but had been stripped of his seat in the house and in fact had lost most of his political power. He moved his family to Texas for a new beginning, and appears on the census of Harrison County with his daughter

Sarah, before her marriage to Caleb Ragin.

Caleb and Sarah lived on the property for six years. Although they sold it to the Stilley's in 1861, the couple and their family apparently stayed in Jefferson. Their family plot can be found in Oakwood Cemetery, with the following four markers:

Caleb Ragin – b. 10/14/1820, d. 9/12/1884
Sarah Ragin – b. 2/24/1828, d. 9/2/1898
Burlee Ragin – b. 8/10/1854, d. 8/10/1880
Arzella Ragin – b. 10/15/1850, d. 11/27/1869

The Ragins both outlived their children, Burlee and Arzella, and when Caleb died, Sarah carved the epitaph on his tombstone:

In Memory of My Husband – We will meet again.

Instead of staying in Jefferson and managing the family business, Sarah decided to move to Mansfield, Texas in 1887. She appointed a trustee to see to the land that she had decided to leave to her grandson, who had been named Caleb. At that time, almost 400 acres had been amassed by Caleb and Sarah, much of which was rental property. In her directive to the trustee, Sarah recorded:

"As I am desiring of settling upon my grandson Caleb Ragin, who resides in Marion County, Texas and who is now a minor, about fourteen years of age, the right and title to all the above (389+ acres). The said J.H. Culbertson, trustee, is hereby conveyed and to let and receive the rents and revenues arising there from and when my said grandson Caleb Ragin shall attain the age of twenty-one years the said trustee J.H. Culbertson, trustee shall make to him a complete conveyance of all the property, and the rents and revenues arising shall be

paid out annually. For the education and maintenance for my grandson Caleb Ragin and in case the said Caleb Ragin shall demise before the age of twenty-one years the said trustee is authorized and empowered to convey all the said property to my sister Pauline Wilson Daniels who now resides in Tarrant County, Texas." (Marion County Records Book A-1, Pages 165-167)

Sarah died in 1898 in Mansfield, and her body was returned to Oakwood city to be buried with the rest of her family. To complete the inscription that had been placed on her husband's tombstone, Sarah had requested that hers be inscribed with the epitaph:

We Met Again

If you continue to follow Webster Street – which becomes Magnolia – until it dead ends, look to your right and you will see a single grave with a decorative iron fence around it. That belongs to Jefferson's favorite daughter, Diamond Bessie. Another chapter in this book tells her tale, but this is a good opportunity to visit her grave.

If you turn around and follow Moss Rose street away from Bessie's grave, take the second left and you'll be going down Central Street. Keep watching the markers on your right, and you'll soon see two black iron posts with a chain connecting them. These are the graves of two men disliked by almost everyone in Jefferson: Jesse Robinson and Bill Rose. In fact, these two rogues were each other's only friend. Rose was a blacksmith, Robinson a bounty hunter who fancied himself a lawman.

Both had dastardly reputations. Just before their relationship came to a bloody climax, Rose had shot and killed Jefferson Marshal Daniel, and Robinson had been arrested for the murder of a popular cobbler in town – supposedly an argument that had horribly escalated.

On April 4, 1871, the two men ran into each other in a Jefferson bar, and one wisecrack remark led to another, and both men became angry. Later in the day, Robinson showed up in the door of the blacksmith shop on Polk Street with a gun in his hand, a threat that Rose didn't take lightly. Rose grabbed his own pistol, and squeezed off a round, but it didn't seem to stop his friend's advance. Robinson shot the blacksmith in the leg, dropping him to the ground, then stood over him and proceeded to empty the gun into Rose's body.

When he was finished, Robinson turned and walked casually across Polk Street. By the time that he reached the other side, he knew that something was wrong. He stopped, vomited up blood, then collapsed to the sidewalk. Tearing open his shirt the bounty hunter saw blood oozing from a small circular wound in his chest. As people from the town gathered around him, he uttered his final words: "That rascal has killed me!"

With both men dead, the citizens of Jefferson couldn't find a single soul who cared enough about the men to bury them. The undertaker brought out two of his cheapest coffins, and a man was placed in each. The two caskets were hauled out to Oakwood Cemetery, where a single grave was dug. As the story goes, before lowering the coffins side by side, they were wrapped together with a heavy chain. The townspeople decided that since they had been linked so closely in life, that they should be linked together in death. The markers that you see were added to symbolize that for all time.

If you're standing on Central Street looking at the black iron posts, lift your gaze a little higher to the next street over. Just beyond it you will see two uniform rows of markers, usually decorated with flags. These are the gravestones of the Union soldiers who served in Jefferson after the Civil War.

During the War Between the States, Jefferson was a shipping port for Confederate Army supplies, and even more importantly, gunpowder that was manufactured in Marshall. When the South surrendered, a garrison of Union troops – the 11th U.S. Army – was stationed in town to make sure that the river port was no longer used to supply any of the Rebel brigades who were still running rampant in the old Confederacy. During the occupation, some fell victim to disease, others incurred the wrath of nightriders in town who still rebelled against the Union occupation, and a few even took their own life, distraught by being stationed in an atmosphere where they were ostracized and hated.

There are many more stories from Oakwood Cemetery, tales that would fill a book of their own. If you'd like, just park your car and walk along the rows of markers. You'll find interesting epitaphs, fascinating headstones, and intriguing ironwork that dates back many decades. It is literally possible to lose your sense of time here.

Enjoy your visit to Oakwood Cemetery, and please, help keep it clean and intact. Respect those whose bodies are interred there. And most of all, please be aware that the gates are locked at dusk. While you could probably make it over the fence, your car would be in for the evening!

The Historic
Haywood House

Jefferson, TX

When visiting Jefferson, one of the most entertaining things to do is to join The Jefferson Ghost Walk on a ghostly stroll through the city after darkness falls. Your host, Jodi Breckenridge, gathers the group in front of the Historic Jefferson Museum; for current information and times simply check in with the Chamber of Commerce when you get to town.

As the sun sets, Ms. Breckenridge lights an old-fashioned gas lantern and leads you on a journey through the old riverport city of Jefferson. You will stroll by some of the city's most historic buildings, and will be treated to the tales of their history and hauntings.

Walking along the old bricked streets of the city, Ms. Breckenridge will tell you ghostly tales from The Jefferson Hotel, The Haywood House, The Excelsior Hotel, The Grove, and The Schluter House, to name but a few. It's an entertaining evening that you won't want to miss... but sometimes, the stories aren't all that you encounter on the Jefferson Ghost Walk.

Take the Haywood House, for example. It has served as a home, a hotel, and even a museum for a period of time. The Haywood House was built after the Civil War by Confederate

General Hinch P. Mabry, about 1865. It was originally conceived as a hotel, a four-story structure that was called the "finest west of the Mississippi River." The Haywood House, named for General Mabry's brother-in-law Joe Haywood, was truly a Jefferson showplace.

Federal troops were stationed in Jefferson after the war to insure that the river port was no longer used to supply any renegade rebel troops. While the Union soldiers established camps along the river, the officers reportedly lived at the Haywood House. One story says that there were several attacks on these officers, and Mabry was targeted for retaliation. Another says that he learned that he was a marked man because of his rank as a Confederate General . No matter which story is correct, Jefferson became an uncomfortable place for him and he fled to Canada for his own safety. His brother-in-law returned to his home in Tennessee because of his association with Mabry.

The hotel changed hands several times, closed, opened, then closed again, until finally a Jefferson citizen named Clarence Braden inherited the building. By then, it had been reduced to the two-story structure as it stands today. Braden was known around town as an eccentric person, and when he made any sort of purchase, he always asked for as much of his change as possible to be in coinage.

Clarence died on June 14, 1962, after a lengthy illness. When he checked into the Terry-DeWare Clinic, he brought with him a suitcase that was so heavy that it had to be carried in by two men. After his death, the case was opened and inside were several boxes of coins... and so the mystery began.

For almost a year he'd lived in a boardinghouse, and when the administrator of his estate began inventorying his room, shoeboxes and cigar boxes were found stuffed with every denomination of U.S. coin – pennies, nickels, dimes, quarters, halves, and silver dollars. Word spread, and all eyes turned toward the Haywood House.

The place was opened, and found to be filled with containers of coins: large glass jars, urns, baskets, and more. Thousands of dollars in bills were found to be stuffed between the pages of almost three tons of books, magazines and newspapers.

A two-ton truck was enlisted to move the money from the Haywood House to the First National Bank, and the more money they moved out of the house, the more the workers found. There were even piles of coins on the floor that were too heavy to sweep up – a shovel had to be used.

When the truck rolled away from the building, its load was so heavy that it could only move in its low gear. The coins were delivered to the local bank, and the counting process began. Over the next week, though, something like an Easter egg hunt exploded in Jefferson; anywhere that Clarence Braden had ever lived or stored items was searched: attics, closets, you name it – and more of his boxes of coins began to turn up. A cousin found a wicker basket of coins. Boxes, crocks and churns were found in J.H. Benefield's attic. The city of Jefferson was flooded with reporters from all across America and many foreign countries as word of the curious fortune began to spread.

The exact amount of Braden's coins may never be known, but at one point the bank declared the total of the coins to be $55,337.82 – 73,602 pennies; 125,907 nickels; 84,273 dimes; 63,890 quarters; 31,213 halves; and 3,322 silver dollars, all according to Fred Tarpley's book *Jefferson: Riverport to the Southwest*. These figures continued to grow, however, and many people in town contend that all of Braden's stash has yet to be discovered.

Haywood House became an antique store, and later, the Texas History Museum. When its doors closed, another owner purchased the building and more renovations began, which brought the next chapter in the mystery of the Haywood House.

During these renovations, a tight, bricked, underground passage was found running away from the house and out toward town. No one knows were it ends, or what its purpose was. The tunnel was lined with brick, about one foot wide, and two feet tall.

Speculation on the tunnel included secretly moving treasure and even slave smuggling, but the only clues found at the Haywood House end of the tunnel were some miscellaneous artifacts: a plate from New Orleans, a belt buckle from the 1800s, and an aluminum cola can from the 1970's. These clues don't give any definitive answers to the tunnel, and it was re-sealed without further investigation.

But that is only one of the mysteries of the Haywood house. During one of the Jefferson Ghost Walks, a lady took a picture of the front of the building, and since it was a digital photograph she was able to look at the results immediately. No one was in the Haywood House at the time, yet in the photo was a woman standing out on the balcony. She was wearing a white blouse and a long skirt, reminiscent of old-fashioned clothes from Jefferson's past.

While I've personally never had an experience at the Haywood House, I saw some of the most compelling footage on video that I've found in quite a long time. I ran into a fellow in town who'd visited the Haywood House during the time when it was a museum. While shooting random video inside, he caught a white, ghostly figure breezing by in front of the camera. I'd never seen anything like it before, nor have I since. While I don't know what spirits might be lurking in and around the old structure, there seems to be quite a bit of activity there. Members of the Ghost Walk have screamed and squealed as they walked by, because some unseen hand has brushed the back of their neck, or given them a gentle tap on the shoulder.

Ms. Breckenridge continues to take her tours by the

Haywood House. Not only are there many stories to tell about the historic old building, but apparently new tales continue to unfold.

A Ghostly Well at Twin Oaks Plantation

Jefferson, Texas

The first time that I had the opportunity to visit Twin Oaks was during one of Jefferson's Historic Pilgrimage weekends. Every year on the first weekend in May, the city celebrates its heritage by selecting four historic homes to put on tour. Docents in period costumes guide you through each house – it is an event well worth experiencing.

At Twin Oaks, owner Vernon Randle met us outside to give the history of the house. It wasn't the first home on the property, because the earlier one had succumbed to fire, a fate that wasn't uncommon to houses during the 1800s. The owner at that time rebuilt, though, so a magnificent home has always been standing on the grounds.

It is easy to close your eyes and imagine a horse-drawn carriage arriving at the front door of Twin Oaks, carrying visitors who had just arrived at the riverport of Jefferson after a long journey by steamship.

Today, the main house is a private residence owned by Vernon and his wife Carol. Beside it, however, is a 115-year-old home carefully moved onto the Twin Oaks property and lovingly restored. Guests of the B&B can select one of its five rooms, or a separate bungalow out by the pool.

So, is this historic old property haunted? Vernon seems

fairly certain that it is – at least, there are some strange goings-on in the main house.

During the Pilgrimage tour, Vernon proudly displayed a large room at the back of the house that he explained would someday be his "lake front" room. The Randles hoped to build a lake behind the house one day, so that they could sit in the wicker furniture in the large observation room and look out across the water.

When Vernon and Carol were adding that room to the house, the workmen found an odd concrete slab in the ground. They removed it, an even more surprising discovery was made – there was a large, round cistern in the ground beneath it. Not to be confused with a well, which has a continuous underground source for water, a cistern is basically a big tank. It is usually underground, and is filled with water that is often collected from rain, a temporarily diverted stream, or simply hauled to the cistern and dumped in.

Vernon remembers a very strange feeling when the concrete cap was removed, and the sweet scent of flowers flowing from inside. This was quite an enigma, because the light from a handy flashlight revealed that there was nothing inside, only the bricked walls and dirt floor.

A ladder was retrieved from the workmen's truck and lowered into the cistern – Vernon climbed down to the bottom of the ladder, and later said that he felt an overwhelming peace and calm in the cistern.

Once the cistern had been uncovered, many strange things began to happen on the property. When he was sitting in the "lake front" room where the cistern was located, Vernon heard water flowing, even though the well-like hole was empty.

He also heard music playing out in the inn, as did several guests staying there, but he couldn't explain any of the unusual sounds.

When I was visiting with him, Vernon told me that he wasn't sure that he and his wife agreed on the "ghost thing", but that they certainly had something going on that was worth looking into.

Twin Oaks is a wonderful bed and breakfast to spend the weekend. While you're there, keep your ears open for the melodic strains floating on the wind. They may be coming from an unexpected source: an old cistern uncovered several years ago.

Twin Oaks Plantation Inn
Hwy. 134
Jefferson, TX 75657
903-665-3535
www.twinoaksplantationinn.com

The Catacombs of Fuller Park

Athens, Texas

I've had the same wonderful person cutting my hair for the last hundred years or so, and she never fails to ask about whatever book I've just sold or project that I'm currently working on. We were talking about *Ghosts of North Texas*, my last book, and I was boring her and everyone else in the shop with stories of spirits from the northern part of the Lone Star State.

I had a great time answering questions and telling tales, and finally she asked me, "So what are you working on now?"

"A book about haunted places in East Texas and the Pineywoods area," I said with a shrug. She immediately stopped working on my hair and stepped around the chair.

"You're kidding! My husband grew up in East Texas – Athens, in fact." She was thrilled by the coincidence, but then a serious expression crossed her face, and she confided, "You've *got* to write about Fuller Park. It's *really* haunted!"

As soon as I got back to my desk, I wrote a note to check the place out, taped it to my monitor, then forgot about it. Of course, you have to realize that I have about a dozen notes taped to my monitor, so it was easy to lose.

A month or so later I was interviewing someone for another chapter in this book when they mentioned, "By the way, you may want to check out a place named Fuller Park in Athens." I immediately remembered that first tip that I'd received, and set out to uncover whatever mysteries might be lurking there. Before too long, I was up to my word processor in a city recreational area, a potential zoo, a small graveyard, something called the "monkey cage", mysterious underground passageways, all at a place called "Fuller Park" – not bad for a brief mention of a haunted place during a haircut!

It wasn't hard to find the park and a little bit about its background. It is overgrown, and the once-majestic fence around it is starting to crumble. The place was named for a local Baptist minister, the Reverend Melton Lee Fuller. You'll find his and his wife's graves in a family cemetery there, and not far away, is a small pavilion-looking structure that people call the "monkey cage".

Now at this point, I could go into stories about strange

lights in the park at night, noises emanating from the graveyard and the money cage, but in reality I think that these are all products of local legend that have been handed down through the years. Grand tales, to be sure, and certainly ones that would chill the air around a campfire on a summer evening. I had pretty much abandoned the idea about putting them in this book, until I remembered something just before I deleted the notes that I had. Back in my haircutter's chair, when she first told me about Fuller's Park, I remembered that she'd said something about underground tunnels. This intrigued me, so I decided to delve a little deeper into the subject.

Now, I can't say that what I found was any more than the same type of local legend that I'd run across in the park itself. It was certainly interesting enough to hold my attention for a while, so I wanted to include it to give you a chance to enjoy as well.

If you go looking for stories about the underground passageways, you'll likely not find a person who can tell you their origin – or at least, the origin of their legend. I went back through my files on haunted places that I've kept for decades, without a single trace. Turning to online resources, the only clue that I got was from *UFO Magazine*, Vol.7, No.6, 1992, which indicated that there was some joint venture between the United States Government and some alien race to build a network of tunnels under the surface of the earth to allow them to move more freely, without being detected by the general population above. It went on to say that one of the entry points to this network of tunnels was at Athens, Texas. I wonder if the local city council knows that? Oh well, I was about to give up completely when I got a little help from a friend of mine, Olyve Abbott. Olyve is a fellow writer of ghost books, and quite a thorough paranormal researcher. I've known her for some time, spoken on the same program with her at paranormal conferences, and had the pleasure of reading most everything of hers that I've found. In her outstanding work on cemetery haunts *Ghosts of the Graveyard,* Olyve gave me a clue about the tunnels penned by an Athens resident.

As it turns out, the *Athens Review* published an article in 1989 by Brian Spurling who mentioned that an entire network of tunnels was said to be located beneath the city. In his research, he found a resident of the city who said that she remembered tales of the tunnels as part of an escape network for slaves who were making their way up north to freedom in the 1800s. The lady recalled her aunt telling her about venturing out to one of the catacomb's openings one day with a group of family and friends. They found the entry door level with the ground, and as they pried it open, she was too scared to enter and waited on the surface for the rest of the group to emerge. When they did, her friends described the tunnels as being very much like those in coalmines, dug out through the dirt with huge, bracing timbers to hold them up. Some were terrified, because they had found strange, illegible markings on the walls, and bones scattered about the floor.

So, what are these mysterious catacombs that are said to wind about beneath the surface of Athens? Perhaps they're a sterile network of concrete and steel, with security checkpoints and military patrols, and a few closed doors that no one is allowed behind.

On the other hand, maybe some old mining shafts were appropriated for helping enslaved men and women get a few miles closer to their freedom, away from the watchful eyes of those who would do them harm.

Or could they be ancient catacombs, here long before the City of Athens was ever established? Since the stories of the tunnels are nothing more than legend, there's no way to know for certain. Maybe my friend Olyve Abbot has it more accurate – her research indicates that the tunnels would have to pass through very sandy soil with a high water table, something that makes their existence very unlikely. But assuming that it's even possible that they might have existed at one time, it's fun to hypnotize about them, and what their use might have once been.

While I was walking down one of Athens' streets near Fuller Park, I could have sworn that I felt a rumbling under my feet. I couldn't help but laugh and think of a Government truck driving below me, carrying a load of gray-skinned, almond-eyed tourists from another galaxy. Looking around, I saw a farm truck rumbling by on a nearby highway. I laughed again at my own imagination, and headed out for a leisurely stroll around the quaint little city.

From the Courthouse in Athens, take Highway 19 South to Gibson Road. You will turn left onto Gibson road and go down about 1/4 to 1/2 mile. Fuller Family Cemetery is located within Fuller Park. The graves of the two people buried there are enclosed with an iron gate with a large iron fence around them.

The Legend of the Lady in Blue

Caddo Lake – Uncertain, Texas

Caddo Lake – you'll not find a more impressive body of water in the state. Cypress trees rise majestically from its waters, their branches draped with Spanish Moss like wedding veils. Cypress knolls ring the bases of the trees, adding to the mysterious beauty of the lake. On a typical boat trip, you're likely to see alligators, snapping turtles, a huge variety of waterfowl, and maybe even a gar the size of your boat.

Now, most people would dispute the existence of a gar that big, but be sure to stop into *The Bakery* restaurant in Jefferson – you'll see a photo of one right there on the wall.

Caddo Lake is truly a place shrouded in mystery, but then, it has been like that since it was first created. As to that aspect of the lake, you'll hear that it is the only naturally-formed lake in the state of Texas. There are two theories as to how it actually came to be: from an earthquake or divine decree.

Let's first take a look at the more scientific of the two. Three earthquakes occurred in 1811 and 1812 in the area around New Madrid, Missouri. These quakes are counted among the most powerful in known history – in fact, they affected the topography of the region more than any other earthquake on the North American Continent has. Scientists estimate that they were of a magnitude of 8.0 or higher on the Richter Scale, based on the amount of sheer damage and destruction. The shock was felt over the entire United States. Over 150,000 acres of forestland were destroyed in the quake. The Mississippi River's course was changed, and the elevation of the land changed drastically in many areas. Tennessee's Reelfoot Lake was created in the aftermath, and many speculate that Caddo Lake on the border between Texas and Louisiana was created as well. Scientists hypothesize that the massive earthquake caused a thundering along the banks of the Red River, where literally thousands of trees were toppled, and fell into the river. A logjam formed that was hundreds of miles long, and the water began to back up. A collapsing riverbank swelled, apparently forming present-day Caddo Lake. It rose to the point that the water became navigable for steamships, and the port city of Jefferson was opened up for trade on a route that started in New Orleans.

The Caddo Indians tell the story a little differently, though. In their legends, the Chief of the Caddo Nation was warned in a dream that a great flood would soon decimate his people, and that he had to move them immediately. He rushed every man, woman and child to higher ground, and within a single day the waters rushed in to cover their old settlement. It is said that even today there are priceless archeological relics beneath the shallow waters of Caddo Lake from the tribe's hasty exodus.

Whether the lake was created from the earthquake, the movement of the Great Spirit's hand, or a combination of the two, the fact remains that the mysterious Caddo was formed a couple of centuries ago on the border between Texas and Louisiana. The Indians adapted to it, and quickly became masters of its waters.

Now, before we even mention ghosts on this body of water, it's important to point out the lake is composed of literally miles of boat roads that weave through the cypress thickets and islands. These places have wonderful names like Mossy Break, Hog Wallow, Alligator Bayou, the Government Ditch, Turtle Shell, Old Folks Playground, Goose Prairie, Whistleberry Slough, Red Belly, Hay Rake, Whiskey Slough and many, many more. Don't let these colorful monikers fool you, though. Unless you are familiar with the lake, or have a good map, it's very easy to get lost – especially at night. A fellow at Caddo Grocery told me that it occasionally happens, and you'll faintly hear someone yelling across the lake through the darkness. The locals refer to this as "spending the night in the Caddo Motel", something that doesn't sound very appealing at all.

I visited Caddo Lake while I was working on this book, and discovered that everything that I'd heard about its beauty was true. It was like no place that I've ever seen before. I just couldn't stop staring at the Cypress tress, and when the wind blew, it stirred the Spanish moss just enough to make it wave like a fragile curtain. My first stop was Caddo Grocery, where I signed up for a guided tour of the lake. While I was waiting for the time to arrive I had the opportunity to visit with several locals who were there eating lunch at a table in the store. I asked them about any ghost stories that were associated with the lake. They laughed a little, exchanged glances like I was a little crazy, and one fellow finally said, "Well, some folks claim to have seen a canoe with a few Caddo Indians paddling just on the other side of a stand of Cypress trees."

I made a note of that and asked, "So do you think that really happens?"

"Never happened to me," he said back with a smile.

"Probably not to anyone else, either," another gentleman added.

We talked about that for a few more minutes, and I asked about any other ghostly tales associated with the lake. The fellows mentioned two specific tragic events that had occurred there in past years that often caused speculation about the lake being haunted.

The first was the killing of Robert Potter out at a part of the lake known as "Potter's Point". There are many stories about Potter, some showing him to be a good man, and others painting a less attractive picture of him. Whatever else that he may have been, he was a signer of the Texas Declaration of Independence and the first Secretary of the Navy for the Republic of Texas. When he moved out to Caddo Lake with his wife Harriet, he became involved in the Regulator-Moderator War in Harrison County. The Regulators were a vigilante band that was enforcing their own brand of the law in the area, and the Moderators were formed by people who opposed the Regulators' over-zealous practices. Potter sided with the Moderators, and quickly became one of their leaders. On the evening of March 2, 1842, a band of Regulators surrounded his house out on Potter's Point. Robert tried to escape by running out into the lake, hoping to swim away, but a Regulator shot him through the back of the head and left him floating lifeless in the lake.

The second tragedy occurred about twenty years later on the evening of February 12th, 1869. A side-wheeler steamboat named the "Mittie Stephens" had made its way from New Orleans, headed for the port of Jefferson, Texas, when a spark from the boiler blew into part of the ship's cargo – 274 bales of hay. A fire broke out that spread rapidly through the ship, and although the crew tried to steer it toward shore, passengers were forced to leap from the sides. As people struggled to tread water, the churning paddlewheel pulled them in and killed the majority of those who had tried to escape the flames. When it was all over, sixty-one out of the one-hundred-seven people on board had perished, most of them violently in the blades of the wheel. The grand old lady burned down to the water line on the hull. Contrary to many local legends, the safe from the steamship was quickly recovered, along with the bell, boilers, and machinery. In fact, you can see the bell in the Jefferson Historical Society's Museum today.

Let's get back to Caddo Grocery, though. Even with the two tragic tales of the lake, no one was ready to tell me about any ghosts associated with the events. I noticed that our guide was looking for us, so I said thank-you and goodbye to the fellows at the table, then headed out of the restaurant and down toward the lake.

The next hour or so was amazing. As we cruised down the Government Ditch, through Hog Wallow, and along many of the mysterious passageways of Caddo Lake, I immediately fell in love with the place. While I was admiring its beauty, I couldn't help but think that it would be the perfect place for a haunting experience. With the Cypress knolls reaching up from the water, and the Spanish moss draping down from the trees, the lake had a very mystifying quality to it. I listened intently for the sound of a Caddo Indian paddle dipping into the water, or the sound of splashing from a phantom survivor of the Mittie Stephens catastrophe, but there was noting more than the low hum of the boat's motor. Still, it was a trip that will forever be burned in my mind – what a way to get an up-close and personal look at the lake!

Our guide took us down many byways and passages through the Cypress trees, finally ending up back at the dock. We thanked her, tipped her, and stopped back by Caddo Grocery for a soft drink. There was another view of Caddo Lake that we were looking forward to, so we drove back to Jefferson for the night.

We spent the next day antiquing in Jefferson, and as sunset neared we made the short drive back out to Uncertain, Texas, and went straight out to the dock for the Graceful Ghost. This 1800s style steamship is extremely accurate to detail, and has a wood-fired boiler, a steam whistle, and a working paddle wheel. We weren't worried about any Mittie Stephens type accident, though, because our captains seemed to be well in control. Captain Jim McMillen was a U.S. Naval officer during the Vietnam War and is licensed by the Coast Guard as a Master of Steam and Motor Vessels. Captain Lexie Palmore McMillen is the only woman in America to hold an Unlimited Inland Master's License and First Class Pilot's License on the Mississippi, Ohio and Tennessee Rivers. According to the statistics on their website, she has piloted America's major riverboats, including the Delta Queen, the Natchez, the Mississippi Queen, and the President. We felt like we were in the best hands possible, so we settled in on the top deck for a very different view of Caddo Lake.

Sure enough, we were treated to a wonderful trip around the lake. The gentle thump-thump-thump of the paddlewheel striking the water was soothingly erythematic, and the occasional sound of the steam whistle blowing felt very nostalgic. I could almost close my eyes and imagine myself on a steamer running on the Big Cypress Bayou path through the lake on a trip from New Orleans to the riverport of Jefferson. Our two captains narrated the excursion well, and everyone on the boat had a great time. When I brought up ghost stories of the lake, however, I stuck out. No one had a story to tell – at least that they would admit to.

As wonderful a time as we had on our excursions onto Caddo Lake, I was extremely disappointed that I didn't come away with any tales for the book. I happened to be explaining this fact to a friend of mine who is Catholic, and she said, "Caddo Lake – hey, didn't the Lady in Blue appear to the Caddo Indians somewhere around there?" I stood there for a second, and was then off and running.

Now I'm not sure that this can be classified as a "ghost story" per se, but I found it nestled enough in the supernatural realm to include it in this book.

It all began back in the town of Agreda, Spain, long before

the Caddo chief was warned of the great disaster that would befall his village, before the area that would become East Texas was explored by European adventurers, and a couple of centuries before the ground around New Madrid, Missouri would shake in the devastating earthquake. On April 2, 1602, a girl was born in the small Spanish town to a couple that were devout Catholics, and they named her Maria after the Holy Mother. The girl seemed to have a very spiritual presence even at an early age, and when she was eight years old she took a vow of lifetime chastity. At the age of sixteen, her parents felt led to go into the service of the church, so her father took the vow of a monk, and her mother became a nun. The next year, Maria became a nun herself and joined the Poor Clare order. She took the name Maria de Jesus de Agreda, donned a nun's habit, and went inside of the convent at Agreda.

The Order of Poor Clare was cloistered – that is to say, they rarely, if ever, left the walls of their convent. Those that did were easily recognized by their bright blue habits.

Maria started exhibiting extraordinary behavior at the convent. She would sometimes fall to the ground and convulse wildly in what the other sisters described as "fits of ecstasy". When the seizures passed, she would tell stories of having traveled to a far-away land where she was able to minister to the native people. Maria described the countryside and the people that she had met there in vivid details, even recalling the names of the natives that she spoke to.

During the time that she was mystifying her fellow nuns over in Spain, European explorers had started moving into the area of Texas and Louisiana. Of course, some of the first people to settle there were priests who were tasked with converting the natives to Christianity. These priests were sometimes shocked to enter an Indian village for the first time and find Catholic-style alters, Indians wearing crosses, and some tribal leaders that reportedly knew Catholic liturgy in their native tongue. These villages had never been visited by the French or Spanish before, so imagine how surprised the priests were. As they worked out the difficulties of communication, the Indians would tell them that they had been taught the religion by a beautiful woman dressed in blue who descended from the clouds. The woman told them that a day was coming when white-skinned priests would come to their land to teach them more, but until that time, they should continue the worship practices that she shared with them.

This started happening enough that it caught the attention of Fray Alonzo de Benavides, a high-ranking church official of New Mexico. Of course, at the time that included most of the southwest, including Texas. Father Benavides became curious, and launched an investigation into the mysterious appearances of the Lady in Blue. He personally visited several of the villages to speak with the Indians and get their stories first-hand. The Poor Clare order was the only one that wore the blue habits that were described by the natives, so he took a painting of a Poor Clare nun and took it on one of his visits. When he asked some of the Indians who had spoken to the Lady whether it looked like her, they replied that the woman in the picture was wearing the same color and type of dress, but that she was older and plumper than their Lady in Blue, who was young and beautiful.

Since the only Poor Clare orders were back in Spain, Father Benavides wrote letters to his fellow Clergy there and told them the story that he had heard from the Indians. Some of the priests visited the Poor Clare convents and passed the story along. When a priest happened upon the one in Agreda, Maria listened to his story, and said, "I am that woman."

Word got back to Father Benavides, who traveled back to Spain in 1631 for the sole purpose of meeting with Maria de Jesus de Agreda. There in the Poor Clare convent, he came face to face with the much-acclaimed, beautiful young woman that the natives knew as the Lady in Blue.

She not only told him of her visits to the Indians, but

described them perfectly. She was able to give exact details of their customs, their appearance, and their clothing. Maria was even able to describe the Texas countryside where she visited. It would have been impossible for her to know these facts unless she'd actually been there – as a cloistered nun, she was basically cut off from the rest of the world. More than that, however, the facts about the Indians and the Texas landscape were still being documented by the Spaniards there, and were not common knowledge back in the homeland.

Father Benavides asked her how she was able to communicate with the natives, and she replied that she simply spoke to them – she could understand them, and they could understand her. He was truly amazed, but sailed back to New Spain – or Texas, as we know it – secure in the belief that he'd met the same Lady in Blue that the Indians had.

During her life, Maria wrote many manuscripts that came from visions revealed to her by God. Two that remain today are "The Mystical City of God" and "Devine History of the Virgin Mother of God." Maria died inside the convent that she loved so much on May 24, 1665, never having set foot outside its walls since that day forty-six years earlier. At least, not physically.

The legend of the Lady in Blue became known throughout the Spanish world at the time, and even after Maria's death the Spaniards in Texas would run across instances of her mysterious appearances. One priest, Father Damian Massanet, was traveling through Texas in 1690 when he penned a letter to a Spanish Official in Mexico. Along with the other information that Father Massanet passed on, he included the following paragraph:

> *"While we were at the Tejas village, after we had distributed clothing to the Indians and to the governor of the Tejas, the said governor asked me one evening for a piece of blue baize to make a*

shroud in which to bury his mother when she died. I told him that cloth would be more suitable, and he answered that he did not want any color other than blue. I then asked him what mystery was attached to the blue color, and he said that they were very fond of that color, especially for burial clothes, because in times past they had been visited frequently by a very beautiful woman, who used to come down from the heights, dressed in blue garments, and that they wished to be like that woman. On my asking whether this had been a long time since, the governor said it had been before his time, but his mother, who was aged, had seen the woman, as had also the other old people."

As the Indian cultures faded away in Texas, so did the story of the woman who first brought Christianity to the tribes there. It is now recorded only in Spanish correspondence and documentation from the time period, and in the writings of Maria de Jesus de Agreda – the mysterious Lady in Blue.

Caddo Lake straddles the border between Texas and Louisiana, a few miles out of Jefferson at the town of Uncertain.

From One Haunted Theater to Another

Commerce, Texas

Alumni of East Texas State University – now Texas A&M University at Commerce – can tell several spine-tingling stories of haunted buildings on campus. One place whose spirits were seen by many students through the years was the old Drama building. Originally, it had been used as the enlisted men's club at Camp Maxie, an Army base in Paris, Texas. The building was donated to the university, though, where it was converted to the theater for the performing arts department.

As the thespians moved in, people immediately began to see the ghost of a man in full soldier's uniform. According to the April 2001 issue of the Texas A&M – Commerce *Pride*, "This apparition liked to whistle as he walked the hallways, occasionally opening doors to check inside. At least that's the story people would tell the department head at that time, Dr. Pat Pope. An old *East Texan* story reports Dr. Pope as saying he didn't believe any of it until the night he himself looked up from his desk to see the figure of a man wearing combat boots and a field jacket standing there. 'He just stood there, turned and left,' the *East Texan* reports Dr. Pope as saying. 'I know there was a ghost. I saw him.' The same story reports that there were actually two ghosts in the theater, the second one a beautiful woman dressed in a Grecian-style gown who was usually seen near the theater seats, which had come from an old theater in downtown Commerce. While the seats were still in the Commerce Theater, one of them already had a reputation for being haunted, with patrons who sat in it claiming it enveloped them with a chill and overwhelming sense of dread."

As the university continued to grow, the time eventually came to replace the old theater in favor of a new Performing arts Center. Dr. Pat Pope, the department head that was so loved and respected by the theater students, eventually passed away – but not before getting to direct many projects in the new theater.

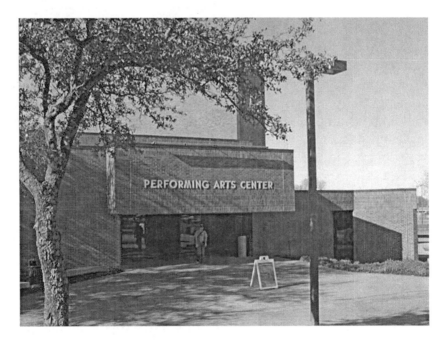

The same April 2001 issue of the Texas A&M – Commerce *Pride* reports, "Not to be outdone by the old theater, the new one comes with its own uncanny drama, according to alumnus Jim Anderson, who currently teachers in the theater department. (Keep in mind, he says, that all theaters are supposed to be haunted. Else why would a perennially burning stage light be called a ghost light, and why else would actors say on the day they get paid that 'The ghost walks tonight.') For the past several years, Jim recalls, students rehearsing late at night will notice one theater seat is folded down. It's the seat that Dr. Pat Pope, longtime department head, always did his directing from. 'No matter how many times that seat gets pushed up, it's always back down when we look out over the theater,' Jim says. And students have often said that they've seen out of the corner of their eye a white-haired gentleman. It's not a threatening experience, they say, just the feeling that someone is watching over the department. And oh, says Jim, Dr. Pope had a habit of hiding the face of a cat or a clock in his painted sets. Today stagehands frequently find cats and clocks bleeding through their painted backdrops. Says Jim: 'We're very fond of our folklore about Dr. Pope, who put so much of himself into this department. If it isn't true, it ought to be.'"

I've come to believe that most theaters do have a ghost – in my travels, I've seen many examples. This was the first time, however, that I've seen a new theater that came with its own spirits to replace those of the old one.

Performing Arts Center
Texas A&M University at Commerce
Commerce, Texas

The Sad Tale of Cry Baby Bridge

DeKalb, Texas

Ready for a good ghost story? Well, grab a cup of hot chocolate, drop in a few marshmallows, and have a seat around the campfire. It all starts back when I was a teenager, more years ago than I want to add up, in the wonderful East Texas town of Hooks. One of our favorite activities was "riding around" – that is to say, piling in a friend's car and driving from one end of town to the other, then back again. We'd stop at the Dairy Queen just to see who was there, maybe see if anyone was hanging around at the church, turn around on Precinct Line Road, and start the circle all over again. Conversations ranged from how the football team was going to do on Friday night, to where the bass had been biting the most out at Texarkana Lake. It was a fantastic time – and place – to be a kid.

I remember one night vividly, although I'm not exactly sure when it took place. I think that it must have been in the fall, because the weather was just chilly enough to run the car's heater on low. A couple of us had been cruising around and we stopped to get a cola and see what was happening at the DQ. No one was there at the moment, but it wasn't long until a carload of friends showed up and ordered a basket or two of fries to munch on while we visited. In the course of conversation someone mentioned having gone out to "Cry Baby Bridge" in DeKalb the week before. She said that it had frightened everyone so badly that they'd practically flown back to Hooks, pushing the speed limit for all that their car would go.

"What is Cry Baby Bridge?" someone asked. "Did you see something that scared you?" another guy joined in. "Where is it?" still another fellow asked. Everyone was chattering at once. The girl who'd brought up the topic just sat back and smiled, waiting for the questions to subside.

When we were all sitting there on the edge of our seats, she began her story: "Twenty or thirty years ago a woman who lived out in the countryside around DeKalb was coming home from the store. She had her three babies – triplets – in the back seat with the sacks of groceries. The lady ran into one of her friends at the store, and they stood in the aisle and gossiped for almost half an hour. Of course, she realized that her husband was going to be coming home from work to an empty house, so she quickly checked out and started home. She didn't want him to be mad because his dinner wasn't ready, so she was driving much faster than usual to try to beat him home. When the car rounded the corner right before a little country bridge, the rear end started sliding and she over-steered to compensate. By the time the woman got to the bridge, the car was hopelessly out of control, and careened over the side and crashed into the creek. Someone found her unconscious behind the wheel about an hour later. They rushed her to the hospital in Texarkana, and although the doctors fought hard to save her life, the lady passed away. Right before she died, she looked up at a nurse and asked, "Are my babies all right?" The nurse immediately notified the County Sheriff that there might have been infants involved in the wreck, and the officers scoured the creek bed for the rest of the night. They pulled the car out, of course, and even got volunteers with hunting dogs to assist in the search. The bodies of the three infants were never found."

She stopped her story, and looked around at her audience. We were all sitting there in rapt attention, and even in the normal din of the hamburger joint, you could have heard a pin drop. Taking a deep breath, the girl continued the story. "People forgot about the wreck over the next few years, until two cars met at the small bridge on a summer evening. Since only a single car could fit safely on the bridge, one driver honked his horn three times to get the other fellow's attention to wave him on across. Now, since it was so warm, both cars had their windows open. As one slowly eased over the bridge, there was the unmistakable sound of babies crying in the night. The drivers stopped and looked over into the creek bed, but the only thing that was there was the tiny stream trickling under the bridge." Our storyteller's voice dropped to almost a whisper. "That's how it started. People soon realized that if you stop on the bridge at night, turn off the engine, and honk the horn three times, you will hear the crying voices of the three tiny babies who were never found."

Now, there is absolutely, positively, no way on the face of the Earth that you can tell a story like that to a group of teenagers and not anticipate the response. Everyone uttered the same words in unison: "Let's go!"

The remaining French fries were wolfed down, the colas were drained, and we all piled into one car. To this day I can't imagine how nine or ten of us managed to cram into a modest sedan, but we did. It was a short drive over to DeKalb, and the girl who'd spun the story for us was giving directions: turn left here, slow down and turn right, look for the next road, and so forth. I will never forget the sight of the headlights cutting through the night, and eventually hitting a small bridge on a dark, lonely, country road. "That's it," the girl whispered.

The fellow who was driving stopped the car on the dead

center of the bridge, and we slowly rolled the windows down. "Kill the car," someone said, and when he did, the night was deathly still. He pushed the headlight control, and we were then parked on the bridge in total darkness. For a moment, while we were waiting for our eyes to adjust, it was like being in some kind of sensory deprivation chamber. "Do it," I heard someone whisper from the back seat, and suddenly the three loud retorts of the automobile's horn split through the night.

Like I said at the first of this chapter, that was more years ago than I really want to count up, but I remember it like it was yesterday. When I finished my book, *Ghosts of North Texas*, and set out to do one on East Texas and the surrounding area, I could hardly wait to write this Cry Baby Bridge chapter.

As I do with all of the information, I launched a huge research campaign to uncover the facts of this story. I was immediately overwhelmed with the information that I found. Consider just a few of the stories:

"The story of Cry Baby Bridge takes place in Union County, South Carolina. Just before you get to the historic Rose Hill Plantation, there is an old bridge with rusted steel frames at the top. The local legend has it that if you park on the bridge and cut off your car, that you can hear a baby crying and then see the mother looking for it. One day in the 1950's a woman threw her baby off the bridge to spite her abusive husband, and she has been doomed to walk the creek in search of her child."

"One rainy night in Oklahoma on a small dirt road, the story behind Cry Baby Bridge was born. A young woman was leaving home to head for work, with her small baby safely strapped into the car seat. When she crossed the small wooden bridge, the dam on the lake next to the road suddenly broke from the pressure of a rainy season. It wiped out the bridge, and swept the car downstream. The mother's body was found washed up on the lake's shore the next day, but the baby's body was never found. Local officials dragged the lake and the

stream, but never found the baby's body. The bridge is still washed out to this day, and it is said that if you go there on a rainy night you can still here the baby cry, and the frantic mother will appear and ask you if you have seen her baby."

"*A number of people have heard the story of Cry Baby Bridge here in New Hope, Pennsylvania. The accident took place at least fifty or sixty years ago. Legend has it that a woman became pregnant with twins, but after the babies were born the father wanted no part of the new family. With no husband, and no way for her to support herself or her children, the young lady decided that it would be best if she took the lives of herself and her children. She carried both of the babies out onto the bridge, climbed over the side, and plummeted herself and her children to their deaths. The people who have been out to the bridge have walked near the center and heard the cries of what sounds like two screaming infant children coming from below, near the water.*"

"*Cry Baby Bridge is a place in Faison, North Carolina that is truly haunted. It all started when a woman and her baby were going home from church one late, rainy night on Highway 403. The lady was driving across the bridge a little fast when her car slid and plunged into the river below. Both the mother and the tiny baby drowned. Some people say that if you go to the church, ring the doorbell, and run back to the bridge, you will soon hear a baby crying beneath the bridge. If you do hear the baby cry, then your car will not start – you will see a greenish glow in the water, which is the spirit of the baby watching you. Your car will not start because the infant wants you to help him and his mother.*"

"*Cry Baby Bridge is located in Genesee County near Flint, Michigan. There was once a young, practicing Satanist woman who had given birth to a bastard child. She thought that she could gain power into the spirit realm by sacrificing her baby's life to the Devil. One night she placed the baby on a railroad trestle next to a cemetery, and lit two white candles.*

The baby was then hit and killed by a passing train as it crossed the bridge. Now, if you go there in October during a full moon, and light two white candles, you will hear a baby crying and see a ghost train passing by in the night."

"In a little town named Doylestown Ohio, a pregnant woman was driving to the hospital to have her baby back in 1963. The baby came before she could get there, and she had to stop and give birth on a small country bridge. While holding her tiny baby, she became distraught over the fact that the father had left town months before, and threw the newborn over the bridge. She couldn't get the final cries of the baby out of her mind, so she went down to the train tracks near the bridge and stood there so the train would kill her that night. As the story goes, if you go to the bridge at Midnight you can her the baby softly crying, and some people have even seen a ghost train going by on the tracks."

I could go on and on with the stories that I found about "Cry Baby Bridge", from one coast to the other, and from Canada down to Mexico. The story is apparently an urban legend that has been spread to small towns across America – my version was one that was based in DeKalb, Texas, but it could have just as easily been anywhere else. I should have known – when I was telling someone at school about my experience at Cry Baby Bridge, they lit up like a lantern and said that they'd already been there, a week before. When they started telling me where it was, though, their bridge had been on the opposite side of town from the one that we visited. It was an urban legend in the making, way back in the 1970's.

So what happened to me and my car-full of friends that dark, fall evening? Well, I hesitate to tell you now, especially in the light of the many Cry Baby Bridge stories that I found. Through the still of that night, however, when the last blow of the horn was echoing off of the trees around us, everyone in the car would probably swear to this day that we heard the cry of a baby – the imagination is a fantastic thing. The driver fired the car to life, sped away, and we rode back to the Dairy Queen with a mixture of screams and howls. Back under the bright florescent lights, with a cold cola and order of fries in front of us all, we laughed and accused and doubted and dared. It was wonderful being a teenager back then.

Cry Baby Bridge is somewhere near DeKalb, Texas, depending on whom you talk to.

The Apache Ghost of Lyday Fort

Dial, Texas

Just outside of the small community of Dial, Texas, is the site of a fort constructed in the early 1800s to protect East Texas settlers from Apache raiding parties. This place is different from most forts in that it was constructed privately by a man named Isaac Lyday.

Mr. Lyday saw the need for protection for the families living along the north Sulfur River. He and several others built a small fort, approximately one-forth acre in size, with a typical wooden picket fence around the perimeter. A well was dug in the middle of the fort to supply water, with storerooms and living quarters built around the inside perimeter. On the outside of the fort was a livestock corral, which is where the ghost story of Fort Lyday originates.

In 1838, the fort was occupied by the Red River County Rangers under the command of Captain William B. Stout. Several families were also inside the fort, and some had brought their cattle with them to store in the corral outside.

That evening everyone had fallen asleep, including the sentry stationed on duty. In the dead of night, an Apache warrior crept up to the fort in the hopes of stealing the cattle and bringing them back to the tribe for much-needed food. He opened the door to the corral, then went inside and started silently driving the cattle outside. The noise of the cows moving woke the sentry, who quickly saw what was going on.

He woke the other Rangers stationed there, and they quickly rode out in pursuit of the Indian. It wasn't long until they caught up with him, and one of the Rangers leveled his rifle and shot the man in the back of the head, killing him instantly. The cattle were rounded back up and most were returned to the corral, but the body of the Apache man was left lying on the ground as food for the predatory animals, as a warning to his fellow tribesmen.

It must have worked, because the fort was reportedly never attacked again. Strange reports began to surface soon afterward, however, of the sound of phantom hoofbeats and the ghostly figure of an Indian on horseback.

The fort was abandoned in 1843, when problems with the Indians began to subside. The fort fell into ruins, and few people know its exact location today. Still, visitors to the area around nightfall have heard the thundering hoof beats of cattle, and have seen a solitary rider herding at full gallop.

That unfortunately didn't happen to me, but I do know someone who professes to have had that experience. Some supernatural activity that we find seems to be merely a replay of a past event, like a cosmic DVD stuck on rewind-play-rewind-play – perhaps this is an occurrence such as that.

The exact location of Lyday Fort has been lost to time, and is now simply East Texas pastureland.

Daphne the Theater Ghost

Henderson, Texas

I've mentioned coincidences that have occurred in the course of writing this book, and one in particular happened while my wife and I were waiting for a morning meal at a Bed & Breakfast in East Texas. We were in the parlor talking with two other couples, and the inevitable question went around the room of what everyone was doing on their weekend getaway. I mentioned that I was researching a book on haunted places in East Texas, and one of the others said, "Wow, you've got to mention Daphne in your book!" We talked about it for a few minutes, and I was making notes on napkins, business cards, or anything else that I could find. So began my research into the Henderson Civic Theatre, and its resident ghost Daphne.

It's been a long-standing premise of mine that every theater has a ghost, and the one in Henderson is no different. According to people that I spoke with, she's more of a mischievous lady than a scary apparition. She's become the de facto mascot of the theater, and in fact, their annual theatrical award is called "The Daphne", and it's given out in categories much like its national cousin Oscar[tm].

Of course, I was drawn to learn more about this theater and the spirit that visits there. As far back as I could dig, theatrical productions in Rusk County began in 1886. The

Henderson Dramatic Club launched the area into the world of culture with a production named, "The Social Class" in an opera house that bad been constructed for them. They went on to do plays for the next few decades, until the advent of World War I changed the face of the country. Resources were redirected to wartime efforts, and the theater group went their separate ways.

A century later, a group of local citizens with a love of the arts drew together to revive the Henderson Civic Theatre like a phoenix from the ashes. Their first production was in a city park, and from there they moved to a local school facility where the plays continued for two years. Next they rented an old building downtown, and during the renovation process, soon discovered that it was the original 1886 Opera House. Funded by donations by supporters throughout the area, they purchased the building and made it their own. They inherited more than the physical structure, however, and the story is best continued from their website:

"When the Henderson Civic Theatre purchased the Opera House, they were unaware they were also getting a ghost. No one knows who the spirit is, but apparently she is female and obviously loves theater. She was named 'Daphne' because she made her presence known on stage when 'Blithe Spirit' was being performed. While no one in the audience saw her, the actors on stage were well aware of her presence as she walked among them during the séance scene in Act I."

"Daphne has become a part of HCT, and anyone who spends much time in the building becomes aware of her in one way or another. She is particularly fond of whispering in the wings and more than one director has scolded the cast and crew for making too much noise backstage, only to find out no one was there at all. She also likes to follow people up the stairway located backstage, and has been known to pace back and forth down the hallways on the upper floor. She isn't limited to any one area and has been seen or felt all over the building. Some think that many years ago there was a doctor's office in the building, and she may have some connection with it."

"While some may not feel comfortable knowing of her attachment to the Opera House, we have become quite fond of her and she is considered an asset to the theater. Every time she has made her presence known, especially during Grand Dress, the play has been a rousing success. So, on that night in particular, the cast and crew watch for her to make herself known."

The Tyler Morning Telegraph gave an interesting account of the spirit from Mrs. Lynda Trent, theatre group member and director, from an interview with reporter Kenneth Dean: "Walking up the creaky steps into the dimly lit upstairs area, where stage props are kept, the age of the building shows. Brick walls half-covered in plaster, squeaky floorboards and the ambience of a turn-of-the-century warehouse all help to prepare someone as they peer around corners in search of

Daphne. Mrs. Trent, who said she has seen the ghost, said Daphne does not perform acts of mischief, but rather does things when they are least expected. 'She (Daphne) has turned on and off one of the spotlights during a show, whispered loudly during rehearsal, followed people up the stairs, been seen on the catwalk. She has basically been seen everywhere in the building, except the lobby. Why that is, I don't have a clue,' she said. Mrs. Trent said the story she believes explains Daphne's presence is the tale of a young woman in the 1930s, who went into premature childbirth and died on the second floor of the building in the doctor's office. 'I don't know if there is an inch of truth to the story, but it seems the best explanation for her presence,' she said. The theatre company gave Daphne her name after a performance of 'Blithe Spirit' in which a young woman was named Daphne. 'Daphne's haunting is more of a teasing. Nothing ever really malicious. She loves to move things the actors put down and then put them back in the same spot, but never anything really mean,' Loyce Radford said."

The Henderson Civic Theatre has enjoyed many successful seasons, and continues to thrill theater-goers with every performance. When you attend a show there, keep one eye open for Daphne – if she is pleased with it, you just might see her lurking there in the shadows of the stage.

Henderson Civic Theatre
122 E. Main
Henderson, TX 75652
903-657-2968
www.hendersoncivictheatre.com

The Howard-Dickinson House

Henderson, Texas

The historic Howard-Dickinson House is poised stately on a hill overlooking South Main Street in Henderson, Texas. Although it is now a world-class museum, it was once the home of a couple of brick-mason brothers who made it the showplace of Rusk County.

James and David Howard came to Texas from Richmond, Virginia and brought with them a talent for construction. They designed their home in Italian architectural style, and built it from 1854 to 1855 using handmade brick and their masonry skills. It was the first brick house in Rusk County, in fact. The house was also the first to use an iron-reinforced structure, and the first to have plaster walls. When it was complete, it was definitely the talk of the town.

For warmth in the winter months, the brothers included six chimneys with fireplaces in the first and second stories, and the basement as well.

With their reputations as master craftsmen in place, the Howard brothers went on to do many of the buildings in Henderson, including the Rusk County courthouse.

David's wife Martha Ann had a cousin of some note named Sam Houston, hero of San Jacinto and the first President of the Republic of Texas. Whenever he was passing through the area, Houston would stay as a guest in the Howard home.

The Howards occupied the house until 1905, at which time Miss Kate Dickinson purchased the home and turned it into a boarding house – for more space, she had the rear wing added to the house. Miss Kate's place served the community until 1950, when she closed the doors.

The house sat empty for the next fourteen years. As any empty building will do, it began to deteriorate during that period. This was aided by an unsavory element, people who broke into the house and did even more harm. It seemed like the wonderful old place was doomed.

In 1964, however, Mr. and Mrs. Homer Bryce came to the rescue. They purchased the house and property, and then donated it to the Rusk County Heritage Association. It took the organization three full years to restore the home to its original beauty, but when they finished, it had every bit the elegance of its bygone days. The Association furnished the house with period antiques, including a trunk that belonged to Sam Houston, and an organ that was the first one of its kind in Rusk County.

There are many displays for visitors to enjoy: historical books, significant papers, paintings, manuscript collections, antique clothing, linens and lace, unique dolls, and beautiful china, glass, and silver. There is a two hundred forty-volume library of medical books, a wealth of genealogy material, and many other references that can be viewed on premises.

Of course, you know by now that I wouldn't be going into this much detail about the house if it didn't have a ghost story associated with it... and it does. Workers and guests there have reported a woman who walks into the house and climbs the stairs. Joan Hallmark, a reporter for KLTV 7 News in Tyler, Texas, tells that the late Mata Jaggers described the incident as follows:

"Mrs. Howard is the spirit most often sensed in the house, perhaps because of the late Mata Jaggers who saw a woman in white enter the house and then disappear as she climbed the stairs.

"Jaggers was convinced she was seeing Mrs. Howard and descriptions by relatives seem to confirm the sighting. When forks are carried on plates out of the Howard-Dickinson dining room, they often jump to the floor. It's thought that Mrs. Howard's spirit is a stickler for proper dining etiquette. Lights that come on in an upstairs bedroom when no-one is in the house have been seen by a number of people.

"A bloodstain on a bedroom floor, coming from a shooting between the Howard brothers, cannot be removed – though many have tried."

While I didn't experience the spirit of Mrs. Howard when I saw the museum, I was definitely impressed with the old place. There are so many things to see there that it's no mystery to me why Mrs. Howard might be coming back for an occasional visit. It's a wonderful old home, and since I didn't even begin to see everything there, I'll be back again... perhaps my visit will coincide with Mrs. Howard's.

Howard-Dickinson House Museum
501 S. Main St.
Henderson, TX 75654
903-657-6925

The Walls of

Huntsville Prison

Huntsville, Texas

I once visited a bed and breakfast where the spirits of young girls would appear to the owner and guests. As it turned out, the building was once a dormitory for a young ladies' college, and the ghosts were simply the girls stopping back by to pay an occasional visit to a place that was very important to them in life. There were never any deaths there, nothing traumatic, only the memories of the times that the girls spent there in school. I'm therefore convinced that ghosts aren't always attached to bad events or deaths.

On the other hand, there is some evidence to indicate that strong negative events can be the source for hauntings as well. Take for example the famous "Walls" Unit of the Huntsville State Penitentiary, a location that has housed prisoners in one form or another for over a century and a half. It is certainly a place that has seen its share of misery. From its inception, it has been the home of execution: hangings, "Old Sparky" – Texas' electric chair, and in modern days, the deadly intravenous needle with its chemical cocktail. Many people have lost their lives there, and many more are scheduled to do so in the near future.

The one thing that I can say is that, with all of the places in this book that I've visited and stayed, I am delighted to have

133

never been a guest there.

The roots of the prison go all the way back to 1848, when the Texas legislature saw a need for organized incarceration and passed a bill to establish a state prison. The governor appointed three committee members: John Brown of Henderson County, William Palmer of Walker County, and William Menefee of Fayette County. Together they selected Huntsville as the home for the new prison facility; their reasoning in selecting that city is a mystery to this day. Perhaps the fact that there was a local rally to attract the prison played a major part, or even that the town was the home to Sam Houston, but no matter what the reason, Huntsville was chosen.

Construction began late in 1848 and proceeded smoothly, except for a brief dispute over the quality of some of the materials being used. By late spring 1849 workers had finished most of the ground floor of the first brick cellblock and expected to complete the entire structure later in the year. In anticipation of possible construction delays, prison officials had erected a makeshift jail of heavy logs and iron bars to house any prisoners who might arrive before the permanent structures were completed. In these temporary cells the first prisoners were confined when they arrived on October 1, 1849.

But what about the ghosts there? Well, most of the activity is in the east and south wings of the unit – both are part of the first building constructed at the prison. Although empty now, those wings were reportedly prime real estate for most of the prisoners. The cells were slightly larger than average, and were also cooler in the summer and warmer in the winter due to the heavy construction of the unit. It may be that with those comforts came a spirit or two. An inmate named Sam Houston (not the hero of Texas, but someone named for him), who was in and out of Huntsville State Prison for different crimes, apparently encountered several apparitions during his tenures there.

On one instance, for example, a guard was escorting Houston between the east and south wings, where a heavy armored door separated the two sections. Houston is said to have seen a spectral form in prisoner's garb step right through the door. As the story goes, he turned to the guard and asked if he'd seen the sprit. The guard said, "I sure did."

Another spirit said to frequent the Walls unit is the "Ax Man", a ghost who strolls down the hallway carrying a head in his hands. Sam Houston swears to have seen him, as have other inmates through the years.

The ghost of Chief Satanta of the Kiowa Indian tribe lingers in an area between the Walls unit and the walkway to the Death Chamber. On October 11, 1878, while the Chief was serving out a life sentence at the prison, he complained of a pain in his chest to the prison physician. He was taken to the prison hospital on the second floor, and when the doctor left him alone briefly the eerie strains of the Kiowa death song were heard issuing from the room. Satanta leapt headfirst from the second-story balcony to the ground below, killing himself rather than remaining imprisoned. A flowerbed marks the place where he died, and his presence has been reported there throughout the years by prisoners and corrections officers alike.

The haunting of the Walls Unit isn't restricted to specific ghosts, though. Guards have heard the clanging noises of cell doors opening and closing, when it would literally be impossible for that to occur.

The South Wing has its own special haunts. Directly below it is the old "Death Row" of the prison, containing nine small cells where prisoners spent their last days on Earth. The area is no longer used – the cell doors are open, and the death chamber where many inmates fell prey to the terrible electric chair has been sealed. The Death Row section is basically underground, and visitors there report a feeling of doom and dread. This area of the prison seems to be especially haunted, and probably with good reason. In an October 29, 1999 story in The Austin American-Statesman, the reporter tells the story of a Prison Supervisor who placed a voice-activated tape recorder in the old death row section: "When he played it back later for several correctional officers, they heard the clanging of cell doors and at the very end an unidentified voice saying 'Hey captain, hey captain...'"

Since there will always probably be a need for Huntsville State Penitentiary, the ghost stories from the Walls unit will probably continue to be told as well. This is one place, however, that I hope I never get to investigate!

A Monument to the Killough Massacre

Jacksonville, Texas

When I first started researching this chapter, I wasn't quite sure about it being a bona fide ghost story. I had been told about the spirit of an Indian in full battle dress appearing on a horse, and a mysterious fog that appeared even on warm, sunny days.

I thought that I'd investigate anyway, and it turned out to be one of the most interesting journeys that I made during this book.

It all started when I was putting together some information for another chapter. I heard about a huge monument in the pineywoods of East Texas that marked one of the worst Indian massacres in the history of this part of the state.

The story starts in December of 1837, well over a year after Sam Houston and his men soundly defeated General Santa Anna at the battle of San Jacinto, which won independence for Texas.

Issac Killough, Sr., moved his family from Talladega, Alabama to East Texas and purchased land from the newly formed Republic. The property had originally been part of a treaty settlement between the Texas Revolutionary Government and the Cherokee Indians negotiated by John Forbes, John Cameron and Sam Houston. In December of

1837, however, the Senate of the new nation of Texas nullified the treaty. The Cherokee weren't all that happy with the treaty because it greatly reduced their lands – since they were led to believe that it would give them a permanent home, however, they accepted the terms. Some bitterness still existed among many tribe members, and the nullification of the treaty only exacerbated those feelings. The stage was set for an inevitable clash between the Texans and the Cherokee.

On Christmas Eve of 1837, Issac Killough didn't know about this rising animosity with the natives. His four sons, two daughters and their husbands, and two single men, Elbert and Barakias Williams all settled on the land. Over the next several months they built houses, and planted crops to sustain their families.

The corn was ready to harvest by August, but word had reached the settlers of a growing threat by the Indians. The Killough party joined with other settlers and fled to Nacogdoches for safety.

In a month or so, the threat seemed to have dissipated, or so the Killoughs thought. They struck a bargain with the Indians to allow them to return to the land to harvest their crops, promising to leave before the first frost of winter.

Apparently not all of the Cherokees respected the arrangement, however, because on the afternoon of October 5, 1838, a renegade band attacked and killed or kidnapped eighteen unarmed members of the Killough party, including Issac Killough, Sr., himself.

The survivors, which included Issac's wife Urcey, began a harrowing journey to Lacy's Fort, forty miles south of the Killough settlement. When they arrived there safely, an enraged General Thomas J. Rusk organized a militia and rode out in search of the Indians. Rusk's men caught up with them near Frankston, and defeated them in a skirmish in which eleven of the Indians were killed.

The Killough Massacre was the largest Indian depredation

in East Texas. The bodies that were found were buried at the site, and in the 1930s the W.P.A. erected an obelisk made of stone to mark the location. In 1965 the cemetery was dedicated as a Texas Historical Landmark, and the area is now enclosed by a fence with a small parking lot beside it.

Before I actually visited the monument, I'd heard quite a bit about supernatural activity there, including the aforementioned sighting of a Cherokee warrior and the mysterious fog. Several paranormal investigators who'd been there had regaled me with stories of odd temperature readings, electric fields, and other scientific measurements often associated with ghosts. I wanted to see the place for myself, though, both for the historical aspects, as well as the spirits that might be showing up there.

I drove through Jacksonville, then headed north on highway 69. It wasn't long until I saw a sign that said,

"Killough Monument" with an arrow pointing to the west. I followed FM 855 a short distance until I came to an identical sign pointing south to FM 3405. I turned my vehicle in that direction, and started looking for the monument. Almost an hour later, I was still looking for it. There was a maze of little Farm/Market roads and I covered most of them; more than a few times I was sure that I was lost. I even stopped and asked people how to find the Killough Monument, but those few that had even heard of it couldn't tell me where it was. One gentleman offered the observation that, "I think it's around here somewhere, though."

I finally gave up, and pressed on to other destinations. By then it had become a quest for me, though, so I knew that I'd return with a more detailed map and much better instructions.

In a few weeks' time, I'd found someone to give me precise driving directions, and I followed them on an online map before ever leaving home. If the monument was where they said it was, I'd been all around it on my previous visit, and had even driven past the turn-off road.

Armed with that information, I set out for Jacksonville once again. Sure enough, I drove straight to the monument.

I have to say that when you first see it, the stone obelisk is quite impressive – the stone composition has the same look as W.P.A. buildings from the 1930's. The graves of those who were found dead are around its base, and the entire area is surrounded by a fence with a historical marker near the entrance. It is beautifully kept, and on that particular day, very serene.

When I got out of my car I noticed one thing that truly turned my stomach – someone had spray-painted a pentagram on the parking lot. If I live to be three hundred years old, I will still never understand how some people can bring themselves to vandalize property like that... especially at a sacred place such as a cemetery.

I just shook my head, sighed, and continued on. I walked

through the gate, and walked around to take a good look at the place. As I walked around inside the fence, a rush of emotion hit me – it was as if I was feeling an overwhelming sense of fear. I think that this was one of the strongest impressions that I had in the course of writing this book. It was literally all that I could do to keep from running back to my car and locking the doors.

There was certainly no rational reason for the feeling. The place seemed to be very safe, and although it was far out in the country, there were many homes within a short distance. I simply couldn't explain the feeling that I was experiencing, and the longer I stayed, the more intense it became.

The scientific side of me was questioning whether or not my imagination could simply be getting the best of me, but I dismissed that notion immediately. It was too strong a sensation, and try as I wanted, I couldn't get rid of the sense of dread.

As I snapped a few photos, I realized that I'd had as much as I could stand. Something was urging me to get away from there very quickly, so I did. I managed to keep from running, but I did walk rather quickly. I also couldn't help but look back over my shoulder again and again, since I was sure that something was coming for me.

I almost jumped into the car, slammed the door shut, and then hit the electric locks. I felt better, but not *that* much. It wasn't until I was several miles down the road that I was feeling like myself again.

Whether I had been influenced by supernatural forces at the massacre site, or I'd just picked up on the residual feelings from that terrible event, I'll probably never know. I want to go back though, if for no other reasons than to pay my respects to the settlers who are buried there. It was an experience that I want to explore further.

If you visit Killough Monument, please remember that is a memorial to a family who died in a very tragic way. As with any cemetery or sacred ground, be respectful, and please do not take anything out with you but photographs.

Killough Monument is not the easiest place in the world to find, so here are the directions to make it a little easier on you:

1. From the intersection of Highway 69 & Farm/Market (FM) Road 855 go west on FM 855 until you reach FM 3405. There is a sign there (or was at one time) that reads "Killough Monument" and points to the left.
2. Turn left on FM 3405 and go just about .4 miles to FM 3411.
3. Turn right on FM 3411 and go .6 miles until you reach a road with a green gate with a huge boulder on either side. That is actually FM 3431, but there is no sign there.
4. Turn left and proceed through the gate – the monument and cemetery are at the end of the road.

Of Moving Statues

and Other

Late-Night Frights

Jacksonville City Cemetery, Jacksonville

A recurring theme in the world of haunted places is cemeteries with statues that actually move – usually at midnight, and often after some harmless ritual is performed, such as the honking of your car horn or flashing of your automobile's lights.

As you probably know if you've read any of my books before, this is a sure sign of an urban legend. One golden rule of ghost hunting is that spirits never, ever show up on schedules that we dictate, and any legend that has some element like that in it is probably not true.

So while I'm usually cautious when I hear stories like that, I happed to be driving through Jacksonville and remembered one about a particular cemetery there. I found the cemetery, and with only a little bit of driving around, I ran across the statue itself: a stately portrayal of Mother Templeton.

The local legend says that on a night when the moon is full, Mother Templeton changes her stance on the pedestal where she looks out over the Templeton family plot.

Normally, her right hand is placed softly just below her heart, and her left hand hangs down by her side. If you believe what some people say, however, at various times she has been seen holding a bouquet of flowers, and at others clutching an open bible.

Now, keep in mind that this only occurs during a full moon – when I visited the cemetery, I only saw Mother Templeton in her normal stance.

Is this an urban legend? Of course it is! I do have to add one explanation for it, though, and it comes from the days of my youth. There was a cemetery near where I grew up that had a stature of Jesus standing out in front. His arms were outstretched as if welcoming in his flock. In those days, the story was told that if you went to the cemetery at night, turned off your headlights, and honked your car horn three times, something magical would happen. After performing that ritual, you would follow the road through the cemetery, and when you got back to the statue, the Lord would be holding his arms out in front of himself, instead of stretched out to the sides.

Know what? It worked. Really. I've seen it myself!

Okay, okay, you probably know me enough by now to guess that I'm being a little tongue-in-cheek. Jesus' arms weren't really moved out in front of his body, but at night – especially from the angle of the road that takes you back to the front of the cemetery – it certainly looked that way at a glance.

The way that the whole routine went is as follows. You would drive into the cemetery from the main entrance, and stop directly in front of the stature of the Lord. He was there in a classic pose, with arms outstretched to welcome you in. After doing the light flashing, horn-honking nonsense that was prescribed by other teenagers who'd been there in the past, you would take the winding drive through the cemetery with your lights off. When you came back around, you were approaching the statue from the right-rear, and as you came upon it, in the darkness, there was an illusion that the arms were stretched out in front.

Of course, at that point in the exercise no one drove back around front to take a better look. Instead, there was a lot of yelling from the guys, squealing from the girls, and the driver would floor the car and get out of the cemetery as soon as humanly possible. And from there, the story would spread... and every time it was told, a little more would be added.

I'm sure that the statue of Mother Templeton has some similar trait. Certainly, I'm dubious of the fact that ghosts are causing the stone to actually move. While I'm positive that spirits manifest themselves all the time as full-form apparitions, and that they can move objects around whenever they choose, I don't believe that they can actually twist the molecules of stone – something that they could have never done in life.

In fact, one of the most famous faked ghost videos was of

a graveyard where the statues were literally turning and looking around. It received a lot of notoriety, but close analysis showed a few tell-tale points that indicated a fabrication. The film-fakers finally confessed, and the ghost enthusiasts who were raving about it felt a little foolish.

In the case of Mother Templeton, the scenario is probably much the same as my own statue-story from my youth. As to her actual identity when she was alive, and the things that she did to warrant having a statue erected to her honor, that all remains a mystery. I'd absolutely love to know, though – that story would be infinitely more interesting than the tale of her moving statue.

Jacksonville City Cemetery
Jacksonville, Texas

The Shocking Lady of the Brick House

Karnack, Texas

I was digging through some archives in East Texas, hoping to find any leads for the book that I could follow, when I ran across an article from August 4th, 1974 in the "Marshall-News Messenger," entitled "Karnack's Good Ghost". It told the story of an old haunted mansion that was once the home to the distinguished First Lady of Texas, Mrs. Lyndon Baines Johnson, or as the whole world knows her, "Lady Bird". The brief mention in the article fascinated me, and I was off and running.

The place in question is called "Brick House". It is a ten room, two-story antebellum mansion that is located 2½ miles southwest of the city of Karnack on Highway 43. It was built in 1854 by Milton Andrews, who would go on to become a Colonel in the army of the Confederacy. While he was away fighting the war between the states, his nineteen year old daughter Eunice Andrews was seated alone in a rocking chair in front of the fireplace in her bedroom. As the story goes, there was a thunderstorm roaring outside, so she was probably reading or sewing by the fire for warmth. A freak of nature occurred that would leave its mark on the house forever: a bolt of lightning struck the chimney, and made its way down to the fireplaces, including the one in Eunice's room. She was struck by the killing fingers of the lightning, and fell forward into the fire. It was a tragic, horrible death.

At the turn of the century, a merchant named Thomas Jefferson Taylor came to Karnack from Alabama and established a general store. Out front was a sign that said, "T. J. Taylor – Dealer in Everything", and he meant it. The gentleman was an aggressive businessman who served the community well, and soon began to prosper. He and his wife, Minnie Patillo Taylor, lived in the apartment over the store where their two male children were born. Minnie was missing her family back in Alabama, and was growing tired of the cramped life above the store. She packed up the kids and took them back home for a visit, then sent word to T.J. that they would not return until he provided them a proper home. Since the business was thriving, he was able to purchase the Brick House from the Andrews family in 1902. Minnie returned with the boys and set up housekeeping there, not realizing that their new home came with an unseen occupant: the spirit of Eunice Andrews.

While strange things happened around the house, Eunice's presence was not specifically documented during the years that immediately followed. A decade from the time that Mr. Taylor purchased the mansion, the family was blessed with the birth of a baby girl on December 22, 1912 – Claudia Alta Taylor. Tragedy struck just five years later when Minnie Taylor died, leaving the family without a mother. The young girl would be raised by her father, an aunt, and the family servants.

Claudia remembers her childhood as being very lonely. She immersed herself in reading, especially about the flora and fauna of East Texas, and swam in the waters of Caddo Lake. As to the moniker by which we all know her, one story is that her nurse, Alice Tittle gave her the nickname when she was two years old when she described the little girl as being, "pretty as a lady bird." Another story indicates that it was her father, T.J. Taylor who bestowed the nickname on her, not the child's nurse. When Claudia was born, Taylor supposedly repeated the nursery rhyme, "Lady Bird, Lady Bird, fly away home, your house is on fire and your children will burn." No matter what the origin of the name was, it stuck, and Claudia became "Lady Bird" forever.

Now, Lady Bird's story could go on to how she attended the University of Texas, met Lyndon Baines Johnson in Austin and married him in November of 1934, or became First Lady of the nation on a fateful day in Dallas, Texas. None of this adds to the ghost story about the Brick House, though, because Lady Bird has never gone on record as having encountered the spirit of Eunice, although she admits feeling a sense of apprehension and unease in the house as a child.

Ghostly activity has been encountered by many people who have lived there over the years. The article in the Marshall News-Messenger that I mentioned earlier reported, "No one stays in her room, not since Mrs. Ray Aulding, a cousin of present occupant Jerry Jones, spent the night there only to be awakened by shutters banging, wind howling through the room and curtains moving as though someone were behind them. During storms one can hear the ghost's soft weeping, bemoaning her fate."

The article quotes Mr. Jones as saying that a family servant was outside on a balcony just off of Eunice's room, when he felt someone tap him on the shoulder. The man spun around to see that a woman was standing there that he'd never seen before. What happened next is a point of confusion; the servant was either pushed off of the balcony, or fell off himself, but he ended up on the ground with some minor bodily injuries. The man swore that he would never enter the house again.

The News-Messenger says that the lady of the house, Patricia Jones, was familiar with the spirit. "I can feel her... sometimes standing behind me, and when I turn there's no one around. I hear glass breaking and things falling to the floor at night." Of course, nothing broken was ever found. The article also indicates that the Jones' daughter, Angela, would not go into the room that had once belonged to Eunice. "She picked up my toothpaste one night, then threw it across the room," she related, "Then she started throwing everything." Jerry Jones told the paper that when his daughter ran down the stairs screaming, her eyes were as big as saucers. "She definitely saw something."

Apparently, since Jerry and Patricia Jones have owned the house, Eunice has settled down somewhat. They seemingly attribute that to their son Jett, who was six years old when the News-Messenger did the story on their family in 1974. Jett reportedly spoke to the ghost often, calling her "Oonie", short for Eunice. Jett described the girl as "white all over with black hair sticking straight up."

The Lubbock Avalanche-Journal did a story that included

the Brick House on October 2nd, 2001. Entitled, "A Tale of Texas Ghosts", Marjie Mugno reported that legendary Texas writer Frank X. Tolbert said that Lady Bird's brother, Tony, "has heard soft sobs coming from the room during storms. He even says he's seen the girl." The article goes on to report that, "Other relatives corroborate the presence of a spook. Mrs. Pauline Ellison of nearby Jefferson, a sister of T.J. Taylor's wife, Ruth, once said, 'I've spent many a night in the room and nothing has ever happened, except that one night, when all the windows were closed, the curtains began to move as if someone were walking around disturbing them. I don't believe in ghosts, yet how could the curtains move without air current?'"

The house is a private residence, so I would hope that everyone respects the current owners' privacy. For that reason, I didn't try to contact them, but I did find descriptions in several publications about Eunice's appearances. When she is seen, it isn't a transparent apparition – witnesses believe that they're seeing an actual person. The specter is a slightly built girl in a white dress with long sleeves. One feature that is always reported is her blond hair, which seems to be standing out away from her head. I picture someone from a science fair that I saw once, who was touching one of those big silver-lightening balls. Her hair was standing out from all of the static electricity, and maybe that's how Eunice appears in her old bedroom. From all reports, she isn't there all the time, but just makes an occasional appearance. Perhaps she's just looking back in from time to time to see how things are going in her old room, or maybe when a storm comes up she makes her presence known to warn others away from potential danger. Whatever the case, at times this childhood home of Lady Bird Johnson seems to be frequented by a spirit from its past.

The Ghostly Girl of Kilgore College

Kilgore, Texas

In all my wanderings, as I've gone about studying and documenting haunted places around the Lone Star state, I have noticed that most college campuses have a ghost story or two as part of their lore. Kilgore College is no exception, with a haunting tale of a young student who continues to inhabit one of the dorms there.

When I first arrived in Kilgore, I did a little digging into the background of the city itself. I had no idea whether or not any of the information would be pertinent to the ghostly girl, but it was fascinating nonetheless.

The City of Kilgore was founded in 1872 when the International & Great Northern Railroad established a rail line between Palestine and Longview. Even though the area had been settled by farmers long before the Civil War began, the railroad company formalized the town and named it for the man who'd sold the land: Constantine Buckley Kilgore. There is some speculation that the founding of a new town that would bear his name was part of the real estate negotiations, but there's no concrete evidence of that fact. It makes some sense, though – I could see Mr. Kilgore setting the price with the railroad company, then calling them back to the negotiating table, with a smile and the words, "Oh, there's one more thing that I'd like…"

No matter how it came to be, the town began to grow with the support of the railroad. A Post Office was opened there in 1873, followed by several businesses and a school to serve the children of the families there. Soon there were a couple of churches, a town newspaper, a hotel, a drugstore, two gristmill/cotton gins, and several stores – including an ice cream parlor. The farmers in the area focused on cotton crops, since their harvests could be ginned in town, and then shipped out on the railway. By early 1930 the Great Depression took its toll, however, and the downspiral of the cotton market dealt a harsh blow to the town and its people.

Kilgore seemed destined to dwindle away to a ghost town, until something happened that pumped a wave of much-needed life into the city: oil was discovered in East Texas in the fall of 1930. Thousands of people descended into Kilgore, looking for oil-field jobs and new starts for their families. Much of the town became a "tent city" for the workers, and over the next five years the population grew from 500 people to over 12,000. Oil wells sprouted up all over town, and one particular downtown block dubbed the "World's Richest Acre" had the most dense concentration of derricks in the entire world.

The oil boom finally waned, but its duration had provided Kilgore with the time and money that it needed to become an established East Texas city.

In 1935 when the petroleum business was in full swing, residents of the city decided that it would be advantageous for a local college to be established. Killgore College was founded under the supervision of the Kilgore Independent School District, and it operated under their guidance for the next decade. It became known statewide as a two-year school with programs in business, science, and the arts. In 1940, the Kilgore Rangerettes were organized; they are a nationally known precision drill corps of sixty-five girls who have entertained millions and can be seen in many national events, including the annual Macy's Thanksgiving Day Parade.

The College is a fascinating place to visit; along with all of the academic facilities on campus, Kilgore College is also home to the East Texas Oil Museum and the Kilgore College Rangerette Showcase & Museum. On-campus living is a feature that is provided to the students, even though most community colleges aren't residential facilities – something else that makes Kilgore College special. One of these is Cruce Stark Hall, a typical corridor-style dorm, but there's something very atypical about the place as well: Stark Hall has a spirited resident that refuses to leave.

Stories about the ghost of Stark Hall all seem to center around a female resident committing suicide there back when the dorm was an all-girl facility. She has never chosen to show herself to the residents through the years, so the fact that the spirit is considered to be feminine goes back to the legend of the Hall. Reports of her activity there continue semester after semester.

One of the most authoritative reports comes from the Magazine of Kilgore College, The Flare. Its October 25, 2002 issue recounts the legend of Stark Hall: "Many students who reside in Stark Hall believe that the ghost of a deceased student haunts the eighth floor of the hall. There is no single story as to who she is or how she died. Several students claimed that she committed suicide by jumping from the eighth floor window. Others say she hanged herself in her closet; still others believe she shot herself in her room. While the story surrounding the spirit is vague, students say her activity is very apparent. One student said he hears noises in the elevator throughout the night. Another said his belongings go missing on a regular basis. While no one said they have seen her, many believe she exists."

Students have reported walking into sudden pockets of icy air in the dorm, when the temperature is warm throughout the rest of the building. Others have heard footsteps, only to look out into the hallway to see that it is empty. Another of the spectral girl's habits is to tap on the hallway wall as she strolls along in the quiet, early hours of the morning.

Could she have been jilted by a boyfriend and decided to take her own life? Or perhaps she was failing her classes and couldn't bear to tell her family. It's even possible that she was with child and felt that taking her own life was the only way out of the humiliation. Who knows – maybe the spirit is really someone else, and not even that of a girl from the college's past. No matter who the ghost is that inhabits Stark Hall, reports of unexplainable noises, cold spots, and rapping on the walls along the hallway continue to be a part of the legends of Kilgore   College.

The Glowing Grave

Kilgore, Texas

As long as I was going to be visiting Kilgore to learn more about their famous college ghost, I started doing some investigation for any other haunted places in the city. One story that was told to me reeked of an urban legend, but I decided to look into it just to find out what the truth behind the tale was.

The basic plot of this ghost story is as follows: a young woman spent her life working in a nuclear power plant, but because of the poor safeguards at the plant, she was bombarded by radioactive rays every single workday. When she finally died, her body was buried at Danville Cemetery in Kilgore. The people of the town began to notice something very strange after her interment, however. A ghostly, green glow could be seen at night emanating from the ground where she was buried. Some people believed that it was the aftereffects of a career of radioactive exposure, while others who witnessed the phenomena were certain that it was her spirit still showing its presence as a warning to those who worked around hazardous material.

There were just too many things wrong about this story for me to take it seriously. First of all, if by some physical possibility her body was still glowing – which is not really a possibility – then it would certainly be shielded by the coffin and the concrete vault, not to mention six feet of East Texas dirt. On the other hand, if it was some type of apparition that just lied there and glowed, it would be the first that I've ever heard of that presented itself in such a manner. I just didn't buy the story, but my curiosity got the better of me, and I set off to find out what was behind the tale of the Glowing Grave.

This story could very well hold the record for the quickest investigation that I've ever conducted. Information about the radiation-lady and her burial in Kilgore was abundant, so I'll just summarize it here before moving to the real ghosts of East Texas.

The woman who is the basis for the tall Texas tale was actually born on February 19, 1946 in Longview, Texas. After graduating High School, she went on to study medical technology at Lamar State College in Beaumont, although she dropped out of the program after the first year. She married, had three children, and in 1972 discovered that her husband was having an extramarital affair. It was more than she could deal with, and she simply walked away from the family on a Saturday morning when her kids were watching cartoons. Her oldest daughter would later tell People Magazine in a 1999 interview that, "I was five, Michael was three and Dawn was 18 months. She said she was going out for cigarettes and would I watch my brother and sister. 'Keep an eye on your brother and sister.' That's all she said."

She found herself in Oklahoma, where she landed a job as a metallography laboratory technician at the Cimarron River plutonium plant of Kerr-McGee Nuclear Corporation, located in Crescent, Oklahoma.

Soon thereafter she joined the Oil, Chemical and Atomic Workers Union, and even participated in the union's strike against Kerr-McGee. The union lost the strike – and most of its members – but the woman had made an impression on her co-workers. In 1974 she became the first female member of the Union Bargaining Committee in Kerr-McGee history.

Since she was a member of that powerful union committee, she was re-assigned from her original responsibilities of grinding and polishing plutonium pellets for use in fuel rods to a position to study health and safety issues at the nuclear power plant. In carrying out her daily duties, she discovered evidence of spills, radiation leaks, and missing plutonium. When her employer was summoned before the Atomic Energy Commission, she testified that she herself had suffered radiation exposure over the course of employment at the plant.

During her testimony, she went on to say that the quality control on the fuel rods used in the reactor was faulty at best, and that reports of inspections had been falsified to allow all rods to be used, no matter what there physical state. Critics of the company have been quick to say that were it not for a bit of blind luck, the United States could have had its own Chernobyl.

All of this was big news, and she was contacted by a reporter from the New York Times who wanted to do a story on the Kerr-McGee plant and its irresponsibly in the manufacture of radioactive plutonium rods. The reporter got her to agree to a meeting where she would lay out some of the evidence that she'd gathered and turn the documents over to him. Also invited to attend was a member of the Atomic Energy Commission, since they were very interested in her findings as well.

She left the Hub Café in Crescent bound for Oklahoma City on November 13, 1974 at about 7:30 PM, driving her 1973 white Honda Civic. At 8:05 PM, the Oklahoma State Highway Patrol received a report of a single car accident. The State Trooper classified the accident as a driver who'd fallen asleep at the wheel, and the case was closed – at least for the moment.

Several other things point to a conspiracy in the death of the woman, not the least of which are suspicious dents on the rear of her car, as if she'd been forced off the road. Also, the documents that she was bringing to the reporter were never found. They should have been there in the car with her body and personal effects. She was 28 years old at the time of her death.

Her body was returned to Texas, and was buried in the Danville Cemetery in Kilgore. The headstone on her grave simply reads:

Karen Gay Silkwood
Feb. 19, 1946
Nov. 13, 1974
Rest in Peace

Does the name sound familiar? It should – just think back to the movie "Silkwood" where Meryl Streep portrayed her character, and Cher played her best friend.

Trying to be a thorough journalist, I went out to Danville Cemetery as dusk fell one early spring evening, and paused at the grave of Karen Silkwood. The cemetery plot wasn't glowing green, and I found no indication that her restless spirit might be roaming the graveyard. Instead, I found a little solace in the fact that even though the mysterious circumstances surrounding her death will probably never be solved, Karen seems to be resting peacefully underneath the East Texas sky.

Danville Cemetery
On FM 2087, south of highway 349

The Light of a Loving Mother

Kilgore, Texas

As long as we're talking about ghostly graveyards in Kilgore, there is a legend that is associated with Pirtle Cemetery there.

Visitors to the cemetery in the evening have reported seeing a glowing light, dancing and flickering like a small flame.

While I didn't see it during my visit there, the story of it has been passed down for generations. The tale goes back to the pioneer days of log cabins and oil lanterns. A couple lived in the Pirtle community near Kilgore with their small son.

Although he was a normal child in every way, the boy had the same phobia that many children do – a fear of the dark. When his parents put him to bed every night, he would cry and cry until his mother would light a lantern and put it in his room until he fell asleep.

The child fell ill, and since doctors were few and far between in those days, he became worse and worse. Tragically, the son died, and the parents were inconsolable – especially his mother.

After the funeral, the woman couldn't stand the fact that her little boy was buried out in the cemetery where it was so dark every evening. On the evenings when she couldn't stand the pain of losing her son, she would take a lantern out to the graveyard and put it on the tombstone.

Eventually the parents died, and were buried beside their boy. According to the legend, people who were passing by the cemetery in the evening would occasionally see a light shining out among the headstones. The locals assumed that the spirit of the mother was still providing a light for her little boy, so that he wouldn't be afraid in the dark.

I'm the first one to say that this story has all the trappings of an urban legend. There is no specific name mentioned, so it is impossible to find the exact marker. Also, I couldn't find anyone who had actually seen the light for themselves.

Still, I hate to dismiss ghost lights so quickly. There are many places around the state where they have not only been documented, but also filmed and studied. There is some argument as to whether such lights are swamp gas, reflections of other light sources, and so forth, but the fact of such lights remain.

As to the loving mother who is reported to be providing a light for her afraid-of-the-dark son, who knows. I'd be tempted to go back to the cemetery at dusk a few times, just to see for myself. True or not, however, it's a wonderful story!

The Lady of Fort Boggy

Leona, Texas

Fort Boggy is a place lost to time – very few people have ever heard of it nowadays. In fact, as I was researching this book I would ask folks, "Have you ever heard of Fort Boggy? It's an old place built on Boggy Creek."

Everyone had the exact same reply: "I've never heard of Fort Boggy, but I saw that movie about the bigfoot monster on Boggy Creek!"

Close, but as they say, no cigar. All of the hoopla surrounding the Fouke Monster, subject of the 1970-something movie named *The Legend of Boggy Creek*, took place just over the border in Arkansas. This is a different Boggy Creek – the one in East Texas.

To get a little more information, I consulted the Handbook of Texas Online (www.tsha.utexas.edu/handbook/online/). I found out that Fort Boggy was actually a two-story log structure, and had been constructed in 1839 by a company of Texas Rangers. It was located about two miles north of the present-day town of Leona on Boggy Creek, and was built to offer settlers in the area protection from Indian attacks.

A community soon began to grow around the fort, including a general store and a sawmill that would be instrumental in milling the wood to build new structures.

Although the settlers were afraid of being wiped out by an Indian attack, something entirely different sealed their fate. A Cholera epidemic swept through the people of Fort Boggy, killing almost everyone there. Soon Fort Boggy wasn't even listed on maps, and was well on its way to being forgotten.

So why is all this so interesting? Well, it goes back to when a friend of mine, Elaine Coleman, visited the site of Fort Boggy. Elaine is a talented author, and wrote the wonderful book, *Texas Haunted Forts*. If it's not a part of your collection, it definitely should be.

Ms. Coleman tells the story of Dr. Whitehead and his wife Martha, who lived around the two-story blockhouse fort that was built in 1839. Established as a fort to protect the settlers, it soon supported a settlement that grew up around the fortress. The settlement sported a general store, a sawmill, and a doctor... Dr. Whitehead, in fact.

There were Indian attacks on the fort that certainly took their toll, and it was a drain on the settlers' morale and supplies. To make matters worse, in the spring of 1841 a cholera epidemic nearly wiped out the entire settlement.

When they moved to Fort Boggy, Martha had fallen in love with an ancient oak tree that was outside of the walls of the fort. When life would get too tough for her, she would stroll under its branches to find solace.

Martha fell ill to cholera, and her fever soared. Her husband tended her as best as he could, but she was slowly slipping away. Her last wish was that her body be buried under the oak tree that she loved so well, and her husband Dr. Whitehead promised to do so.

When she slipped away, a grave-digging detail went outside to honor her last wish – to dig Martha's grave under the oak tree. As they dug down, however, the hole started to fill with water. The diggers reported back to Dr. Whitehead that his selected site was not practical; the water table was just too high.

The gravesite was moved to a knoll overlooking Fort Boggy and the massive oak tree – interesting things began to happen around the fort after that.

The most chilling occurrence was a wailing that was heard when the night was clear and still – the sounds seemed to be coming from up on the knoll. It was assumed to be the voice of Martha Whitehead, who was mourning the fact that she wasn't buried under the oak tree that she loved so much. The stories persisted as long as the fort was standing.

In today's world, nothing is left of the fort or the old oak tree. The only remnant of Fort Boggy is the name that persists through the ages, and stories of Martha that continue on.

The Starr Home of Maplecroft

Marshall, Texas

One interesting thing about writing this book is that once people find out about it, they come out of the woodwork with ghost stories. Occasionally, I'd hear the same one from a couple of different sources, which made the place in question worth checking out – such was the case with the stately Starr Home of Marshall, Texas, otherwise known as "Maplecroft".

I was looking forward to visiting Marshall, because I already knew a bit about its history. The town was founded in 1839, and in 1842 became the seat of Harrison County. One of the most fascinating things about this Texas town is that it was once the capitol of Missouri, believe it or not! As Civil War loomed across the country in the mid-1800s, states began to choose sides. Texas seceded from the Union on February 2, 1861, and at that time, Marshall was a thriving metropolitan area. It was the center for the manufacture of many goods that were used to supply the Confederate troops: black powder, ammunition, clothing, saddles, and harnesses. Many of these items were shipped out of the riverport of Jefferson – in fact, the powder magazines where the explosive was stored awaiting shipment can still be seen standing on the shores of the Big Cypress Bayou there.

Back in Missouri, though, there was a lot of controversy.

The state itself favored secession, so the people put a Secessionist government in place, then prepared to join the Confederacy. Union troops were quickly dispatched to occupy the border state, because the President feared that it would be strategic in the upcoming conflict. The Secessionist government fled to Texas, and established Marshall as the capital in exile.

That's just one of many interesting things about Marshall – but certainly the crowning jewel of the city is Maplecroft, the mansion built by the Starr Family, and the next place on our agenda to go ghost-hunting.

The building of the house was commissioned in 1870 by James Franklin Starr, and was constructed by shipwrights and other craftsmen using materials from the East Texas area and as far away as New Orleans. It was built on the site of an antebellum plantation named Rosemont, and although the plantation home was demolished to make way for Maplecroft, a portion remained and was converted into a schoolhouse for the Starr family children, and then later into a laundry.

In 1976 Maplecroft and the surrounding buildings were donated to the Texas Parks and Wildlife Department, and stands much as it has though the ages. My wife and I arrived at the home on a warm summer's day, ready for a tour and a few ghost stories on the side.

The first thing that I noticed was the sunburst front gate – if it was an indication of how ornate the house was going to be on the inside, I knew that we were in for a treat.

Since it is a Texas State Park, we were met at the door by a park ranger in uniform who played a short film on the history of the house. There was a nominal charge for admission – not much at all. Since we were the only ones there that weekend, we were granted our own private tour, and we stepped into the hall to explore Maplecroft.

The inside of the house reminded me of Greek Revival architecture. There was a hallway in the middle, with rooms on both sides. A large stairway going up to the second floor dominated the front part of the hall, and my wife couldn't help but ask the obvious question: "Do we get to go upstairs?"

Our guide smiled and replied, "I'll be showing you the entire house."

Next it was my turn. "So, I've heard that the place is haunted by the spirit of a woman – have you seen anything like that?"

This time she stopped, turned around and looked right at me. "There aren't any ghosts here!" she said with a scoff. "And I'm usually here quite a bit by myself. You'd think I might notice something like that."

As she resumed our tour, my wife and I just looked at each other and shrugged. If there were anything there, hopefully we'd run across it.

We walked through the formal dining room, the breakfast

nook, and the other downstairs rooms. The antiques were beautiful, the décor made you feel like you were back in the 1800s, and our guide told some wonderful stories about the house and the Starr family. There was nothing about the downstairs that seemed haunting or mysterious, though.

When our guide stepped away to turn on some air conditioners, my wife asked me about the stories that I'd heard about Maplecroft. I quickly relayed the accounts that had been given me: Footsteps are sometimes heard in the hallways of the house, people catch the glimpse of a woman walking through the hallways out of the corner of their eye, and an occasional whiff of perfume lingers on the air when no one else is present in the house.

We'd seen nothing of the kind so far, but we still had high hopes as our guide re-appeared and led us upstairs. The bedrooms were palatial and extravagant, and whoever was handling the decoration of the house had it perfectly appointed. On every bed was an antique gown from the family laid out on display, and there were family photographs hanging on the walls of most every room.

There was also a different feeling to the house upstairs. It seemed quieter, yet more intense. I can't report that we encountered the female spirit of Maplecroft during our visit there, but *if* she were to be found walking through the empty rooms of the house, I feel certain that it would be upstairs. It just felt, well, *different* up there.

We're definitely going back for a visit. On a different day, who knows what we might find there.

One thing is certain – it is a wonderful old home, very representative of the time period, with a history that anyone will be fascinated to hear. And maybe, just maybe, there is a ghostly woman who still visits the house when everything is still and quiet.

Starr Family Home State Historical Site
407 W. Travis St.
Marshall, TX 75670
903-935-3044

Chester, the Thespian Ghost

Nacogdoches, Texas

Why do spirits seem to always be found in theaters? I certainly don't know. Maybe it's the emotionally charged plays that are performed there over the years that attract a ghost or two. Or perhaps it is the strong devotion to the craft that thespians seem to have that causes them to return to the stage for an occasional visit. Whatever the case may be, show me a theater, and I'll show you a ghost.

One legendary example is a fellow known only as "Chester", a lively specter who takes an occasional curtain call at the Turner Auditorium at Stephen F. Austin State University in Nacogdoches.

The William M. Turner Auditorium is a part of the Griffith Fine Arts Center at the university. The complex is a wonderful place for both academia and visitors alike – it has been host to some of the world's most famous touring companies, yet it offers students a place to hone their craft with two lab theaters, classrooms, and the offices and facilities for the College of Fine Arts and the Department of Theatre.

Talk to any student who's spent time there, and you'll hear several legendary tales about Chester. One of the most common descriptions of him is simply a feeling that occurs when there are only a few people in the building. Just imagine being alone in the theater, sitting on the edge of the stage with your feet dangling off. It's dark and quiet, so much so that your breathing seems to echo through the empty hall. If I were to slip in through a side door, take off my shoes, and start sneaking across the stage with as much stealth as I could muster, at some point you'd get that eerie feeling that someone was watching you. We've all had it. Chances are that as I got closer you'd feel it stronger, until you finally turned around to catch me creeping up on you.

That's how people describe Chester's presence, although on some occasions he has made himself known in a more tangible manner. When a few lone actors have been rehearsing on the stage, the curtains have been seen rustling as if someone was walking behind them. Thinking themselves alone, the actors rushed to see who might be passing through backstage, but no one was there.

On other occasions, a solitary person on stage has heard footsteps on the overhead scaffolding as if a stagehand was pacing back and forth to adjust the lighting or prepare a backdrop. Calling up to the person above, there is no answer, because no one is there. There is something about the theater scaffolding, though. At other times dust has gently drifted down in waves to the stage, just like someone was disturbing the matrix of walkways and props overhead. All heads look up, but again, no one is there.

Chester has tapped actors on the shoulder, been blamed for the disappearance and reappearance of countless objects, and has even been heard pacing the backstage area.

Only once has the mysterious Chester been seen, and that was back in 1987 during a performance of "The Scottish Play", which non-thespians know as Shakespeare's "Macbeth". A ghostly scene in the play was represented by a projection of eight spectral faces onto a stage backdrop. Only the actors noticed that there were nine faces there during the play – of course, Chester was blamed.

But perhaps it isn't that odd that Macbeth was the play where Chester manifested himself. A legend has surrounded the play from the time that it was first produced on stage, which may explain why the spirit of the Turner Auditorium chose that time to appear to the audience. In any theater where the play is produced, its name is never spoken aloud, and it is simply referred to as "The Play", "The Unmentionable", or "The Scottish Play" by the staff – to do otherwise would bring misfortune down upon the actors. In many cases, props are destroyed once they are used in Macbeth, because they tend to bring bad luck upon future productions.

Some blame the scene with the witches for the curse, saying that Shakespeare himself wove actual spells into the text of the play. Others point out that because there is quite a bit of physical action in Macbeth, someone inevitably gets injured in most productions. Perhaps the explanation is just that simple.

On the other hand, during its premier on August 7, 1606, the actor portraying Lady Macbeth died backstage during the opening performance. In a 1934 production, three different actors in the role of Macbeth quit within the period of one week, with no explanation. Other injuries and deaths are associated with the play throughout the years, making actors around the globe weary to tempt the fates associated with the play.

Did the staging of a cursed play give the spirit of Chester the chance to play a bit onstage? Who knows. Maybe there is some magic in Shakespeare's words:

> *Round about the cauldron go;*
> *In the poisoned entrails throw.*
> *Toad, that under cold stone*
> *Days and nights has thirty-one*
> *Swelteed venom, sleeping got,*
> *Boil thou first in the charmed pot.*
> *Double, double toil and trouble:*
> *Fire, burn; and cauldron, bubble.*
> *Fillet of a fenny snake,*
> *In the cauldron boil and bake;*
> *Eye of newt, and toe of frog,*
> *Wool of bat, and tongue of dog,*
> *Adder's fork, and blind-worm's sting,*
> *Lizard's leg, and howlet's wing,*
> *For a charm of powerful trouble,*
> *Like a hell-broth boil and bubble.*
> *Double, double toil and trouble:*
> *Fire, burn; and cauldron, bubble.*

No matter what happened on that night when "The Scottish Play" was produced in the Turner Auditorium, the existence of Chester seems to be a reality to the people who work there. He has been called the spirit of an architect who designed the theater, and is so proud of his work that he periodically returns to inspect the building and poke his nose into what is going on there. Others believe Chester to be a former drama student who is coming back for a recurring role at Stephen F. Austin University. Still another theory is that the spirit lingers from a time long before the university was formed, when the area that is now Nacogdoches was part of the frontier. He might be a carry-over from those past times, when the gentle piney woods of East Texas saw bloody Indian battles, brutal conflicts during the Civil War, or patriot's blood shed for the independence of the Republic of Texas.

It really doesn't matter who he is or why he's there; Chester seems to be a very benevolent spirit intent solely on gracing the stage at the Turner Auditorium. Unless you're an actor there, chances are that you'll never cross his path. Unless, of course, a production of "The Scottish Play" is being done, in which case there will be at least one guaranteed presence in the theater – I'll be sitting there in the front row, hoping to catch a glimpse of Chester.

William M. Turner Auditorium
The Griffith Fine Arts Center
Stephen F. Austin State University
Nacogdoches, Texas

LaNana Creek and the Eyes of father Margil

Nacogdoches, Texas

That's an ominous chapter title, to be sure, but I promise you that there are no stories of disembodied eyes floating along this creek in Nacogdoches – in fact, there doesn't seem to be a ghost story here at all. It was so interesting, and did involve a supernatural event, that I decided to tell the story anyway.

In fact, if you were to find your way to LaNana Creek, you would find yourself at the site of a genuine, bonafied miracle.

Most places associated with miracles are visited by pilgrims, especially those involving water. Take the French spring of Lourdes, for example, where three million bathe every year hoping to be healed by the waters that are reportedly the site of an appearance of the Blessed Virgin.

In East Texas, though, the miraculous LaNana Creek is not as famous. It therefore doesn't have the patronage that its distant cousin Lourdes does.

Before visiting the creek, I thought that it was a good idea to first familiarize myself with the perpetrator of the miracle – a holy man of the Franciscan order known as the Venerable Antonio Margil.

Margil was born in Valencia, Spain, on August 18, 1657, and immediately showed a propensity for service to the church. He joined the Franciscan order in 1672. After ten years of dedication to the Catholic Church in Spain, he was ordained as a priest and received an assignment to go to New Spain as a missionary. First he served at the Missionary College of Santa Cruz de Queratero in Costa Rico, then was one of the founders of the Missionary College of Nuestra Senora de Guadalupe de Zacatecas in 1706.

Following in the footsteps of the military commander Domingo Ramon, he journeyed into East Texas to further the cause of the church. Margil always traveled on foot, so the fact that he covered so many miles is truly amazing. In fact, it earned him the nickname "The Wing-Footed Friar" among his peers.

Because of his mode of transportation, Margil had to deal with the harsh extremes of weather, attacks from predatory animals, periods without water or food, and encounters with hostile natives who often beat, tortured, and abandoned the priest. He almost didn't survive the trip into Texas, and in fact, after crossing the Rio Grande Margil had developed such a high fever that his traveling companions were certain that he would not survive. They gave Father Margil the Last Rites, made him as comfortable as possible, then left him there by the river to die.

But he didn't. Instead, he made a remarkable recovery and even managed to catch up with his fellow travelers.

During 1716 he visited four East Texas missions, including one in Nacogdoches, before traveling on to establish several new ones, including Nuestra Senora de los Dolores,

San Miguel de los Adaes, and the most successful mission in Texas, San Antonio de Aguayo in San Antonio... better known as The Alamo.

It was during his visit to the Mission of Our Lady of Guadalupe in Nacogdoches, Texas when the miracle attributed to him occurred. He was traveling with a group from the mission to a village outside of Nacogdoches, when the group stopped to rest. They were severely dehydrated because of a drought in the region, and were having to go without water. The people with him were about to collapse, when Antonio Margil walked into a dry creek bed before them. He turned and addressed his colleagues, saying, "Do not be dismayed – do not be frightened. Trust in God, soon you shall have water." He then raised his walking stick and struck a dry rock twice. Suddenly, fresh water began to flow from the two places where his staff touched. After the group had quenched their thirst with the cool liquid, they pressed on. The story of his miracle began to spread, and the water from the two holes – which reminded people of two eyes – continued to service the mission until the rains came and rejuvenated the creek.

The Venerable Antonio Margil had many more years of service before returning to New Spain, where he fell ill in 1726. The day before his death, he was laying sick in bed and his attendants brought a picture of Our Lady of Remedies to him for inspiration. Margil managed a smile, spoke a gentle greeting, then added "Hasta manana, my dearly beloved Lady, until tomorrow." The next day, on the feast of the Transfiguration, he quietly slipped away.

The Vatican Congregation for the Causes of Saints indicates that the decree for the introduction of the cause of Margil was given on July 19, 1769 and the decree of declaration of the virtues of Margil was given on June 31, 1836. This second decree completed the process towards beatification and canonization except for the required miracles, and granted the Margil the title of "Venerable".

Upon verification of the miracle by the Catholic Church, Margil will be beautified. If a second miracle can be proven, he will be canonized.

As to the stream where the Venerable Margil caused the fresh water to flow forth, it is now known as LaNana Creek in the city of Nacogdoches. The place where the miracle is thought to have occurred is marked on the creek trail. Many people believe that the water from the "eyes" where Margil struck his staff continues to flow into the creek, joining the other water there.

Now, I'm not sure about that story, but I'm not one to trifle with possibilities. Since I have a touch of high blood pressure, I knelt down beside the stream, scooped up a handful of water, and rubbed it on my chest. Who knows, I may have inadvertently discovered what pilgrims who are flying over to Lourdes in France have been missing right here in East Texas.

The Wailing Woman
of Fort Sherman

Pittsburg, Texas

In the early 1800s one of the most serious problems that the early settlers had was Indian attacks. Now, I realize that there are certainly things that can be argued from here to eternity about the Native Americans and the settlers, who was right and who was wrong, and about fifty degrees of political correctness. The fact is, though, that I have blood in my veins from many nations, including the Cherokee, so I have ancestors on both sides of the Indian War. For that matter, so does my wife. If nothing else, I guess that gives me the ability to at least tell this sad story.

In 1838, the settlers in East Texas were having a particular problem. As they were establishing homes, ranchland and farms, the buffalo were slowly being forced westward. Since the Cherokee were so dependent on the animals for the lives of the tribe, they stepped up their aggression in a final effort to drive the settlers back out of the East Texas area. As a result, Captain W.B. Stout was dispatched with a garrison of men to establish a stronghold in the area. His charter was to protect the civilians for as long as necessary, using whatever force was required. Captain Stout and his men built a small, but stout stronghold and named it Fort Sherman.

Today, you won't find much of anything that remains of

the fort – just a cemetery on the ground of Lake Bob Sandlin State Recreation Area, and a campground named after the fort.

In some ways that is unfortunate, because the fort is an important footnote in the history of East Texas.

There were quite a few battles there. Although the many deaths on both sides that resulted from the many skirmishes were all tragedies, one particularly sad tale has been handed down over the years about a young Cherokee woman named Little Creek. During one of the battles, her husband – and the father of her three sons – feel prey to a soldier's bullet. When the other warriors returned with his body, Little Creek sang the Cherokee's song of death for him, grieving for her beloved man.

Little Creek had no family other than her three sons, so the duty of providing for them fell to her. She was an honorable woman, and although she wasn't as versed in the hunting ways as her husband was, she donned his deerskin robe and took his bow and arrows to try and find game. It was a fruitless day, and she was forced to return home to her family without meat. While others in the tribe might have shared, she felt compelled to complete the task herself.

As she walked back to the Cherokee camp, more sad and depressed than ever, a whiff of fresh meat roasting over an open flame drifted to her on the breeze. She followed the scent, and soon spotted Fort Sherman. Little Creek found a hiding place in the brush near the fort's perimeter, and waited for night to fall.

Under a cloak of darkness, she carefully crept into the fort and began a systematic search for the smokehouse where the meat would be kept. It was an arduous task to keep the stillness of the night as she crept from building to building, yet Little Creek managed. Finally, her persistence paid off – she found a store of buffalo meat, and took enough to feed the family for many days.

Coming into the fort she had moved with stealth and speed, but as she left the young Cherokee woman found herself balancing an awkward load, and making much more noise than she should have.

She hadn't quite reached the wall of the fort when a sentry confronted her at rifle-point. He ordered her to stop, and show her hands, but Little Creek panicked and tried to run for her freedom. A single shot rang out through the silence of the evening, and the young widow fell to the ground. As the sentry tried to determine whether or not he'd hit the intruder, she managed to pull herself up and slip away with a good portion of the meat that she'd taken.

It was a long, painful struggle to return to the Cherokee camp, but Little Creek finally arrived. As the legend goes, she laid out the meat in front of her three boys, told each of them goodbye, then stumbled out to the place where the fallen warriors were laid out to rest. She pulled herself to the base of her husband's death scaffold, and through the silence of the night, began to sing the Cherokee song of death as she slowly slipped away.

The Cherokee were slowly pushed back over the next few months, and by 1839 had been forced out of East Texas. Having done their job, Captain Stout and his men packed up their supplies and abandoned Fort Sherman. Soon, the only thing that gave any indication that a settlement had been there was the old cemetery on the grounds of Lake Bob Sandlin State Park.

When I was researching this chapter, I visited Lake Bob Sandlin State Recreation Area to find out a little more about the old fort. The rangers there were very familiar with Fort Sherman. When I asked about its exact location, one of the rangers told me that it is currently believed that the waters of Lake Bob Sandlin cover the original site. He was quick to add that in building the lake, no relics or any other archeological pieces were found, so they don't believe that anything was destroyed in the process. Whatever was once there all those years ago has long been erased.

As I walked the pathways around the cemetery, I stopped to visit with a fellow and in the course of conversation I asked if he had been there before.

He said that his family loved the lake, and camped there whenever they had the opportunity. When I brought up the subject of Fort Sherman, he told me that he'd seen the signs and the graveyard, but didn't know the story behind it.

Of course, I couldn't help but share what I knew. When I mentioned Little Creek, and the fact that some claimed to hear her voice singing through the pines, he just grinned. "Well, I don't know about any of that. Here at night, though, when the wind is blowing across the lake into the trees you do hear some mighty strange things."

Like I said before, it is too bad that nothing is left to commemorate the fort but a cemetery.

That, and a mysterious chant that some say can be heard in the evening hours when the night is still. As I continued to walk the area, I never heard Little Creek's death song on the wind, but I had to stand there in awe of the chapter in East Texas history that had taken place there all those years ago. It reminded me that even though I might find myself on the most innocuous country trail, its history might be something unimaginable by its appearance today.

Lake Bob Sandlin State Park
341 State Park Road 2117
Pittsburg, TX 75686
903-572-5531

The Ghost Road Light

Saratoga, Texas

It's a dark, moonless night in Hardin County. You're driving along the backroads, and turn onto Farm-to-Market Road 787 – or FM 787 as it's known locally – and something very strange occurs. At the end of the road ahead of you there is a soft glow, a hovering light that seems to be taunting you, weaving about as if it is studying you as much as you are watching it.

What is this strange phenomenon? The Ghost Road light, of course, a regular occurrence in Hardin County. It's been called the Bragg Road Light, the Hardin County Light, the Ghost Road Light, and many other names on television shows and in printed media. What the light might actually be has been the subject of much debate over the years, and to be honest, to this day no one knows for sure. It has been well documented in photographs, and studied by many reputable sources such as National Geographic. With all of the stories surrounding it, there is one fact that cannot be disputed: the light exists.

The road itself has its origin back in the logging days of East Texas, long before the timber giants of today established controlled cutting and re-planting procedures. The entire area was known as the Big Thicket because of its wealth and population of native trees, with dense, impassible underbrush.

To this day it is said to be one of the most biologically diverse places around. A large number of bird species stopped there on annual treks, and wildlife inhabiting the Thicket included wild rabbit, deer, wolves, panthers, bears and too many others to list here. They made their home among the trees, and humans who wandered in had to be exceptionally careful to find their way back out. With a simple turn in the wrong direction, one tree would start looking like the next. When you were in the Big Thicket, there were no defining landmarks to guide your way. The darkness of the forest would simply close in on you.

Anticipating the wealth of raw resources there, the Gulf, Colorado and Santa Fe Railway (GCSF) bought a nine-mile right-of-way through the land in 1902. They saw an unlimited potential of hauling lumber out of the thicket off to mills, moving oil as wells spread across Texas, and also hoped to capitalize on the additional revenue from carrying livestock to market. Of course, any passenger trade would be icing on the financial cake. The railroad started at their main line at the small town of Bragg, which had been named for Confederate General Braxton Bragg, and chopped their way south through the forest to the town of Saratoga. The last bit was cleared in January of 1904, and the GCSF begin laying timbers and tracks for the railroad spur.

Rumors of hauntings along the railway line begin circulating almost immediately. One story attributed the ghost to a Union sympathizer during the Civil War. During that time, the Thicket was a natural place for criminals and such to hide out, and Confederate troops would set fire to the forest to flush out the unsavory characters there. As the legend goes, the troops were doing a routine burning when they saw a known Yankee sympathizer running from the flames. Several soldiers opened fire, killing the man, then leaving his body to be consumed by the fire and the forest. His ghost was said to walk through the forest in the form of a glowing light, walking the escape path that he'd taken that fateful day.

Other people claimed that the spirits went further back in time, when Spanish soldiers occupied the area. In their quest for treasure and the legendary "Seven Cities of Gold" the Spaniards actually found very little wealth. What they did find, this story tells, they hid in the Thicket to return and retrieve later. The plan of those scheming conquistadors was discovered, and although the men were executed as traitors, searchers could not find the treasure that they'd hidden in the forest. The mysterious light was supposedly one of those slain solders, vigilantly guarding their treasure even after his death.

One more explanation for the ghostly light seen along the railroad line was that it was the spirit of a hunter who had ventured into the Big Thicket in search of game, even though he wasn't familiar with the terrain there. After a successful day of shooting small game, he headed back toward home, but had become hopelessly lost in the dense forest growth. Because of the abundance of animals and edible plants, he is said to have survived for quite some time before falling prey to one of the perils of the Thicket. In this version of the story, the light is the ghost of the hunter, still wandering the forest in search of a way home.

These stories were all circulating at the time when the GCSF Railway was still in operation, so reports of the mysterious light easily date back to the early 1900s.

After thirty years of operation, the Saratoga Branch ceased to be profitable. Mr. Cowley, the GCSF Gulf Division Superintendent, is quoted as saying, "The Gulf, Colorado and Santa Fe Railway enjoyed a good business out of Saratoga after the construction of the line for several years, but it dwindled away due to the construction of pipelines for the handling of the oil and to the diminution of the lumber traffic. There were several mills on the line, one principal one operated by the McShane Lumber Company, which cut out in 1915. Subsequently, traffic into and out of Saratoga dwindled down to merchandise, flour and feed and gasoline, and outbound logs or stave blocks or staves, but each year the traffic of the branch decreased." In 1933, the railroad spur was abandoned.

Hardin County purchased the right-of-way from the GCSF in 1934 with the idea that it would make a good county road out to Saratoga, and its road crews set about the process of pulling up the rails and digging up the timbers. The road was built, and the sightings of the ghostly light continued.

Throughout the years, the topic of harvesting lumber from the Big Thicket has been broached by several corporations, so to try and preserve the beautiful forest the Big Thicket Association was formed. In 1995, the Association commissioned a study of the bio/ecology of the area around Bragg Road (as the county highway had come to be known). Several different ecosystems were discovered to exist there, including Baygall, Prairie, Palmetto Flat, and Wetland Savannah. According to this study, over forty different types of trees and shrubs were identified, over thirty types of flowering plants, and other vegetative species such as ferns and vines.

Armed with this information, a fight to preserve the area around Bragg Road was launched and on July 28, 1997 the Hardin County Commissioners Court voted to designate the area as the "Ghost Road Scenic Drive County Park", insuring that it would be protected in the future.

The current story that a visitor is likely to hear today concerns a brakeman who was killed in a tragic train wreck. There are several versions of the story circulating around, but the more interesting ones have the poor man getting decapitated in the accident – of course, they only found his body. The brakeman apparently still walks the path of the tracks, looking for his missing head. An addendum to the story goes that a decade after the wreck, another train was rolling down the track on a moonless, stormy evening when they saw a light swinging back and forth on the tracks ahead. The engineer slowed the locomotive, and as it came to a stop the crew saw that a huge tree trunk had been blown over the tracks. It would have spelled disaster had the train hit it at full speed, probably causing a derailment and disaster to everyone on board. When the train crew jumped down to try to move the tree trunk, they began searching for the man whose light had saved their lives, he was no where to be found – they decided that it was the spirit of the brakeman who'd helped them advert danger that night.

As rousing a story as the beheaded brakeman makes, it is probably not an accurate account of what is happening out on Bragg Road. I couldn't find any accounts of train wrecks on the nine-mile spur during its thirty years of operation, and the fact that the light was appearing even as the railroad was being constructed indicates that the mysterious glowing objects pre-dates the first train through that part of Big Thicket.

Skeptics like to write off the light to some kind of luminous "swamp gas", while others say that it is only the reflection of car headlights. Of course, headlights certainly don't translate well to when the light was first reported so many years ago. Still, everyone has an explanation or opinion. The one thing that no one can dispute is that the light is there – just ask National Geographic, because even though they can't explain it, they saw that it was undeniably there.

Ghost Road begins at a bend on F.M. 787, 1.7 miles north of the intersection of F.M. 787 and F.M. 770, near the town of Saratoga. You can get more information on the Big Thicket, or Ghost Road itself, by contacting The Big Thicket Association, P.O Box 198, Saratoga, Texas 77585.

Hauntingly Beautiful Scottsville Cemetery

Scottsville, Texas

While researching this book, I never ceased to be amazed at the coincidences that occurred – one of my favorites happened in the fall when I was just starting to do a little digging on the ghosts of East Texas. My wife and I received a call from some friends of ours who were going on an annual excursion out to a small cemetery in Scottsville, Texas. We were invited to make the drive about ten miles out of Marshall to visit the historical place, so we said "yes!", grabbed our camera, and headed out.

It was a wonderful little memorial park, with old tombstones and breath-taking statuary. We had a fascinating time reading the grave markers and enjoying the peaceful atmosphere of the cemetery. I think that one of the most beautiful pieces was a huge angel that was draped over one of the graves, like she was grieving for the deceased person buried beneath. After exploring the place, we peeked into the old rock chapel at the cemetery, but it was just too dark inside to make anything out. We wandered around a bit more, then climbed into our car and drove back out toward the highway.

We did stop at one area that looked like it was once the site of a home, because it had concrete steps going up into an overgrown hillside. There was also a well, a small bridge and other telltale signs that the property we were standing on had once been an estate of some sort. After snapping a few photos, we headed out, satisfied with a relaxing afternoon's adventure.

The coincidence came about when I was pouring through the archives of East Texas newspapers. I found an article in the *Marshall News Messenger* from August 4, 1974 by Mac Groves entitled "East Texas Ghosts Are Hauntingly Plentiful". Mr. Groves tells many stories, and at one point he said, "At the Scottsville Cemetery a young couple is parked to romance near the historic site. Without warning, the chimes in the old chapel begin tolling – yet there is no movement within or about the church."

This interested me to no end, especially since we'd visited the cemetery just shortly before. I decided that it was time to do a little research on the Scottsville Cemetery.

One of the first places that I found a reference to it was in

Texas Escapes, the Texas Historic Travel Magazine. The good folks there advised: "At the Scottsville community, take time to explore the Scottsville Cemetery, which contains some of the most elaborate statuary in East Texas. Of particular interest is a breathtaking statue of a grieving angel. The gothic revival chapel made of stone was dedicated in 1904 by Pete and Betty Scott Youree in memory of their only son, William." In a separate article, *Texas Escapes* said, "If you would like to confront the ghosts of Christmases past, few graveyards can match the beauty of Scottsville Cemetery, a small family cemetery near Marshall. Founded in the 1840s by Colonel William T. Scott, the cemetery contains a priceless collection of Italian marble statuary standing over the graves of six generations of the Scott and Rose families."

I found several Texas travel guides that gave it a nod, as well. In *The Best of East Texas* by Bob Bowman, for example, the award for "best cemetery" went to none other than Scottsville Cemetery.

I had no idea that the beautiful old place had such a history and popularity, so I decided to look into the past of the city itself. Scottsville was founded by a pioneer-statesman named William Thomas Scott. Scott was born in 1811 in Louisiana, and he moved to Harrison Country in 1840. He was a prosperous businessman, and brought with him his family and slaves. A palatial plantation home was built with slave labor. According to the University of Texas' history archives, the house was reminiscent of Jefferson Davis's Mississippi mansion. Once his family was settled in, the Scotts had a school built for the education of his children, which was watched over by the family governess. During this time the Scott's also established the first church in the community, a Methodist congregation.

A large Laura Mundi tree near the mansion is reported to be the place where Sam Houston conferred with William Scott and other prominent men in the area concerning a conflict between two regional vigilante factions: the Moderators and the Regulators. In fact, Scott was very politically active. He was a member of congress in the Republic of Texas, and served on the Constitutional Convention that ratified the Constitution of Texas in 1845. After Texas joined the United States, he served terms in both the Senate and the House of Representatives for Texas, and his name is on the Ordinance of Secession when Texas withdrew from the Union.

In the 1860's during the Civil War, the Scott Plantation supplied provisions to the Army of the Confederacy. There was no actual fighting in the area, so thankfully the Scott family home never faced destruction during the war.

Scottsville grew in post-war Texas, and was granted a post office on August 4, 1869. As the small town progressed, Colonel William Scott was there to witness quite a bit of it, since he lived for almost twenty more years. He died in 1887, at the home that he loved so much, and was buried in the Scottsville Cemetery.

But what about the alleged spirited activity there? As much as I tried, I couldn't get any first-hand accounts. There are many stories that persist about the place, however. I found many references to glowing balls of light that weave about the rows of headstones and statues at dusk, and more than one mention of the bell in the stone chapel ringing when the doors are locked up tight and the wooded area is otherwise silent.

As I walked on the soft grass paths that led though the tombstones, I didn't notice anything but the lyrical chirping of a bird in the distance, and an awe at the people and history that is commemorated there in Scottsville.

One very sad thing that I saw was on the statue of the grieving angel – some vandal had apparently snapped off an outreached arm to take home for a souvenir. It made me want to strike any reference to the cemetery from this book, but since it was already listed in so many travel guides, I decided to leave it in, but with a personal request to any visitors. This is such a beautiful place, I ask that if you get a chance to go there, please show respect for the people buried there. Don't take anything out but your photographs and memories of the serene little park that is Scottsville Cemetery.

Scottsville Cemetery is located in the community of Scottsville, Texas, on FM Road 1998 north of Marshall.

The Railroad Ghosts

Sulphur Springs, TX

Sometimes the tales associated with ghost stories are truly tragic, and this one is no exception.

It takes place in the city of Sulphur Springs, a city that was originally named "Bright Star". Around 1850, several stores and a hotel were built there; it had become a popular camping place for teamsters hauling commodities west from the riverport of Jefferson.

The city's name was changed to Sulphur Springs in 1871. People there realized that the mineral springs in the area could be utilized to cash in on the "natural spring health resort" craze that was sweeping the country at the time. While it never became the health Mecca that people had hoped, it did begin a steady growth as a center for East Texas commerce. By 1885, several churches had been established including Baptist, Methodist and Presbyterian. A high school, flour mill, saw mill, several factories, foundries and machine shops, tanneries, hotels, banks, two weekly newspapers and even an opera house had been opened.

One of the town's most famous ghost stories comes from that time – around 1890. During that period, the railroad was an important factor in the city's growth. As the legend goes, during that time a railroad worker and his wife were constantly arguing. Their fights were legendary in town, and everyone knew about the trouble that they were having in their marriage.

Late one evening, he invited her out for a buggy ride beside the railroad tracks to show her where he'd been working. She assumed that it was going to be yet another boring journey out with her husband. When they arrived at the railroad, however, an argument between them was already in full swing. The man had been drinking, and as the disagreement escalated, he began to get physical with his wife and hit her several times.

With several terrible blows, the husband thought that he had knocked his wife out, so he tied her across the railroad tracks and sat their beside her to wait for the next train. It was a cliché move, but one that he hoped would terminate the misery of their marriage.

According to the legend, after securing his wife to the tracks the alcohol in his system began to make him drowsy, and he soon fell into a deep sleep there beside her. His wife came to, and sat up as best she could with her bondage. She managed to reach over and tie the laces of his boots to one of the train rails. He woke up when the sound of the train's whistle came blasting down the tracks, and suddenly came to the realization that he had been immobilized by his wife. He couldn't stand up or crawl out of the way, and in the darkness there was no way that the engineer would see them on the tracks.

The locomotive came barreling down on the duo, instantly killing them both. Local stories soon began to surface about sounds in the evening as trains came by: a man screaming, and a woman laughing hysterically.

These stories persist to this day, but I can't verify whether or not they're real. During my visit, the tracks were empty and silent – and to be honest, I wasn't disappointed. I can only hope that this couple whose lives were so tragically ended are now at peace.

About 2 miles off of 19 on hwy. 11 to the right on a little black top road is the desolate patch of railroad tracks. Where the tragedy actually happened is anyone's guess.

The Phantom Killer

Texarkana, TX

I'd like to say that this is a ghost story, but I'm afraid that it is much scarier than that. You see, no matter how many ghost stories I've uncovered, and people I've interviewed on their experiences, I have never once had someone tell me that they have had a negative experience with the supernatural.

On the other hand, back in the 1940s the town of Texarkana was terrorized by a very real horror – a serial killer who took the lives of five people and wounded three more.

So how do the two topics – ghosts and serial killers – tie together? Well, I had contacted a paranormal investigator from Texarkana to ask about haunted places that she had experienced. I was hoping to hear about a specter in the wonderful "Ace of Clubs" house, or the old museum, or even the Post Office that sits squarely on the state line. Instead, she told me a tale from Spring Lake Park, which was the site of one of the killings. "If you can find the right tree," she said, "you'll find one of the most haunted places in East Texas."

Spring Lake Park – those three words brought back a flood of nostalgia to me. I grew up in Hooks, Texas, a mere fifteen minutes from Texarkana, so I was very familiar with the place. As a child, I went with church groups to the putt-putt golf course there. There was also a small zoo, a few baseball diamonds, and of course, the fairgrounds which were transferred annually into an explosion of neon thrill-rides and win-a-prize booths.

When we were dating, my wife and I would go there on a

Saturday afternoon with a sack of burgers and fries for an impromptu picnic. When we were married a few years later, we would meet there at lunch with our sandwiches and chips – of course, we would save the bread crusts for the ducks in the pond there in the park.

I'd heard a story that the large oak tree in the park was where La Salle hanged one of his men as he passed through the Texarkana area, but that was only a speculative tale told by teenagers. Other than that, I had no idea that there had been murders in the park. That was definitely the case, though, as the facts of the matter showed.

Back in the 1940s, Spring Lake Park didn't sport all of the attractions that would be there thirty years later. In fact, it was basically a wooded park that was considered a "Lover's Lane" by local teenagers. On April 14th of 1946, Paul Martin, age 17, and Betty Jo Booker, Age 15, were found in Spring Lake Park, victims of the "Phantom Killer" who was earning a notorious reputation in East Texas. Mr. Martin's coupe was at the entrance to the park, but his body had been dragged some distance away. Ms. Booker's body was found in a different location, just as far away from the vehicle. Both of the teenagers had been killed by gunshot wounds, but at the autopsy it was discovered that Ms. Booker had also been assaulted.

Other people had been attacked by the madman, and it soon became know that an indiscriminate killer was wandering the Texarkana countryside.

My parents were kids themselves at the time, but they both remember the era of the Phantom Killer. There were no lights allowed inside your house after dark – if you did burn a lamp, the shades had to be pulled down tightly. Local men organized into nocturnal patrols, walking the streets with loaded shotguns in search of a man in a white hooded mask.

He continued to find prey, however, in the form of young couple who were sneaking off to a secret lane for a little innocent romance. All in all, the killer had murdered almost half a dozen people and attempted the same fate on others. No one was ever convicted of the crime, and local legend has it that he continued to walk the streets of Texarkana for the rest of his natural life.

I have two additional recollections of the Phantom Killer. One was a movie named, "The Town that Dreaded Sundown". It starred Dawn Wells, of "Gilligan's Island" fame, and she was probably the biggest star to come to Texarkana in memorable years. Everyone loved her, and she seemed to be a delightful person.

In that movie, the murder in Spring Lake Park is depicted by the Phantom Killer taking the girl's trombone, lashing his knife to it, then blowing out random notes from it as he repeatedly stabbed her. There are a few problems with that scenario, since Ms. Booker was a saxophonist, and her instrument was never found after her murder.

The other issue problem is that there is no evidence that she was ever tied to a tree during the process of her assault or murder. That fact alone discredits any ghost stories tied to certain trees in Spring Lake Park.

I mentioned that I have two remembrances of the Phantom Killer, though. The first was the movie, but the second is more up-close and personal. I was riding around the back-roads of Texarkana with some of my buddies one night, when we stopped on a secluded highway.

"Where are we?" I asked.

One of my friends nodded to a house across a small pasture, and said, "See that place? That's where the Phantom Killer lives."

I immediately challenged him, but he said, "No fooling, the guy who lives here was arrested for the crimes, but they didn't have quite enough evidence to convict him. People say that he's just living out his life as an old man."

So what do I believe? Well, I've been to Spring Lake Park hundreds of times, fed the ducks there at lunch on countless workdays, and even played a game or two of miniature golf along the way.

The zoo isn't there anymore, thankfully, since I remember seeing the tiger pacing a small cage back and forth, back and forth.

The fairgrounds of my youth, where I spent all those evenings at the Four States Fair have disappeared as well. I am proud to say that Spring Lake Park is thriving, however. There are playgrounds and ballparks, and people still seem to continue to flock there.

On my last visit, I saw a young couple eating sandwiches out by the lake, and I couldn't help but think about my wife and I two decades ago. I hoped that those folks were saving their bread crusts, since the army of ducks seemed to be descending on them as they sat there.

I also saw a much different park than that of my youth, and figured that it was even more so a few decades earlier. I don't think that the Phantom Killer tied the girl to a tree, and I know for a fact that he didn't murder her with a knife tied to a trombone. I do know that he did strike at least twice in the park, so it is a place of turmoil.

If there is a haunted place in Spring Lake Park, it would probably be the tree where LaSalle hanged one of his party, but its location has been lost to history.

But what of the Phantom Killer? Well, he may have been lost to history as well. No one was ever convicted, and there is a chance that he is still alive today. He probably doesn't move as quickly, nor is he a threat to society anymore, but he may still dwell on those murderous days in Spring Lake Park.

I visit the place every time I'm in town, though, without a single care or worry. Ghosts I can handle, and a truly scary human such as the Phantom Killer – well, I can only hope that he's moved on.

The Past of Parker House B&B

Trinity, Texas

The Parker House B&B in Trinity, Texas is one of those places where you feel like you've stepped into the past. It is filled with exquisite antiques – the kind of furniture that your grandmother might have had... if your grandmother was a connoisseur of fine furnishings, that is. The parlor boasts a Victorian Revival rosewood parlor set crafted by renowned cabinetmaker George Henkels. It is very much like the set he exhibited at Philadelphia's 1876 Centennial Exposition.

The inn was recognized by Arrington's Bed & Breakfast Journal as one of the Top 15 B&B's with "The Best Antiques" for 2003. If that wasn't enough, Antique Appraiser and Art Conservator Robert C. Norman observed, "The Tyler's [owners of Parker House] have put together a very fine collection of antiques that fit the Parker House very well."

The house also has a rich, historical background, and of course, a ghost or two to go along with it.

The Parkers, for whom the house is named, refer to Isaac Newton Parker and his wife Mary Ashley Parker. Long before the house was ever built, Isaac served in the Civil War as a private in Company D of Hood's Fifth Texas Infantry. When the war ended in 1865, he returned home and worked the family farm for another decade. He eventually began to look beyond the farming trade, and decided to try his hand as a merchant. As with everything else in his life, Isaac reportedly became very successful in the mercantile business.

Isaac and Mary eventually moved their business to the city of Trinity in late 1889, and purchased a house that had been built the previous year. They had eight children, and enjoyed a wonderful life in the community. Isaac's success as a businessman continued, and the family thrived.

Although everything was going very well, tragedy befell the Parker family in 1905, when Mary passed away. About a year later, in 1906, Isaac remarried. His new bride, Lou Palmer, was a younger woman – 40 years old, compared to his age of 65. Lou was a store clerk who from all accounts was quite a beautiful woman. Now, whether she was an employee at Isaac's store will be left to speculation, but it is certainly something that has been discussed over the years.

The house was reportedly remodeled in 1911 by the Parkers, who changed the original Victorian decor of the structure to a simpler, classical style. Isaac passed away in 1918, and Lou – or Miz Lou, as she was called – continued to live in the home for thirty-seven more years. She died in 1955.

The house went through several owners, until in 1988 it was purchased by Steven and Mary Ann Tyler, who performed a restoration of the house and opened it as a Bed & Breakfast – one hundred years after it was originally built.

After all that time, it appears that some former owners of the house are occasionally returning to their home to pay a visit. Doors that were closed have been found open and doors that had been standing open seem to close by themselves. Visitors to the bed & breakfast have felt the touch of an unseen hand, or seen a misty figure walking through the inn.

An article on the Parker House on the Trinity, Texas Chamber of Commerce website by Vanesa Brashier quotes the owner, Steven Tyler: "She (the ghost) tends to communicate with very small children and new or expectant mothers." When a friend of the owners came to Parker House for a visit along with her 3-year-old son, Tyler explained, "Everyone else was in the other room and our friend heard her son talking to someone. When she found him she asked him what he was doing, and he said he was talking to the lady in the wall."

Tyler has more stories to tell, however. "One morning, a young mother from Seattle came to breakfast. She was obviously puzzled and asked me if we had spirits in the house. Never knowing exactly how to respond, I asked her what happened." The young mother explained that she had awakened to the feeling that a person was stroking her forehead and saying, "Good mom, good mom."

Mary Ashley Parker may have been made uncomfortable by the presence of Ike's second wife, Miz Lou, Tyler continues. "The thinking is that Mary was upset about this other woman being in her house," he said. Tyler also believes

Mary's spirit may have lingered following her death, which occurred at the home. Who knows – whether it is Mary or Miz Lou, a female spirit seems to frequent the inn, and if you stay there you just might make her acquaintance.

The Parker House is a beautiful, classic B&B, where guests are treated to snacks and soft drinks all day, fresh gourmet coffee or juice served to their room upon waking in the morning, and a delicious home-cooked gourmet breakfast in the dining room. The visits from the spirits are just an added bonus.

The Parker House Bed & Breakfast
300 N. Maple at Elizabeth Street
P.O. Box 2373
Trinity, Texas 75862
(936) 594-3260

The Ghostly Blue Light of Barrett Cemetery

Winfield, Texas

Ah, finally a story that sounds like an urban legend, but instead has a very interesting twist. When I first heard about the mysterious blue light that had been reported in the area around Barrett Cemetery, I thought of other phantom fireballs like the one that has been so successfully documented at Ghost Road in Saratoga.

As the story continued about the light, tales surfaced about how it taunted teenagers on a "lover's lane" near the cemetery. Once I heard that, I rolled my eyes, sat back in my chair, and said, "Uh-oh." It reeked of urban legend – a celebrated story that was handed down from the Senior Class to the upcoming Juniors throughout the last few decades, that featured a wonderful place to bring a girl for a little kissing and snuggling on a dark Saturday night. I can just hear the guys whispering, "Better sit a little closer; you've heard about the ghost light that is lurking just beyond the lane."

Still, I'm a leave-no-stone-unturned kinda guy, so I set out to find exactly what was happening at Barrett Cemetery.

To start with, the place has certainly earned its historical merits. One of the oldest graves there belongs to Mary Barrett, a five-year-old girl who died in 1856. She was the daughter of Calvin and Edith Barrett, a family who would come to know much sorrow.

The couple moved to East Texas in 1853, and deed records indicate that Calvin purchased 320 acres near the present-day Winfield in the Thomas Ripley Survey from Benjamin Porter in 1854. His brother William took the land where the Cherokee Trace and "The Jefferson Road" intersected. The Cherokee Trace was a thousand-year old trail that ran from present-day Nacogdoches up into Oklahoma. It was first used by the Cherokee Indians, but was later adopted by the Caddos as they traveled between their settlements on the Red River and Angelina River. The Jefferson Road was a well-worn trail that led down to the Riverport of Jefferson, Texas, where steamships regularly traveled upriver from New Orleans bearing cargo and passengers.

Records indicate that the couple had ten children, three of which, Burl, Bud and Thomas, served in the Army of the Confederacy with their father, Calvin. Burl was the only one of the three boys to return home – Bud was killed in a firefight with the Union Army, and Thomas fell ill with measles as it swept through the unsanitary conditions of his army camp. He died of the disease far away from his family and home. Only Burl came back to East Texas and lived until March 17, 1921. His marker stands there in Barrett Cemetery, emblazoned with the emblem of the Confederate States of America. He is listed as being a Private in Sutton's Texas Calvary.

The railroad came through the area in the 1880's, and William Barrett donated some land for a town to be established. It was known as "Barrett" for some time, named after the families that had initially settled the area, but its moniker was changed to "Winfield" in 1892 in honor of the general passenger agent for the railroad, W. H. Winfield.

The tiny Barrett Cemetery continued to grow as the population of the town rose and fell over the years. In 1890 there were forty-seven there, but by 1896 the town had three churches, several stores, a pottery operated by J. S. Hogue, and approximately 150 in town. By 1914 Winfield had added a brick company, a newspaper, several stores and cotton gins, and two banks – 700 people lived there by then. By 1925 Winfield had dropped to a population of 629, and by 1940 it was only 350, which isn't far from where it is today.

There were several hundred graves in the cemetery by then, and rumors were starting to be told about mysterious goings-on in the area. The fact that it was a couple of miles out of town made it a popular hang-out for teenagers, which is what made me a little leery of any reported ghosts stories there. Something that I found in the May 1998 edition of the *East Texas Journal* impressed me, though. Reporter/publisher Hudson Old interviewed Glenda Ross, someone who grew up in Winfield and actually witnessed the blue light. According to the *East Texas Journal*, Ms. Ross gave the following account:

> *"My boyfriend and some other guys had a friend who was kind of jumpy," she said, "so they decided to give him a scare."*
>
> *They spent the afternoon fixing up one of their friends to look like a werewolf, and "a good while after dark they went out to the cemetery.*
>
> *"They wouldn't let the girls go with them the first time they went out, but the plan was to hide the werewolf in the cemetery, then return with the scardy-cat friend," she said.*
>
> *Instead, the boys were back in town shortly with wild reports of a blue light that had chased them from the cemetery.*
>
> *"They said the light appeared as soon as they crossed the fence going into the cemetery," she said.*

"When it started moving toward them, they broke and ran; one of the boys was so scared he ran through the fence and was cut up some."

Arming themselves with clubs, the boys loaded up their dates and returned to the cemetery.

"We pulled up to the fence and didn't see anything, but nobody wanted to get out of the car," she said. *"Finally, a couple of the guys got out and crossed the fence. They hadn't been there very long when I saw the light appear. I've never seen anything like it, before or since. The boys broke and ran for the car with the light following."*

Tales of the light shot around the town.

"The next night we went back and my mother went with us," Glenda said. *"She was skeptical until the light appeared again. She was so scared she got down in the floorboard in the back seat and begged the boys to get us out of there. I could still see the light when we went peeling out of there."*

With word of the phenomenon loose on the streets, *"Blue Light Cemetery"* became a regular route on local law enforcement patrols back then, Glenda said.

"Some people would go out there and see it, some people never saw it. Some said it was a reflection from a tombstone, but what we saw wasn't a reflection," she said.

The stories about the blue light at Barrett Cemetery don't come up very much these days. A local energy company has purchased most of the land around the cemetery, so it is secured as private property. The graveyard itself is behind a locked steel-pipe gate. The local teens don't go parking there anymore, and nocturnal visitors are rare.

People who have ancestors in the cemetery can pick up the key at the security office down the road and go there to visit, but the company does not want to have random strangers going through their property, for both security and safety reasons.

You probably won't find any company representatives who are anxious to talk about the cemetery and its legendary blue light. While the company respects the sacred ground and those buried there, they don't want to encourage the local teens that used to frequent the property as a "lovers lane".

What the blue light was, and whether it still winds its way through the tombstones of Barratt Cemetery, is a mystery that will remain forever shrouded in the lore of East Texas.

A Few Words In Closing...

Well, this is it – the last few pages of this little travel guide to the spirited places of the Pineywoods of East Texas. It's been a blast for me, and I hope that you enjoyed reading it as well. If it were up to me, I'd go back to page one and start writing this book all over again. I'd love another plate of Chicken Diavolo at Lamache's in Jefferson – one of my favorite places to eat Italian food in the entire world. While in town, of course I'd have to spend a night in the Jay Gould room of the stately old Excelsior House, or get deep under the covers in Room 19 of the Jefferson Hotel. Or stay a night or so at Falling Leaves B&B, just for the hospitality and the great food that awaits a visitor every morning.

Or perhaps a relaxing massage treatment at Claiborne House's "Touch of Class Day Spa", or an evening at the famous McKay House.

There were a couple of dead ends that I ran across; Cry Baby Bridge for one, the radioactive grave for another, but part of the fun of ghost hunting is doing research and separating the true stories from the tall tales. There were many that I didn't even get to visit, like the statue of Jesus whose arms move at a Catholic church in Texarkana. At some point, I had to stop chasing those stories!

The true hauntings that we've talked about in this book were great fun to research, explore and document. I can't tell you exactly what the Bragg Road Ghost Light is, I just know that it's there. There's no denying it – you can go see it for yourself. I also know that the folks at the Jefferson Hotel have seen enough to know that something supernatural is going on there; they even have journals where people have recorded their own experiences.

Oh, and before closing, I could use one more stroll through the tranquility of Scottsville Cemetery. What a beautiful, peaceful place.

Unfortunately, I have to put this manuscript to bed. I ended my last book, "Ghosts of North Texas", with the statement:

"As I write these last words, I'm sitting at desk in a notoriously haunted room where a particular ghost has been experienced by many people. After the final word is typed, I'm just going to shut down my computer, turn off the light, sit here for a few minutes, and see if anyone shows up..."

I was actually in a wing-back chair at The Grove in Jefferson, in the Blue Room with a makeshift desk pulled up beside it. I knew that I'd be writing about The Grove in this book, so it seemed to be a good transition point for me.

In that same vein, I'm writing this closing chapter in Room 218 of a haunted hotel overlooking a beautiful mountain valley. It's a historic old place, and the years have given it a lot of character. Gazing out of the window, I see a beautiful Catholic Church below, and a unique one at that – the only entry is through the very top of the bell tower. I could tell story after story about this place, but it's getting late. After I've packed up my computer, I wonder if one of its supernatural visitors will drop by. Who knows – this is a wonderful place to put a big red ribbon on *The Ghosts of East Texas and the Pineywoods*, though. I'll save any details about the hotel and Room 218 for my next book.

So that's it. I do have to say that in my travels across the Pineywoods area of Texas, every mile was exquisitely scenic. The pine trees always gave the roadsides a lush, green backdrop, and as the seasons changed during my travels I saw flowers and foliage of every hue. This part of the world is genuinely beautiful.

But as much as I enjoyed the scenery, I think that the history was even better. Who would have thought that the serene city of Jefferson was once Texas' second-largest riverport? Or that Bragg Road had once been a railroad spur used to haul timber and oil? How about the idea that a Spanish Nun visited the Caddo Indians in spirit form long before Europeans ever contacted them? Well, I never ceased to be amazed at the true, historic tales from this area – the Texas Pineywoods, the place of my birth, and if I have any say, I'll be there until I die. By then, someone else will own The Grove, but Lord willing, I'll get the chance to go back and visit it occasionally. Patrick, the former owner of The Grove, told me to look for him in the parlor just inside the front door. Me, I have a different place picked out. I think that I'll be sitting out on the front gallery rocking, just listening to the birds and watching the squirrels. Many years from now, perhaps some other writer will be putting together his or her own book on the ghosts of East Texas, and he'll include a footnote to The Grove chapter:

"The current owners of The Grove are adamant that early in the morning, there's often the smell of freshly-brewed coffee out on the front gallery even though none has been made in the house, and the old wicker rocker seems to move back and forth by itself. It eventually stops, but not before they hear a heavy, satisfied sigh and a few gentle laughs."

Until we meet again,

Mitchel Whitington
mitchel@whitington.com

JESSIE ET LE
TERRIBLE SECRET

61

JESSIE ET LE TERRIBLE SECRET

Quatre gardiennes fondent leur club

Ann M. Martin

Adapté de l'américain par
Marie-Claude Favreau

Donnnées de catalogage avant publication (Canada)

Martin, Ann M., 1955-

Jessie et le terrible secret

(Les baby-sitters; 61)
Traduction de: Jessi and the Awful Secret.
Pour les jeunes de 8 à 12 ans.

ISBN: 2-7625-8402-7

I. Titre. II. Collection: Martin, Ann M., 1955-.
Les baby-sitters; 61.

PZ23.M37Jec 1996   j813'.54   C95-941814-8

Conception graphique de la couverture: Jocelyn Veillette

Jessi and the Awful Secret
Copyright © 1993 Ann M. Martin
Publié par Scholastic Inc.

Version française
© Les éditions Héritage inc. 1996
Tous droits réservés

Dépôts légaux: 1er trimestre 1996
Bibliothèque nationale du Québec
Bibliothèque nationale du Canada

ISBN: 2-7625-8402-7   Imprimé au Canada

LES ÉDITIONS HÉRITAGE INC.
300, rue Arran, Saint-Lambert (Québec) J4R 1K5
(514) 875-0327

*L'auteure remercie chaleureusement Suzanne Weyn
pour son aide lors de la préparation de ce livre.*

*Un grand merci au docteur Adele Brodkin pour
ses judicieux conseils dans l'appréciation de ce récit.*

CHAPITRE 1

Le regard fixé sur moi, madame Noëlle donne des petits coups secs sur le plancher avec son bâton. Elle n'a pas besoin de prononcer une parole. Instantanément, je lève la jambe plus haut derrière moi et je pousse les épaules vers l'arrière.

— Beaucoup mieux, mademoiselle Raymond, dit-elle en hochant la tête.

Elle s'éloigne et va observer les autres élèves à la barre.

— Tu es beaucoup trop raide, dit-elle à Marie Bernard. Détends tes épaules. Respire !

Mais avant d'aller plus loin, laissez-moi me présenter.

Je m'appelle Jessie Raymond, j'ai onze ans et, entre autres choses, je suis des cours de ballet dans une école spécialisée. Madame Noëlle est assez âgée et plutôt sévère, mais, comme professeure de danse, elle a très bonne réputation.

J'ai une classe le mardi et le vendredi, après l'école. Mon père travaille dans les environs et vient me chercher en auto, une fois le cours terminé. Il nous faut environ une demi-heure pour rentrer à la maison.

Madame Noëlle tape dans ses mains et nous fait faire des *grands battements*. Ce sont des exercices de réchauffement conçus pour délier les muscles des hanches et des jambes.

Invariablement, le cours débute par ce genre d'exercices préparatoires, sans quoi on risquerait de se blesser en exécutant des mouvements plus complexes.

— Avant de commencer le travail au centre, nous dit madame Noëlle, je vous annonce que l'école donnera six semaines de cours gratuits à certains enfants défavorisés. Les classes auront lieu chaque mardi à cette heure-ci. Nous avons besoin de volontaires pour assister madame Dupré.

— Et nos cours à nous? demande Marie-Claude Perrault.

— Les volontaires auront six cours gratuits pour rattraper le temps perdu, explique madame Noëlle.

— Mais ça risque de nous retarder, non? fait Karine Saint-Onge.

— La décision vous appartient. Pour celles d'entre vous qui prévoient devenir professeures un jour, c'est une expérience enrichissante. Bon, y a-t-il des volontaires?

Je lève la main sans hésiter. J'adore travailler avec les enfants. Je fais même partie d'un club de gardiennes, le Club des baby-sitters. (Le club est très important pour moi. Presque autant que le ballet.) Et je n'ai pas peur de prendre du retard. Je suis la plus jeune de la classe. (Avant mon arrivée, Marie-Claude était la plus jeune, mais elle a un an de plus que moi. Je pense que ça lui fait quelque chose.) En plus — n'allez surtout pas le crier sur les toits — je suis une des meilleures. Je ne dis pas ça pour me vanter, c'est juste la vérité. Il n'y a pas longtemps, j'ai obtenu le premier rôle dans *La Belle au bois dormant*, une production de l'école. J'ai aussi dansé le rôle principal dans d'autres ballets.

Marie Bernard est la seule autre à lever la main.

Franchement, je suis étonnée qu'il n'y ait pas plus de volontaires. Donner des cours à des enfants me semble amusant et je ne comprends pas qu'on puisse refuser. Je suppose que mes compagnes craignent de perdre trop de temps. (Je sais que les danseuses doivent être sérieuses et compétitives, mais je trouve qu'elles exagèrent parfois.)

Et que Marie se soit proposée est tout aussi étonnant. Elle est très gentille, mais elle recherche tellement la perfection qu'elle en est maniaque. Ce qui n'en fait pas une des plus douées de la classe pour autant. À son grand regret, elle est raide quand elle danse. Comme si elle s'inquiétait trop pour pouvoir se laisser entraîner par la musique. Je ne m'attendais pas à ce qu'elle accepte de retarder ses cours réguliers, et je trouve ça encore plus généreux de sa part.

— Très bien, nous dit madame Noëlle. Présentez-vous mardi prochain à madame Dupré.

Elle fait un signe à notre nouveau pianiste, un jeune homme avec des lunettes qui se met à jouer pendant que nous prenons place au milieu de la salle pour faire une *arabesque penchée*. (Il s'agit de lever une jambe haut derrière soi tout en inclinant le corps vers l'avant et en plaçant les bras de façon à garder l'équilibre.)

Marie est juste devant moi, et je remarque que la jambe sur laquelle elle repose tremble énormément. Je voudrais bien lui suggérer de déplacer son poids un peu vers l'arrière, mais madame Noëlle ne tolère aucun bavardage durant les cours.

Ensuite, nous passons aux pirouettes et aux sauts. Puis vient le moment que je préfère : à la fin de la classe, chacune d'entre nous danse seule en exécutant une série de pas dictés par madame Noëlle. Aujourd'hui : *pas de bourrée* avec *port de bras*, suivi d'un *pas de chat*, et enfin *arabesque penchée* à la première position.

C'est moins compliqué que ça en a l'air quand on sait ce que les termes signifient. Le *pas de bourrée* avec *port de bras* consiste à faire de tout petits pas sur pointes, en levant et en descendant gracieusement les bras. Le *pas de chat* est très amusant. Il faut sauter, joindre les orteils, puis retomber souplement.

Mon tour venu, je m'élance au milieu de la salle. Quand je ne fais pas juste les mouvements, mais que je danse vraiment, c'est comme si mon corps pensait pour moi. Tout ce que j'ai appris semble inscrit dans mes bras et mes jambes, pas dans mon cerveau.

— Avec toi, ça semble si facile, me dit Lise Jordan quand j'ai terminé.

— Merci.

Lise a dansé avant moi. Elle s'en est bien tirée, sauf qu'elle a légèrement basculé vers l'arrière après son *pas de chat*.

Lise est une des filles les plus gentilles de la classe, mais je ne la connais pas mieux que les autres. Je me suis toujours sentie un peu à l'écart du groupe.

Étant la plus jeune et la plus nouvelle, ça n'a rien de surprenant. En plus, le fait que je sois Noire me rend différente. Personne ne me passe de remarques, mais dans le grand miroir sur le mur, ça fait bizarre de voir une seule tête foncée parmi tous ces visages blancs.

Avant d'arriver à Nouville, je n'avais jamais ressenti à ce point ma différence. Dans notre quartier du New Jersey, où j'ai grandi, être Noir ne comptait pas. Mais lorsque nous avons emménagé ici, ça a pris soudain une grande importance.

Nous sommes venus à Nouville parce que mon père y a été muté, avec une bonne augmentation de salaire. Ma sœur Becca (qui a huit ans) et moi étions presque aussi excitées que lui. Quant à mon petit frère Jaja qui est encore bébé, il se sent à l'aise partout.

En plus de quitter la parenté et nos amis, il fallait nous habituer à une nouvelle école et à un nouvel environnement. Et croyez-moi, certains habitants de Nouville n'étaient pas ravis de voir des Noirs envahir leur quartier bien blanc. Au début, ç'a été difficile. Mais nous avons tenu bon et, à présent, tout se passe plutôt bien.

Malheureusement, je n'ai pas encore réussi à m'intégrer à mon groupe de ballet. J'essaie de ne pas m'en faire. Après tout, j'ai des amis à l'école et au CBS (le Club des Baby-sitters). J'ai même une très grande amie : Marjorie Picard. Je me dis souvent que je n'ai pas besoin d'autres copains, mais, en fait, je me sens parfois un peu seule à l'école de ballet.

À la fin de la classe, nous applaudissons madame Noëlle, puis nous allons nous changer au vestiaire.

— C'est gentil de t'être portée volontaire, me dit Karine en sortant avec moi. Je l'aurais fait aussi, mais je dois me consacrer entièrement à mes cours.

Karine est la plus âgée de la classe. Elle est nerveuse ces temps-ci parce qu'elle n'a jamais tenu de premier rôle et ça risque de bloquer son entrée dans une école plus importante. C'est dommage, parce qu'elle danse bien. Malheureusement, bien danser ne suffit pas. Il faut être exceptionnel.

Pour que Karine ne se sente pas trop mal à l'aise, j'essaie de prendre les choses à la légère.

— Oh! moi, si j'ai accepté d'être volontaire, c'est seulement pour me distraire un peu. Et je crois que ça va être amusant.

— Oh non! rétorque Marie-Claude en fronçant le nez. On ne me fera pas enseigner à une bande de petits braillards.

— Ils ne sont sûrement pas tous débiles, dit Marie. C'est très généreux de la part de l'école d'offrir ce programme. Aider, c'est le moins que je puisse faire, je trouve.

Je pense bien que je vais aimer travailler avec elle.

Dans le vestiaire, nous ne perdons pas de temps. C'est très intéressant de voir comme dix filles toutes pareilles en maillots noirs, collants roses, chaussons à pointes et chignons serrés deviennent si différentes une fois changées. Marie-Claude, par exemple, porte des *leggings* avec un grand chemisier, et Lise ne met jamais autre chose que des jeans et des chandails.

— Je n'arrive pas à sauter assez haut dans les *pas de chat*, dit Marie à Mireille Houle en retirant ses chaussons.

— Je te comprends, fait Mireille en passant un t-shirt. J'ai eu le même problème. Mais quand j'ai perdu cinq kilos, ça s'est réglé.

Marie se lève et s'examine dans le grand miroir.

— Je pourrais perdre un peu de graisse autour de la taille, dit-elle.

Quelle graisse ? Elle n'a pas un gramme à perdre, encore moins cinq kilos !

— Le poids fait toute la différence, affirme Mireille. Tu verras.

Moi, je trouve que Mireille ne saute pas si haut que ça et sa théorie ne tient pas debout. D'ailleurs, ça ne réglera pas le problème de Marie. Si elle veut sauter plus haut, elle devrait simplement s'exercer. C'est ce que je lui dirais si elle me demandait mon avis. Mais je ne veux pas m'imposer.

Marie tourne le dos au miroir et tord le cou pour se voir.

— J'ai aussi de grosses fesses, marmonne-t-elle.

Pas du tout !

— Ça t'alourdit, continue Mireille comme si elle était experte en la matière.

Je n'en crois pas mes oreilles.

Pourtant, entendre Mireille parler comme ça ne me surprend qu'à moitié. Dans le ballet, le *look* compte énormément. Les danseurs doivent être minces, avoir les épaules carrées et le visage ovale. C'était, paraît-il, l'opinion du grand chorégraphe George Balanchine qui exigeait que toutes les danseuses du corps de ballet (celles qui ne sont pas des vedettes) forment un groupe homogène. Depuis sa mort, ça commence à changer, dit-on. C'est peut-être vrai.

Beaucoup de filles sont obsédées par l'allure qu'aura leur corps quand leur développement sera terminé. Elles pourraient ne pas avoir la silhouette idéale pour devenir ballerine. C'est dur à accepter quand on danse depuis l'âge de quatre ans. On voit soudain son rêve s'écrouler et il faut

13

reconsidérer son plan de carrière !

Moi, je ne m'inquiète pas trop. J'ai la chance d'être naturellement mince, comme tout le monde chez moi. (Sauf tante Cécile, qui habite avec nous pour s'occuper de Becca et de Jaja. Je croise les doigts pour ne pas tenir d'elle.)

Bien sûr, c'est facile de ne pas m'en faire : j'ai encore quelques années de sursis avant que mon corps ne change vraiment. Quand ce moment-là arrivera, j'espère ne pas être aussi obsédée que Mireille et Marie.

CHAPITRE 2

Le vendredi m'offre toujours un véritable défi. Je sors du cours de ballet comme une flèche en espérant que papa soit à l'heure pour me prendre (d'habitude, il l'est) et je dois me retenir pour ne pas rouspéter quand je trouve que nous ne roulons pas assez vite. Si je suis si pressée, c'est que j'ai une réunion du CBS à dix-sept heures trente précises. Et je dis bien précises !

Christine Thomas, notre présidente, tient à la ponctualité. Si on n'est pas à l'heure, elle nous jette des regards foudroyants. Des regards qui me paralysent tellement que je serais prête à tout pour les éviter. Malheureusement, je les subis souvent le vendredi lorsque j'ai une ou deux secondes de retard. Parfois, avec la circulation, ce n'est pas facile d'être à temps. Mais essayez donc d'expliquer ça à Christine.

Ce vendredi, j'arrive à dix-sept heures trente pile. Ouf ! J'entre en coup de vent dans la chambre de Claudia et je me dépêche de m'asseoir à ma place habituelle sur le plancher.

— À la seconde près, encore une fois, me chuchote Marjorie. (Elle connaît l'horaire surchargé de mes vendredis.)

Je lui souris et je pose la main sur mon cœur qui bat à coups précipités.

— On a eu tous les feux verts, dis-je en haletant. Un seul jaune et c'était fichu. (Mon père s'arrête toujours au feu jaune au lieu d'accélérer pour passer. Quand je suis pressée, ça me rend folle.)

— La réunion est ouverte, déclare Christine, assise dans le fauteuil de Claudia.

Claudia, Anne-Marie et Diane sont installées sur le lit. Sophie est à côté du téléphone.

Mais avant d'aller plus loin, je voudrais vous décrire mes amies du CBS et le fonctionnement du club.

Puisque Marjorie est ma meilleure amie, commençons par elle. Elle a des cheveux roux bouclés, des taches de rousseur plein la figure, et elle porte un appareil orthodontique et des lunettes. (Elle meurt d'envie d'avoir des verres de contact, mais ses parents disent qu'elle est encore trop jeune.) Marjorie ne se trouve pas jolie. Elle déteste son nez, surtout. Mais elle est d'une telle gentillesse qu'on oublie facilement ses petites imperfections physiques.

Elle est l'aînée d'une famille de huit enfants ! Il y a les triplets, Bernard, Antoine et Joël, qui ont dix ans. Ils sont identiques, mais quand on les connaît, ce n'est pas difficile de les différencier. Vient ensuite Vanessa, qui a neuf ans et qui partage la chambre de Marjorie. Puis Nicolas, qui a huit ans, Margot, qui en a sept, et Claire, qui en a cinq.

Marjorie se plaint toujours du bruit et du désordre qui règnent chez elle ; mais, moi, j'adore aller lui rendre visite. Sa maison est toujours animée. Mais peut-être que je n'aimerais pas y vivre. Marjorie n'a pas beaucoup d'intimité et elle trouve ça dur. Surtout qu'elle en a encore plus besoin qu'une autre, car elle veut devenir écrivaine. Une de ses histoires a d'ailleurs remporté un prix à l'école. Marjorie rêve d'écrire et d'illustrer des contes pour enfants. Elle a tellement d'imagination que je suis sûre qu'elle va y parvenir.

Elle et moi avons beaucoup de choses en commun. Nous sommes toutes les deux en sixième année et nous aimons lire (surtout les histoires de chevaux, mais aussi les mystères). Je ne pourrais pas souhaiter avoir de meilleure amie.

Maintenant, laissez-moi vous parler de Christine. Elle est présidente du club parce que c'est elle qui l'a fondé et qu'elle a le tempérament qu'il faut. Elle nous arrive toujours avec de nouvelles idées. Elle sait comment les réaliser aussi ; même si elle a la langue bien pendue, ça ne l'empêche pas d'agir.

En dépit des apparences, Christine n'est pas cassepieds. Elle a beaucoup d'humour et c'est une fille très « pratique ». En fait, c'est grâce à son comportement de chef si le club fonctionne si bien.

Bien qu'elle sache s'imposer, elle est toute petite de taille. Elle a treize ans comme toutes les autres membres (sauf Marjorie et moi), mais elle a l'air plus jeune. Elle a de longs cheveux châtains et des yeux bruns. Pour elle, la mode se limite à un jean, des chaussures de sport, un t-shirt ou un chandail. Christine est ce qu'on appelle un garçon manqué. Elle adore le sport et elle entraîne même une équipe de balle molle composée d'enfants : les Cogneurs. Les garçons sont le dernier de ses soucis (sauf qu'elle aime bien Marc Tardif, l'entraîneur des Matamores, l'équipe de balle molle rivale).

17

Malgré tout ce que je viens de vous dire, vous ne devinerez jamais la suite : Christine est millionnaire. En fait, c'est son beau-père, Guillaume Marchand, qui l'est.

Mais Christine n'a pas toujours été riche. Ce qui est arrivé, c'est que monsieur Thomas, son père, a abandonné sa famille juste après la naissance de David, son petit frère. Et madame Thomas a dû élever seule Christine, ses deux frères aînés et David. Mais elle est comme sa fille : réaliste et énergique. Elle a trouvé un boulot (dans les affaires, je crois) et c'est justement au travail qu'elle a connu Guillaume.

Quand Christine était en première secondaire, madame Thomas a épousé Guillaume, et, avec toute sa famille, a emménagé dans le manoir de ce dernier. Au début, Christine n'était pas emballée. Ni par le déménagement, ni par Guillaume, ni même par le manoir. À présent, elle aime bien son beau-père et elle s'est habituée à sa nouvelle maison. Elle adore les enfants de Guillaume, André (qui a quatre ans) et Karen (qui en a sept). La plupart du temps, ils vivent avec leur mère, mais ils passent chez leur père une fin de semaine sur deux, la période des fêtes et une partie des vacances d'été.

La famille de Christine ne s'arrête pas là. Sa mère et Guillaume ont adopté une petite Vietnamienne de deux ans et demi qu'ils ont appelée Émilie. Puis la grand-mère de Christine, Nanie, est venue vivre avec eux pour aider. Si on ajoute le chiot de David, le chat de Guillaume et les poissons rouges de Karen et André, ça fait toute une maisonnée !

Et maintenant, passons à Anne-Marie Lapierre, la meilleure amie de Christine. Même si physiquement elles se ressemblent, elles ont des personnalités bien différentes. Anne-Marie ne parle pas beaucoup, mais elle sait écouter et elle est très sensible. (Elle pleure pour un rien, surtout quand quelque chose de triste arrive à quelqu'un d'autre.)

Comme Christine, Anne-Marie fait partie d'une famille reconstituée. Au départ, elle était fille unique. Sa mère est morte alors qu'elle était encore bébé et, pendant longtemps, elle n'a vécu qu'avec son père (un homme très strict). Puis, un jour, sa vie a basculé. Diane Dubreuil est arrivée en ville. Elle est devenue la seconde meilleure amie d'Anne-Marie et… sa demi-sœur !

Voici ce qui s'est passé. Diane, qui a grandi en Californie, est venue habiter Nouville quand ses parents ont divorcé et que sa mère a décidé de revenir dans sa ville natale.

Diane et son jeune frère n'aimaient pas Nouville, au début. (Ce n'est jamais facile de s'expatrier.) Leur père était resté en Californie, ainsi que tous leurs amis. Même aujourd'hui, Diane a du mal à s'acclimater à nos hivers. Son frère ne s'est jamais habitué et il est reparti vivre avec son père.

Comme je le disais donc, Anne-Marie et Diane sont devenues amies. Anne-Marie a présenté Diane aux autres membres du CBS et celle-ci s'est jointe au groupe. Un jour, en regardant un album de photos, les deux amies ont découvert que la mère de Diane et le père d'Anne-Marie sortaient ensemble alors qu'ils fréquentaient le même collège.

Anne-Marie et Diane ont donc décidé d'essayer de réunir à nouveau leurs deux parents. Il a fallu un peu de patience, mais leur plan a fonctionné et tout s'est terminé

19

par un mariage. Diane et Anne-Marie sont donc devenues demi-sœurs !

Les Lapierre ont emménagé dans la vieille maison de ferme de madame Dubreuil (qui comporte même un passage secret menant à la grange !). Au début, les deux filles étaient très emballées, mais elles se sont vite rendu compte que vivre ensemble ne se fait pas toujours sans heurts. Par exemple, la mère de Diane n'aime pas tellement le chat d'Anne-Marie, Tigrou. Et que dire des repas ! Diane et sa mère sont végétariennes et ne mangent que des salades, du tofu, des aliments naturels, alors qu'Anne-Marie et son père mangent de tout. La planification des soupers est un vrai casse-tête. Mais tout a fini par s'arranger et ils sont heureux. Anne-Marie et Diane sont généralement ravies d'être sœurs.

Maintenant, Claudia Kishi. Une fille fascinante. Elle est unique dans son genre. D'origine japonaise, elle a de beaux traits délicats et de longs cheveux noirs soyeux. En plus, elle a une façon très « artistique » de s'habiller. Elle agence les styles et les couleurs de façon extrêmement personnelle. (Sur toute autre, l'effet serait plutôt bizarre, mais sur Claudia, c'est superbe.) Aujourd'hui, elle porte un gilet vert émeraude sur une chemise d'homme blanche, et un pantalon fuseau fuchsia. Elle a roulé ses manches et passé une ceinture tressée multicolore. Pour finir, elle a mis des boucles d'oreilles en perles de céramique qu'elle a confectionnées elle-même. Claudia est une artiste accomplie. Elle peint, dessine et sculpte.

Mis à part l'art et les vêtements tape-à-l'œil, ce que Claudia aime par-dessus tout, ce sont les friandises. Mais ses parents n'apprécient pas la voir grignoter des bonbons, alors, elle est contrainte de dissimuler jujubes et tablettes de chocolat ici et là dans sa chambre. Rien d'étonnant de trouver un sac de croustilles sous son oreiller ! Et elle adore les romans policiers (qu'elle doit aussi cacher, car ses parents n'approuvent pas ses choix de lecture).

Mais Claudia déteste les livres « intellectuels ». D'ailleurs, l'école ne l'intéresse pas. Elle n'est pas idiote ; n'empêche que ses notes sont catastrophiques. Elle est tout à fait le contraire de sa sœur Josée, considérée comme un génie. (Elle a un Q.I. très élevé, ce qui est très frustrant pour Claudia.)

Sophie Ménard est l'autre fille à la mode du groupe. Elle et Claudia sont de grandes amies. Sophie fait permanenter ses cheveux blonds, elle porte des vêtements dernier cri, mais pas aussi fantaisistes que ceux de Claudia.

Comme moi, Sophie a emménagé à Nouville parce que son père a été muté ici. Après avoir fait la connaissance de Claudia, elle est devenue membre du club. Juste comme elle commençait à s'habituer, la compagnie de son père a rappelé celui-ci à Toronto. Alors Sophie a dû nous quitter.

Peu après, ses parents ont décidé de divorcer. Heureusement, madame Ménard est revenue vivre ici avec Sophie. Une chance pour nous !

Sophie a un autre problème : elle est diabétique. Elle doit suivre un régime sans sucre et se faire des injections d'insuline tous les jours.

Un mot maintenant sur le fonctionnement de notre club : nous nous réunissons le lundi, le mercredi et le vendredi, de dix-sept heures trente à dix-huit heures. Claudia est la seule à avoir une ligne téléphonique personnelle et sa chambre est notre quartier général. C'est d'ailleurs pour ça qu'elle est vice-présidente.

Pendant les réunions, les clients téléphonent pour faire appel à nos services. Avec un seul coup de fil, ils peuvent joindre sept gardiennes. Neuf, en fait, puisque nous avons aussi deux membres associés qui n'assistent pas aux réunions, mais qui nous dépannent à l'occasion : Louis Brunet, le petit ami d'Anne-Marie, et Chantal Chrétien, une voisine de Christine.

Marjorie et moi sommes membres juniors. Comme nous n'avons que onze ans, nous ne gardons pas le soir. (J'ai hâte d'être assez vieille pour qu'on cesse de me considérer comme une fillette.)

Donc, les clients appellent pour nous dire quand ils auront besoin d'une gardienne. Et c'est ici qu'intervient Anne-Marie, la secrétaire du club. Elle consulte l'agenda où sont consignés nos horaires (mes cours de ballet, les heures d'entraînement au tir à l'arc de Marjorie, les cours d'art de Claudia, les exercices de balle molle des Cogneurs de Christine...). Nos confions alors la garde à l'une de celles qui sont libres. Anne-Marie est très fière de ne s'être encore jamais trompée.

L'agenda renferme aussi les coordonnées de nos clients et les renseignements utiles sur leurs enfants : allergies, peurs, heures du coucher...

La seule section de l'agenda dont n'est pas responsable Anne-Marie, c'est celle où est noté l'argent gagné et dépensé. Ça, c'est le boulot de Sophie, notre trésorière (et génie des maths). Nous gardons chacune l'argent que nous gagnons, mais Sophie inscrit quand même les sommes reçues dans l'agenda pour la bonne marche du club. Elle recueille aussi nos cotisations qu'elle conserve dans une grande enveloppe.

Personne n'aime le jour des cotisations, mais celles-ci sont très utiles pour dédommager Claudia (nous payons une partie de ses factures de téléphone) et Charles Thomas (qui vient reconduire Christine en auto), et aussi pour acheter du matériel destiné aux trousses à surprises.

Les trousses à surprises, une autre idée de Christine, sont des boîtes remplies de livres, de crayons, de jouets et de petites babioles pour distraire les enfants turbulents ou maussades. (Christine avait remarqué que les petits adorent ce qui est nouveau. Comme je crois l'avoir déjà dit, elle est présidente parce qu'elle n'arrête pas d'avoir des idées géniales.)

Diane, elle, est suppléante. Elle peut remplacer quiconque est absente d'une réunion, alors elle connaît les tâches de tout le monde. Quand Sophie est partie pour Toronto, Diane a pris la place de trésorière. Comme elle déteste les maths, elle était ravie de voir Sophie revenir.

En plus d'établir l'horaire des gardes et de verser nos cotisations, nous devons aussi écrire dans le journal de bord. (Encore une bonne idée de... vous devinez qui!)

C'est dans ce cahier que nous commentons toutes nos gardes. C'est très utile quand on va garder un enfant de connaître ses goûts, son caractère, les problèmes qu'on risque d'affronter.

Vous voyez donc que, même si le téléphone ne sonne pas, nous avons beaucoup de travail à faire pendant notre demi-heure de réunion. Mais aujourd'hui le téléphone n'arrête pas de sonner. Nous avons toutes accepté une garde, quand, à dix-sept heures cinquante-cinq, madame Mainville appelle. Elle a besoin de quelqu'un le lendemain soir pour garder Jonathan (qui a quatre ans) et sa petite sœur Laurence.

— Personne n'est libre, dit Anne-Marie après avoir consulté l'agenda. Il faut appeler Chantal.

Tout le monde regarde Christine. D'habitude, c'est elle qui appelle Chantal puisque c'est son amie. Mais aujourd'hui, elle fait la grimace.

— Quelqu'un d'autre ne pourrait pas l'appeler pour une fois? fait-elle d'un air embarrassé.

— Qu'est-ce qui se passe? demande Diane.

— Ces temps-ci, elle me téléphone souvent pour me demander de sortir avec elle. Son horaire a changé, elle a plus de temps libre et ses autres amis semblent avoir d'autres activités.

— Chantal est gentille, dit Sophie. Tu n'aimes pas la voir?

— Je n'ai pas le temps! s'écrie Christine. Avec les enfants, les réunions et tout le reste, je n'ai pas une minute à moi. Je ne veux pas lui faire de peine, mais chaque fois qu'elle téléphone, je dois refuser.

— Dis-lui de nous appeler, nous, suggère Sophie. On l'aime bien.

— Mais oui, ajoute Claudia.

— Ah? fait Christine, le visage illuminé. Alors, je lui téléphone. Je vais lui parler de la garde chez les Mainville et je lui dirai de vous appeler.

— Ça fait longtemps que je veux mieux la connaître, dit Diane.

Christine compose le numéro de Chantal.

— Parfait, dit-elle avec un sourire. Voilà un autre problème de réglé.

24

— Bonjour, dit madame Dupré en accueillant les volontaires.

Devant la porte du studio de madame Noëlle, en plus de Marie et moi, il y a quatre autres volontaires venant de classes différentes. Deux d'entre eux sont des garçons.

Madame Dupré est beaucoup plus jeune que madame Noëlle — dans la vingtaine, sans doute. Elle est jolie avec ses yeux bleu-gris et son grand front. Elle a de longs cheveux bruns ramenés en queue de cheval. D'habitude, elle assiste madame Noëlle, mais je suppose qu'on lui a confié ce projet.

Aujourd'hui, plutôt que son ensemble noir, elle porte un collant gris et un maillot assorti, des jambières colorées et une jupe rouge. Elle doit avoir remarqué mon regard posé sur elle, parce qu'elle dit :

— Pour cette classe spéciale, vous pourrez porter des maillots de couleurs vives si vous voulez. Ça mettra les enfants plus à l'aise. Il ne faut pas oublier qu'ils n'ont jamais suivi de cours de ballet.

— Youpi !

Parfois, j'en ai assez de mon maillot noir.

Madame Dupré me sourit.

— Les enfants sont déjà dans la salle de danse. Allons voir ce qu'on peut faire avec eux.

— Vincent Poulin est volontaire. Je n'en reviens pas ! me chuchote Marie à l'oreille tandis que nous suivons madame Dupré.

Elle fait un signe de tête en direction des garçons devant nous.

— C'est lequel ?

— Celui qui a l'air snob.

Je devine tout de suite de qui elle parle. L'un des garçons est Sud-Américain et très beau. L'autre est un grand mince aux cheveux blonds bouclés et au nez aquilin qui se tient tellement droit qu'il en a l'air hautain.

Snob. Le mot décrit parfaitement l'expression de son visage.

— Est-ce qu'il est vraiment snob ?

— Le plus snob au monde, répond Marie. Il va à la même école que moi et il se croit déjà danseur étoile. L'autre, je ne le connais pas, mais tu peux être sûre que je vais m'arranger pour que ça change.

— Tu connais les filles ?

— La rousse s'appelle Danielle. L'autre, je ne sais pas.

En entrant dans la salle, nous tombons en pleine pagaille. Les enfants — ils sont une quarantaine — courent partout en hurlant. La plupart doivent avoir huit ou neuf ans. Marie et moi, nous nous regardons nerveusement. Madame Dupré n'arrivera jamais à les calmer, encore moins à leur apprendre à danser !

Madame Dupré éteint la lumière. Le soleil d'hiver se couche déjà et la salle est plongée dans l'ombre. Elle frappe dans ses mains et dit d'une voix forte :

— S'il vous plaît, assoyez-vous par terre en vous espaçant un peu.

Les enfants prennent place en silence. La professeure rallume la lumière et s'avance au centre de la salle.

— Bienvenue au cours, dit-elle. Tout d'abord, j'aimerais savoir combien d'entre vous ont déjà fait de la danse ?

Les élèves se regardent, mais aucun ne lève la main.

— Moi, je connais la danse des canards ! s'écrie un garçon à la tignasse noire et bouclée.

Il se lève, ramène ses mains sous ses aisselles et se met à sautiller ici et là. Évidemment, les autres éclatent de rire. Je me mords la lèvre pour garder mon sérieux.

— Très joli, dit madame Dupré. Et quel est ton nom ?

— David Ramirez.

— Merci, David. Tu peux te rasseoir, à présent. Quelqu'un d'autre a-t-il suivi des cours de danse ?

Une petite fille à la peau très foncée lève timidement la main.

— Quel cours as-tu suivi ? lui demande madame Dupré.

La fillette parle si bas que je ne l'entends pas.

— Plus fort, s'il te plaît, dit madame Dupré gentiment.

Les yeux de la petite fille s'arrondissent, comme si, soudain, elle se voyait prise au piège.

— Non, je n'ai jamais suivi de cours, répond-elle d'une voix à peine audible.

— Oh ! très bien, fait madame Dupré. Je suis très heureuse qu'aucun d'entre vous n'ait fait de danse auparavant. Nous n'aurons pas à corriger de mauvaises habitudes. Ce sera nouveau pour chacun de vous et vous apprendrez de la bonne façon. (Elle tend le bras dans notre direction.) Voici mes assistants : Marie et Jessie, à ma gauche. À ma droite, Vincent, Raul, Danielle et Suzanne. Je m'appelle madame Dupré. Nous allons commencer par des exercices de réchauffement. Restez assis, placez vos jambes bien droites devant vous. Je veux que vous vous penchiez doucement et que vous alliez toucher le bout de vos orteils.

— C'est de la gymnastique ! gémit David Ramirez. Je pensais qu'on devait danser !

— Il faut se réchauffer avant de danser, répond madame Dupré. Touche tes orteils, s'il te plaît.

— D'accord, mais c'est moins drôle que je croyais, murmure-t-il en se penchant.

Quand toute la classe est penchée, il m'est facile de remarquer deux fillettes qui chuchotent au bout de la salle. Elles ne semblent pas avoir conscience de ce que font les autres élèves.

— Jessie, s'il te plaît, va les rappeler à l'ordre, me demande madame Dupré.

Les filles sont tellement absorbées par leur conversation qu'elles ne me voient même pas approcher. L'une est petite et rousse. L'autre a de longs cheveux blonds et un teint de pêche. Je suis presque collée contre elles lorsqu'elles me remarquent enfin.

— Vous devriez être en train de vous réchauffer comme les autres, leur dis-je gentiment.

— Bof ! réplique la rousse. C'est nos mères qui nous ont forcées à venir. Faites comme si on n'était pas là.

Je ne m'attendais vraiment pas à ce genre de réponse !

— Eh bien, tant qu'à être ici, joignez-vous au groupe.

— Ça ne nous tente pas, répond la blonde.

Je jette un œil à l'avant de la salle et je vois madame Dupré qui me regarde. Comment dois-je réagir ?

— On apprécierait beaucoup votre participation, dis-je.

— On s'en fiche, répond la rouquine, d'un ton plutôt surprenant pour son âge.

Soudain, je comprends mieux ce que doivent ressentir certaines mères.

— S'il vous plaît, faites comme les autres, dis-je d'un ton suppliant.

Madame Dupré s'approche.

— Mesdemoiselles, si vous ne voulez pas participer, veuillez rester dans le corridor, dit-elle.

Les deux filles se regardent.

— Allez-vous le dire à nos mères ? demande la blonde.

— Oui, elles seront avisées de ne pas vous envoyer ici mardi prochain.

En moins de temps qu'il n'en faut pour le dire, les fillettes étendent les jambes et se baissent pour toucher leurs orteils.

— Jessie, passe entre les rangs et assure-toi que tout le monde a la bonne position, me dit madame Dupré.

Il n'y a pas le moindre reproche dans son ton. Heureusement, parce que je me sens un peu gênée de ne pas avoir accompli correctement ma première tâche d'assistante.

Après les exercices de réchauffement, madame Dupré fait jouer une cassette de la trame sonore de *Fantasia*, et demande aux enfants de danser sur la musique. Quelle foire ! Certains des petits se déhanchent de façon grotesque, et d'autres sont si sérieux que c'en est tout aussi comique.

La professeure nous conseille de circuler parmi les enfants, de prendre leurs noms et de noter leurs aptitudes selon une échelle de un à cinq. Cinq pour ceux qui ont un certain talent, et un pour ceux qui sont raides et n'ont aucun rythme. Deux, trois et quatre pour les autres qui se situent dans la moyenne.

— S'il arrivait qu'un même enfant soit noté par plusieurs d'entre vous, ça n'a pas d'importance. Je compilerai les résultats ce soir et je serai bien contente d'avoir plus d'une opinion.

En déambulant parmi les enfants qui dansent, j'attribue à la plupart d'entre eux un deux, un trois ou un quatre. Mais il y a des exceptions. Par exemple, le garçon qui s'appelle David bouge vraiment de façon désordonnée — les bras grands ouverts, accrochant même au passage ses voisins. Pourtant, quelque chose dans sa façon de suivre la musique me pousse à lui accorder un cinq.

Surprise! La petite fille qui a déclaré ne jamais avoir suivi de leçons (elle s'appelle Marthe) maîtrise certains pas de ballet avec beaucoup de grâce. Je lui donne un cinq aussi.

Les deux bavardes du bout (la rousse se nomme Nora et la blonde, Jeanne) ne font que sautiller sur place en papotant. Je leur mets un.

J'accorde un cinq à une petite grassouillette blonde prénommée Yvonne. Son style, très amusant, consiste à bondir en secouant la tête.

Le temps file. Déjà, les parents arrivent pour chercher leurs enfants.

Je me sens un peu malheureuse, mais très satisfaite de m'être proposée pour aider madame Dupré.

Nous remettons notre feuille d'appréciation à madame Dupré qui nous remercie pour notre aide.

— C'était amusant, hein? me dit Marie en nous rendant au vestiaire.

— Oui. Certains des enfants ont du caractère!

— Mais qu'est-ce que madame Dupré va bien pouvoir faire avec eux?

— C'est vrai que, si elle se contente de les laisser danser n'importe comment pendant une heure et demie, ils n'apprendront pas grand-chose.

— On verra bien.

Dans le vestiaire, nous tombons sur les filles de notre cours régulier.

— Comment ça s'est passé? demande Marie-Claude.

— C'est toute une expérience, réponds-je en riant.

Elle renifle.

— Je n'ai pas de mal à te croire! Une expérience dont je me passe très bien!

— Non! non! C'était très agréable, tu sais.

Pendant que je parle à Marie-Claude, je vois Marie retirer son maillot et se regarder en grimaçant dans le miroir.

— Je deviens de plus en plus bouboule, fait-elle d'une voix angoissée.

— Oui, il faudrait vraiment que tu perdes quelques kilos, lui dit Mireille Houle. Tu vas voir, après, ce sera beaucoup plus facile de sauter. Qu'est-ce que tu en penses, Jessie?

— Je ne sais pas. Je n'y ai jamais…

Je suis interrompue par Karine qui entre dans le vestiaire en lançant:

— Alors?… Les enfants sont des monstres?

— Non, mais on va avoir du pain sur la planche, c'est sûr ! dis-je.

— Pour ça, oui ! ajoute Marie.

CHAPITRE 4

Jeudi

Aujourd'hui, après l'école, j'ai gardé les Papadabis, et croyez-moi, je n'ai pas chômé!

Imaginez-vous que Karen (Marchand) et Nadine Dansereau se sont amenées aussi. Avec Sarah, Léonard et Annie, ça faisait beaucoup! Annie, Nadine et Karen sont vraiment la bande des trois mousquetaires. Quand elles sont ensemble, leur imagination ne connaît plus de limites!

Christine n'avait pas prévu avoir deux enfants de plus à garder quand elle se présente chez les Papadakis, mais ça ne la dérange pas vraiment de trouver Karen et Nadine avec Annie. Elle est contente de voir sa demi-sœur (Karen) et elle connaît très bien Nadine. Les trois fillettes ont sept ans et sont pratiquement inséparables. C'est pourquoi elles se sont surnommées «Les trois mousquetaires».

Les Papadakis habitent juste en face de chez Christine, c'est donc elle qui les garde le plus souvent. Ce jour-là, à son arrivée, les enfants, costumés, sont déjà en train de jouer à l'hôtel et aussitôt madame Papadakis sortie, ils entraînent Christine dans leur jeu.

— Youpi! fait Annie. À présent, Sarah ne sera plus obligée de faire la réceptionniste.

Christine éclate de rire en voyant Sarah, qui n'a que deux ans, installée sur une pile de coussins derrière la table basse. Les plus vieilles lui ont mis un petit chapeau sur la tête. Sarah est occupée à gribouiller sur une feuille de papier (le registre de l'hôtel, sans doute).

Karen lui enlève son chapeau.

— Tiens, fait-elle en le tendant à Christine. Sarah était en train de noter ton nom, mais elle n'est pas très douée pour ce jeu. Elle fait n'importe quoi dans le livre de l'hôtel et elle n'arrête pas de faire sonner la clochette.

Comme si les paroles de Karen venaient de le lui rappeler, Sarah se met à taper sur la clochette placée sur la table en criant: «Closse! Closse! Closse!»

— Tu vois? fait Karen.

— Alors, je suis contente de prendre la relève, dit Christine en s'assoyant derrière la petite table. Sarah sera mon assistante.

Elle regarde les enfants déguisés. Karen a passé une robe de satin violette par-dessus ses vêtements. Elle a mis de l'ombre à paupières et relevé ses cheveux. Annie porte un petit chapeau à voilette, des chaussures à talons hauts et un châle en dentelle. Nadine, un voile de tulle blanc autour de la taille, a une perruque blonde sur la tête et une tonne de rouge à lèvres.

— Qui est à l'hôtel, aujourd'hui ? demande Christine.

— Personne encore, répond Nadine. On recommence au début puisque tu viens d'arriver.

— Le groom est déjà au travail, note Christine.

Léonard, qui a neuf ans, a revêtu un veston de son père.

— Je ne veux pas être le groom, se plaint-il. Mais elles disent que je dois. Est-ce que c'est vrai ?

— Pourquoi ne le laissez-vous pas jouer un autre rôle ? demande Christine.

— Qui va porter les bagages ? s'objecte Annie.

— Vous n'avez même pas de bagages ! s'écrie Léonard.

— On fait semblant ! rétorque Annie. C'est juste un jeu, tu sais !

— Moi, ça ne m'intéresse pas de porter de l'air, bougonne Léonard.

— J'ai une idée, dit Christine. Léonard, fais le groom pour les filles et quand elles seront à leurs chambres, tu pourras devenir un client.

— D'accord, répond Léonard, maussade.

Une fois la crise résolue, le jeu commence. Karen est la première cliente de l'hôtel. Elle s'avance et prend un air impatient en tapant sur la cloche.

— Puis-je vous aider ? demande Christine.

— Vous ne savez pas qui je suis ? fait Karen d'un ton sec.

— Oh! à présent je vous reconnais! s'écrie Christine. C'est vous, madame Mystère. Mais vous me semblez un peu changée.

Karen se penche au-dessus de la table.

— Annie n'a pas autant de costumes que nous, chuchote-t-elle. J'ai fait du mieux que j'ai pu.

— Tu es parfaite, répond Christine à voix basse.

Karen reprend son rôle de madame Mystère.

— Je suis épuisée, soupire-t-elle. Je sors d'une réunion avec la famille Addam. Une famille de fous, si vous voulez mon avis.

— À qui le dites-vous! fait Christine. Et comment s'est passée cette réunion?

Karen sourit.

— Merveilleusement bien. Morticia nous a servi des œufs à la diable et des doigts de dame. Les ongles étaient exquis!

— Beuuuuurk! s'écrient Léonard et Annie en riant.

— Signez ici, dit Christine en présentant une page blanche.

Karen se penche sur le cahier et trace un grand X sur la première ligne. Elle se tourne vers Léonard.

— Groom! Montez mes sacs en peau de lézard, dit-elle en pointant du doigt des bagages imaginaires.

Léonard pousse un soupir et fait semblant de prendre les sacs de Karen. Puis ils se dirigent vers l'escalier.

— Groom! lance Karen.

— Quoi?

— Vous avez oublié un sac.

Roulant les yeux, Léonard revient sur ses pas chercher le sac invisible.

À cet instant, on sonne à la porte.

— Pause ! dit Christine en se levant.

Elle court à la porte, pousse le rideau de la fenêtre et aperçoit une jeune fille aux cheveux blonds bouclés. C'est Chantal Chrétien.

— Allô, fait Christine en ouvrant.

— Je suis allée chez toi et ta grand-mère m'a dit que tu étais ici, explique Chantal en entrant.

— Qu'est-ce qui se passe ?

Chantal hausse les épaules.

— Rien. Je voulais juste te dire bonjour et bavarder. Si ça ne te dérange pas.

— Mais non, voyons. Pourvu que tu acceptes d'habiter à l'hôtel le plus bizarre de la planète.

— Comment ça ?

— Viens voir.

Quand elles entrent dans le salon, Sarah s'est remise à taper furieusement sur la clochette et Léonard, la mine renfrognée, a jeté son veston par terre. Les filles aussi ont l'air contrariées.

— Léonard ne veut plus être le groom, dit Annie.

— Pas de problème, dit Christine. Je suis allée au bureau d'emploi et j'en ai trouvé un autre. Voici Chantal.

Chantal lance un regard étonné à Christine, mais elle accepte de jouer.

— C'est mon uniforme ? demande-t-elle en ramassant le veston froissé.

— Oui, répond Christine en reprenant sa place derrière la table. Tu as la charge des bagages de nos chers clients. Ça te va ?

— D'accord ! dit Chantal en enfilant le veston.

Aussitôt, le visage de Léonard s'illumine.

— Je reviens tout de suite ! lance-t-il en courant vers l'escalier.

— Qui est notre prochain client ? demande Christine.

— Dis-lui d'arrêter de taper sur la cloche, gémit Annie en pointant Sarah du doigt.

Christine retire une feuille du cahier.

— Tiens, Sarah, dessine un peu.

Heureusement, Sarah accepte.

Quand Annie s'approche, Christine s'exclame :

— Tiens, bonjour, madame Bigoudi ! Quel bon vent vous amène ?

— Oh ! je vais rendre visite au baron Du Vivoir et à sa femme, la reine Rougette.

— Est-ce qu'un baron peut épouser une reine ? s'étonne Christine.

— Évidemment, répond Annie d'un air hautain. De nos jours, ça arrive souvent. (Elle se tourne vers Chantal.) Groom, j'aurai besoin de ma robe de bal pour ce soir. Voyez-y, voulez-vous ?

Chantal fait un petit salut et se retient pour ne pas rire.

— Bien, madame. Tout de suite, madame.

Quand madame Bigoudi a signé le registre et que Chantal a pris ses bagages, Nadine entre et se présente comme la princesse Véronica du Royaume Harmonica. La princesse, semble-t-il, tente de fuir un sorcier maléfique qui l'oblige à jouer de l'harmonica nuit et jour.

— J'ai mal aux joues, j'ai la gorge sèche, j'ai la figure tout enflée ! C'est horrible ! confie-t-elle à Christine.

Tandis que la princesse signe le registre, une musique rock poussée à fond retentit soudain et tous les regards se

38

tournent vers l'escalier. Affublé de lunettes fumées, d'un t-shirt noir et d'un bandeau rouge sur la tête à la façon des pirates, Léonard descend, un magnétophone à la main.

Arrivé à la dernière marche, il saute et atterrit les bras écartés.

— C'est moi, Johnny Rocket! s'exclame-t-il. J'apporte dans votre hôtel ma musique endiablée!

Il danse jusqu'au centre de la pièce en balançant son appareil à bout de bras.

Les filles entrent dans la danse immédiatement. Christine et Chantal éclatent de rire en regardant les enfants se déhancher partout dans leurs costumes. Même Sarah se met de la partie.

— Ils n'ont plus besoin de nous, je crois, crie Christine à Chantal, au milieu du tintamarre.

— Non, répond Chantal tout aussi fort.

— As-tu téléphoné à Sophie ou aux autres?

— Oui. Je dois voir Sophie et Claudia en ville samedi. Diane sera peut-être là, aussi.

À cet instant, Sarah trébuche et commence à pleurer. Christine court la prendre.

— Personne ne m'en a parlé, dit-elle tout en frottant la petite dans le dos pour l'apaiser.

— On s'est dit que tu étais trop occupée, hurle Chantal. Tu veux venir?

Christine s'assoit sur le canapé, Sarah sur les genoux.

— Je ne peux pas. Je garde, samedi.

— Tu viendras une autre fois.

— C'est ça. Une autre fois.

CHAPITRE 5

Vendredi, je suis bien contente de retrouver ma classe de ballet régulière. J'ai l'habitude d'avoir deux cours par semaine et n'en suivre qu'un seul, ça fait toute une différence ! Heureusement, mes muscles n'ont pas eu le temps de se rouiller, et je n'ai rien oublié. Mais je comprends soudain pourquoi la plupart des filles ne se sont pas portées volontaires pour aider madame Dupré. Manquer un seul cours les angoisse.

Moi-même, tandis que je fais des *pliés* à la barre, je sens l'anxiété me gagner. Je croyais que ça ne me ferait rien de perdre un peu de temps, et voilà que je constate que j'ai tout de même un certain esprit de compétition !

Pourtant, je n'ai vraiment pas à m'en faire. Une fois la classe commencée, je me rends compte que je n'ai pas manqué grand-chose mardi, et que je danse comme d'habitude.

Enfin, presque.

Une fois, je vacille un peu en faisant une *arabesque* et, à la fin du cours, je trébuche en exécutant un *assemblé* (un saut très simple).

Mais ce n'est pas parce que j'ai raté un cours. C'est tout simplement que je ne me concentre pas assez. En fait, je n'arrête pas d'observer Marie Bernard.

Depuis l'épisode du vestiaire, mardi, je n'ai pas réussi à chasser Marie et son régime maigreur de mon esprit. Il y a quelque chose qui cloche dans cette affaire, mais quoi?

À présent, je remarque une foule de détails qui ne m'avaient pas frappée auparavant. Par exemple, Marie se regarde constamment dans le miroir qui couvre tout le mur opposé à la barre.

Bon, d'accord, les danseurs font toujours ça. D'ailleurs, le miroir est là pour nous aider à corriger notre posture. Dans le cas de Marie, cependant, c'est différent. Elle s'observe même quand elle attend en file, ou durant les quelques minutes de la pause.

Peut-être pensez-vous qu'elle est vaniteuse. Non, ça n'a rien à voir avec la vanité. Elle ne semble pas s'admirer. On dirait plutôt qu'elle s'inquiète de son apparence. J'ai aussi remarqué qu'elle se pince toujours la taille et le ventre.

Après la classe, ce jour-là, Danielle (celle qui est volontaire) nous attend dans le corridor.

— Jessie! Marie! fait-elle quand nous sortons du studio.

— Allô! dis-je, un peu surprise. (Je ne lui ai jamais parlé avant.)

— Écoutez, dit-elle. Suzanne et moi, on a décidé avec Vincent et Raul d'aller manger ensemble après la classe, mardi prochain. Pour mieux faire connaissance. Vous voulez venir?

— Bien sûr! dis-je.

J'ai peut-être répondu un peu vite, mais c'est la première fois que quelqu'un de cette école me fait une invita-
tion et je suis trop contente pour refuser.

— Où allez-vous ? demande Marie.

— Au *Roi du hamburger*.

— Je ne sais pas, hésite Marie. Je ne mange pas de
hamburger, habituellement.

— Nous non plus, fait Danielle. En tout cas, pas souvent. Mais c'est le restaurant le plus près et il fait froid. Une
fois n'est pas coutume.

— Tu as sans doute raison.

Marie finit par accepter, mais avec une certaine réti-
cence.

Danielle est dépitée par son manque d'enthousiasme.

— En tout cas, tu es invitée. Viens si tu veux. À mardi !
Elle nous envoie la main et s'en va en courant.

— Ce serait intéressant de faire plus ample connaissance, non ? dis-je à Marie.

— Je connais déjà Vincent et c'est pas un cadeau,
marmonne-t-elle.

— Et Raul ? Je pensais que tu voulais le connaître
davantage ?

— Avec Danielle dans le décor, je n'ai aucune chance.
Elle est tellement jolie. Elle n'a pas un gramme de graisse
de trop.

— Toi non plus.

Marie lance un petit rire amer.

— Si au moins c'était vrai !

Je n'ai plus le temps de bavarder. C'est vendredi et je
ferais mieux de me grouiller. Il y a une réunion du CBS !

Une fois de plus, je réussis à arriver à l'heure. À part le

43

récit amusant de la garde de Christine chez les Papadakis, il ne se passe pas grand-chose.

Je ne prends aucune nouvelle garde et la fin de semaine est assez ennuyante. De toute façon, je ne pense qu'à mardi prochain.

D'habitude, la mode me laisse plutôt indifférente, mais là, j'en suis à me demander ce que je vais porter. Puisque nous ne sommes pas obligés de porter notre maillot ordinaire, il faut que je trouve autre chose. Après y avoir longuement réfléchi, je fixe mon choix sur un maillot vert fluo, un pantalon d'exercice bleu foncé et de grosses chaussettes jaunes. Je n'ai pas envie d'avoir l'air bébé. Même si je suis plus jeune que les autres, je veux qu'ils croient que j'ai leur âge.

Mardi, le cours commence une fois de plus dans l'anarchie. Il y a trop d'enfants. En tout cas, c'est mon opinion. Mais madame Dupré divise calmement la classe en six groupes et en assigne un à chaque volontaire.

Ouf! c'est Raul qui hérite de David et de deux de ses copains. Tant mieux. Malheureusement, je me retrouve avec Nora et Jeanne sur les bras. Ces deux-là sont bien décidées à ne rien faire de plus que le strict minimum. Quand nous travaillons les *pliés*, elles se contentent de fléchir les genoux un tout petit peu. On dirait deux vieilles dames. (Du coin de l'œil, j'aperçois David qui saute comme s'il avait des ressorts aux pieds. Je préfère encore Nora et Jeanne.)

Dans le groupe de Marie se trouve la timide Marthe. (Marie porte une grande chemise blanche et un pantalon d'exercice gris qui camouflent les lignes de son corps. C'est d'ailleurs peut-être pour ça qu'elle s'est habillée ainsi.) De tout le cours, Marthe ne regarde ni Marie, ni personne. Elle est entièrement concentrée sur ce qu'elle fait.

Après avoir montré aux enfants les *pliés*, chaque volontaire mène son groupe à la barre d'exercices. Là, madame Dupré leur montre à exécuter un *grand battement*. Les enfants semblent aimer ça, c'est le premier véritable mouvement de ballet qu'ils apprennent.

Pendant le dernier quart d'heure, madame Dupré remet la musique de *Fantasia* et demande aux enfants de danser en n'utilisant que ce qu'ils ont appris aujourd'hui. Le résultat est comique ; il faut vraiment chercher très fort pour trouver le moindre mouvement ressemblant à un *plié* ou à un *grand battement*.

Malgré cette danse débridée, madame Dupré semble très satisfaite.

— D'abord, il faut briser leurs mauvaises habitudes, nous dit-elle à la fin, puis transformer ces petits en danseurs.

— Si c'est ce que vous voulez, commente Danielle à voix basse tandis que madame Dupré s'éloigne.

— Qu'est-ce que tu veux dire ? dis-je.

— C'est la méthode d'enseignement la plus bizarre que j'aie jamais vue. Moi, quand j'avais huit ans, mes cours de ballet ne ressemblaient pas du tout à ça.

— C'est vrai, dis-je. C'était plus discipliné.

— Évidemment ! fait Suzanne. Je ne vois pas vraiment où va madame Dupré.

— J'ai l'impression qu'elle ne prend pas ces cours au sérieux, dit Raul. Pour elle, ce ne sont que de pauvres enfants défavorisés, et de couleur, en plus.

— Il y a plusieurs Blancs, lui rappelé-je.

— Oui, mais ils viennent tous de milieux pauvres,

alors, à ses yeux, ils ne comptent pas.

— Tu es injuste, objecte Marie d'une voix douce. Elle leur enseigne, non?

— Je suis de ton avis, dit Vincent. Je crois qu'il serait plus opportun de réserver notre jugement pour plus tard.

Je retiens un sourire en voyant Marie rouler les yeux derrière lui. C'est vrai que Vincent a une façon bizarre de s'exprimer.

— Si on parlait de tout ça devant un bon hamburger? propose Danielle en retirant l'élastique de ses cheveux. Je meurs de faim.

Après nous être changés rapidement, nous nous retrouvons devant l'école. Il fait déjà très noir et le vent glacial nous mord les joues. Collets remontés, têtes enfoncées dans nos manteaux, nous nous dirigeons vers le *Roi du hamburger*.

— Je ne sais pas ce que vous en pensez, dit Suzanne en ouvrant la porte vitrée du restaurant, mais moi, je n'aurais pas fait un mètre de plus. On gèle.

— Oui, je suis totalement et irrémédiablement frigorifié, ajoute Vincent le plus sérieusement du monde. (Une fois de plus, j'essaie de ne pas sourire. Il est tordant, ce Vincent.)

Comme je vais souper bientôt, je décide de commander seulement des frites et un Coke.

— C'est peut-être ce que je devrais prendre aussi, dit Marie. Pourquoi avoir choisi ce restaurant? Tout est bourré de calories!

— Essaie une salade, suggéré-je.

— Les vinaigrettes sont très riches, tu sais.

— Tu n'es pas obligée de manger, après tout.

Le regard de Marie se pose sur Raul dont le plateau contient une montagne de frites, un hamburger géant et un grand verre de Coke.

— Non, j'aurais l'air bizarre si je ne commandais rien, décide Marie. Je vais prendre une petite assiette de frites et un petit Coke.

Nous nous assoyons à une longue table.

— Je me demande si on va toujours travailler avec les mêmes groupes, commence Suzanne en développant son hamburger.

— J'espère bien que non, dit Vincent. J'ai cette petite boulotte d'Yvonne. Peu importe ce que je lui dis de faire, elle rebondit. Je dis «plié», elle rebondit. Je dis «lance ta jambe en arrière», elle rebondit. Elle serait meilleure au football.

— Je te l'échangerais bien contre mes bonnes à rien de Nora et Jeanne, dis-je. Elles ne sont pas du tout intéressées par le cours.

— D'ailleurs, j'ai été surprise de voir que tu arrivais à les faire bouger un peu, dit Danielle en riant. Je ne les voudrais pour rien au monde.

— Et toi, comment te débrouilles-tu avec David? demande Marie à Raul.

Raul a la bouche pleine et fait signe d'attendre.

— Il se croit malin, répond-il enfin. Mais je peux le contrôler. S'il tente de sortir du rang, je le démolis.

— Tu ne peux pas faire ça! s'écrie Suzanne.

— Je sais, admet-il. Je ne vois pas vraiment comment agir avec lui. Il distrait les autres.

— Ça ne devrait pas être notre problème, déclare Vincent, une frite à la main. La responsabilité incombe à madame Dupré.

— C'est vrai, fait Danielle. (Elle se tourne vers Raul.) Tu crois réellement que madame Dupré n'attend rien de ces enfants? Tu crois que c'est pour ça qu'elle est si permissive?

— J'imagine, répond Raul. Mais je n'en suis pas sûr.

— Peut-être qu'elle a raison de ne pas trop attendre d'eux, ajoute Vincent. Les enfants sont là pour se distraire, non pas pour devenir danseurs.

— Ils devraient avoir une chance, comme tout le monde, insiste Raul avec véhémence.

— Je pense qu'on leur donne justement cette chance, dit Marie.

— Seulement si le programme est bien suivi, riposte Raul en secouant la tête tristement. Désolé de m'emporter autant, mais quand on fait partie d'une minorité, on s'habitue à être sur la défensive. Tu ne trouves pas, Jessie?

— Non, pas vraiment, réponds-je lentement. Euh… je comprends ce que tu veux dire, mais ce n'est pas ce que je vis. D'une certaine façon, j'ai beaucoup de chance.

— En tout cas, moi, j'en ai fait l'expérience et j'ose espérer que ce n'est pas ce qui se produit ici, dit-il en mordant dans son hamburger.

— Il faudra veiller au grain, dis-je diplomatiquement.

Je me sens à l'aise. Les autres discutent avec moi d'égal à égal, comme si j'avais leur âge. Je jette un coup d'œil vers Marie pour voir si elle se plaît ici.

Mais c'est surtout de la nervosité que je lis sur son visage. Elle n'a avalé qu'une frite. Les autres, elle les casse en deux et les fait tourner dans son assiette. À première vue, on pourrait croire qu'elle en a mangé plus qu'en réalité. De temps à autre, elle porte la paille de son

Coke à ses lèvres. Mais le niveau de liquide dans le verre ne baisse pas vite.

Pourquoi ne mange-t-elle pas ? Elle veut peut-être se garder de la place pour le souper. Ou bien elle déteste ce genre de nourriture. À moins qu'elle ne soit au régime.

La dernière hypothèse m'inquiète un peu. Ce serait trop insensé de la part de Marie. Une autre question me tracasse : pourquoi Marie n'a-t-elle tout simplement pas dit qu'elle ne voulait rien prendre ? Ça n'aurait dérangé personne. Et pourquoi essaie-t-elle de faire semblant de manger ?

Avant que je puisse pousser plus loin mes réflexions, je vois papa entrer dans le restaurant. Je lui avais pourtant dit de m'attendre dehors ! Je n'ai rien contre lui, je suis fière de mon père. Mais il n'y a rien de tel pour rappeler à tout le monde que je n'ai que onze ans.

— À la semaine prochaine ! dis-je aux autres en ramassant rapidement mes affaires. Mon… euh… mon chauffeur est là.

— À bientôt, Jessie, dit Danielle.

— À mardi, ajoute Raul.

— Ces jeunes-là sont plus vieux que toi, non ? fait mon père en montant dans la voiture. (Ah ! la la ! ce qu'il peut être protecteur !)

— Oui, mais ils sont très gentils.

C'est vrai qu'ils sont tous très gentils. Même Vincent. Et je commence à aimer beaucoup Marie. J'ai admiré sa façon d'être en désaccord avec Raul, même si elle le trouve de son goût. Mais son problème de nourriture me laisse songeuse. J'espère qu'il n'y a aucune raison de s'inquiéter.

CHAPITRE 6

Les gens sont souvent difficiles à comprendre. Je ne vois pas pourquoi Marie s'en fait avec sa taille. Et vraiment, je ne sais pas où veut en venir madame Dupré.

Je ne crois pas qu'elle se désintéresse des enfants du cours. Les danseurs de ballet ont tendance à être très intenses, très sérieux dans leur art. Madame Dupré ne fait pas exception. Aucun détail ne lui échappe. J'ai toujours l'impression que, derrière son grand front, ça bouillonne sans arrêt.

Pourtant, ce que disent les autres volontaires est vrai. Jusqu'à maintenant, elle n'a pas été très exigeante pendant ses classes.

En tout cas, si le premier cours m'a étonnée, le suivant me déroute encore davantage. Madame Dupré a complètement changé de tactique.

Tout d'abord, elle a fait installer un piano dans la salle, et un pianiste que je n'avais jamais vu (un garçon dans la vingtaine) y prend place. Madame Dupré tape durement dans ses mains pour attirer l'attention.

— Voici notre pianiste, monsieur Jean Tsuji, un musicien bénévole.

Le jeune homme sourit en saluant de la main.

Puis madame Dupré demande aux enfants de reformer les mêmes groupes que la semaine précédente.

— À présent, nous allons faire des exercices d'étirement et de réchauffement, dit-elle.

Pendant que monsieur Tsuji joue un morceau simple et cadencé, elle donne ses instructions. Une fois les exercices terminés, elle commence le cours sur les cinq positions de base. Nous, les volontaires, nous nous promenons parmi les élèves pour les aider.

À mon grand étonnement, Nora et Jeanne sont concentrées sur leurs pieds. Je crois que madame Dupré les a eues par surprise.

Par contre, David fait toujours le pitre. Il louche, tire la langue, exagère les mouvements de façon ridicule. Évidemment, les élèves autour de lui rigolent.

— David ! fait madame Dupré. Viens en avant. Tu vas montrer les cinq positions au reste de la classe.

Tous les regards sont posés sur lui. Le menton relevé effrontément, il s'avance.

— Première position, dit madame Dupré.

David joint ses pieds l'un contre l'autre.

— Non ! non ! fait madame Dupré. Les orteils en dehors. Plus en dehors. (En première position, les pieds doivent être complètement tournés vers l'extérieur, comme Charlie Chaplin dans ses films.)

David tourne ses pieds.

— Deuxième position, dit madame Dupré.

David lui lance un regard gêné. Il a oublié.

— Les pieds écartés, dit-elle sèchement.

Il écarte les pieds, mais oublie de les garder tournés.

— Non, non. Je te conseille de regagner ta place et de mieux écouter.

La mine contrariée, David rejoint les rangs.

Madame Dupré demande ensuite aux élèves de prendre place à la barre. Ils sont nombreux mais ça peut aller. Il s'agit de faire des *pliés* dans chacune des cinq positions. Ces exercices font travailler efficacement les tendons et les muscles internes de la jambe. Les enfants sont naturellement souples, mais ils se retrouvent ici dans des positions qui ne leur sont pas familières et plusieurs perdent l'équilibre et heurtent leurs voisins. Ce qui produit parfois un effet «domino»: un élève tombe sur l'autre qui fait tomber le suivant, qui fait tomber le suivant...

Les assistants travaillent fort. Il faut pousser les pieds des élèves dans la bonne position, les encourager à s'incliner davantage, à garder le menton haut et à maintenir leur posture. Nora et Jeanne essaient de reprendre leur attitude de petites vieilles, mais madame Dupré s'amène et, fermement (mais gentiment), elle pose les mains sur leurs épaules et les fait se courber.

La petite Marthe exécute tous les mouvements à la perfection. Même ses bras s'étirent avec beaucoup de grâce.

— Beau travail, lui dit Danielle.

La petite baisse les yeux, comme s'il s'agissait d'une réprimande.

Raul accorde un peu plus d'attention à David, mais celui-ci semble bien déterminé à ne pas coopérer. Dès que Raul a le dos tourné, il s'acharne sur la tresse de Mélissa qui est devant lui.

— Hé! crie la fillette en se retournant.

David sourit alors d'un air angélique et regarde au plafond.

Après quelques minutes de ce petit manège, madame Dupré intervient.

— David, viens t'asseoir ici près de la porte.

— J'ai rien fait! proteste-t-il.

— Ici. Tout de suite, dit calmement madame Dupré.

David obéit, mais lui fait une grimace quand elle s'éloigne. Les élèves rigolent. Madame Dupré doit bien se douter de ce qui se passe dans son dos, mais elle fait mine de l'ignorer.

— Continuez, dit-elle aux autres.

David se laisse glisser contre le mur et s'assoit par terre. Les bras croisés, il regarde la classe. Je m'attendais à ce qu'au bout de quelques minutes madame Dupré lui dise de regagner sa place, mais non. Elle montre aux élèves à faire des *demi-pliés* en cinquième position et on dirait qu'elle l'a complètement oublié.

Comme l'a mentionné Vincent, la boulotte Yvonne rebondit même en faisant des *pliés*. Madame Dupré sourit en lui tenant les épaules et la guide pour s'élever et s'abaisser plus lentement.

— Ce n'est pas une faute de bondir, dit-elle gentiment, mais avec élégance.

Je m'occupe d'un élève, quand j'aperçois soudain Marie qui s'arrête et repousse sa frange de son front. Elle est rouge et en sueur. Elle se penche en avant et pose ses mains sur ses genoux.

Je m'approche d'elle.

— Ça ne va pas?

— Je me sens faible. Je dois couver quelque chose, répond-elle d'une voix tremblante.

Madame Dupré nous rejoint.

— Elle ne se sent pas bien, lui dis-je.

Marie se redresse et recule en vacillant.

— Je peux rentrer chez moi ? demande-t-elle.

— Bien sûr. Quelqu'un peut-il venir te prendre ?

— Je vais téléphoner à ma mère.

— Parfait. Jessie, reste avec elle jusqu'à l'arrivée de sa mère.

J'accompagne Marie au vestiaire.

— Fais-tu de la fièvre ? dis-je.

— Je ne pense pas, répond-elle en ouvrant son sac.

Lentement, elle se change et doit même s'arrêter deux fois pour se reposer. Durant ces pauses, elle reste assise la tête entre les mains. Je ne peux pas m'empêcher de remarquer qu'elle est encore plus maigre que je l'aurais cru. On voit parfaitement ses côtes.

— Est-ce que tu ne devrais pas manger un peu ? J'ai des *chips* dans mon sac.

Marie lève les yeux sur moi. J'étais sûre qu'elle allait répondre oui, mais elle secoue plutôt la tête négativement.

— Je n'ai pas vraiment faim, dit-elle.

J'appelle sa mère pendant qu'elle finit de s'habiller. Puis j'attends avec elle dans le hall.

Lorsque je reviens au studio, Suzanne est en train de faire la démonstration d'un *pas de chat* simple sur un air entraînant qu'interprète monsieur Tsuji. (C'est la «danse des chats», tiré de l'Acte III de *La Belle au bois dormant*. Si ça peut vous intéresser.)

David est toujours assis près de la porte, mais le *pas de*

chat semble avoir capté son attention. Il n'est plus avachi. Il a le corps tendu, la mine éveillée, comme s'il essayait de mémoriser le mouvement.

Madame Dupré laisse chaque élève essayer le nouveau pas. Encore une fois, le résultat est tordant. Mais peu importe leurs gaucheries, tous sont ravis de l'exercice. Yvonne, la petite balle, saute très haut. Et Marthe le réussit presque bien. Elle a vraiment un talent inné.

Je jette un œil à David. La tête dans les mains, il regarde faire ses camarades. Manifestement, il meurt d'envie d'essayer.

Nora et Jeanne font tout pour passer les dernières. Quand vient leur tour, elles s'exécutent tant bien que mal, rouges de confusion.

À la fin, madame Dupré s'approche de David.

— David, dit-elle doucement, si tu ne peux pas te tenir tranquille la semaine prochaine, je vais être obligée de te demander de ne plus revenir.

Les yeux de David s'arrondissent. Il ouvre la bouche, mais sans pouvoir prononcer une parole.

— Je ne peux pas te laisser distraire les autres, lui explique madame Dupré. Alors, penses-y bien.

Sur ce, elle retourne s'occuper des autres élèves. David me regarde.

— Est-ce qu'elle peut faire ça? me demande-t-il d'un ton sceptique.

Je hoche la tête.

— Ce n'est pas l'école, ici. Ils peuvent te renvoyer.

— Bof! je m'en fous, marmonne David en se levant. C'est débile, de toute façon.

Les parents commencent à arriver dans le hall. Enthousiasmés par les *pas de chat*, les enfants s'élancent vers eux en décrivant ce qu'ils ont fait. Mais pas David. Les mains dans les poches, il rejoint un homme aux cheveux bruns et aux épaules carrées. L'homme pose sa main gentiment sur la nuque de son fils, et ils partent en silence.

Marthe prend la main d'une belle grande dame au teint très foncé. La femme jette un coup d'œil dans la salle. On dirait qu'un million de questions passent dans son regard. Quand elle me remarque, elle hausse les sourcils, comme surprise de me trouver ici. Une fraction de seconde, nos regards se croisent, puis elle se retourne et part. Qu'est-ce qui a bien pu lui traverser l'esprit?

Bientôt, tous les enfants sont partis.

— Merci de votre aide, nous dit madame Dupré en souriant. Et merci à vous, monsieur Tsuji.

Le jeune homme lui fait un sourire et un petit signe de tête, puis ramasse ses partitions.

— La mère de Marie est venue la chercher? me demande madame Dupré.

— Oui.

— Très bien. Excusez-moi, mais je dois me dépêcher, j'ai un autre rendez-vous, dit-elle en prenant son sac.

— Qu'est-il arrivé à Marie? me demande Raul.

— Elle n'avait pas l'air dans son assiette, fait Vincent.

— Elle pense avoir un virus, dis-je. (Il faut que je me souvienne de dire à Marie que Raul s'est informé d'elle.)

— J'espère que ce n'est pas contagieux, dit Danielle.

Je voudrais bien leur demander s'ils ont remarqué comme Marie avait maigri. Est-ce qu'ils ont noté qu'elle n'a rien mangé au restaurant? J'ai besoin de l'avis de quelqu'un d'autre.

Mais quelque chose m'empêche de parler. La présence des garçons peut-être. À moins que ce ne soit la peur de passer pour une commère.

— On va au restaurant? nous demande Danielle.

— Je veux bien, moi. Mais il faut d'abord que je téléphone à mon père.

Heureusement, papa n'a pas encore quitté le bureau.

— C'est parfait, dit-il. J'ai justement un travail à terminer ici.

— Peux-tu venir me prendre à dix-huit heures dehors?

— Hé! tu as honte de ton vieux père?

— Mais non... c'est juste que je ne veux pas qu'ils croient que je suis... euh... trop jeune... tu sais...

— Alors, si on se donnait rendez-vous devant le comptoir? Je serai le gars avec un lait battu au chocolat.

— Papa! fais-je en grognant. Bon, d'accord.

Ce n'est pas si terrible que ça, après tout. Ils ont tous vu mon père la dernière fois et ça ne les a pas empêchés de me réinviter. Tant mieux, parce que j'aime bien faire partie de ce nouveau groupe. Pour la première fois depuis que j'ai commencé mes cours de ballet, j'ai vraiment l'impression d'être acceptée.

CHAPITRE 7

Pendant la réunion du CBS, je reste silencieuse. Je n'arrête pas de penser à Marie. Ce qu'elle a, ce n'est pas seulement un virus.

— La Terre appelle Jessie Raymond, fait Christine. Allô? Allô? Ici, la Terre…

— Excusez-moi, dis-je en souriant.

— À quoi rêvais-tu, Jessie? demande Diane.

— Oui, tu étais sur une autre planète, ajoute Sophie.

— Je songeais à une fille de mon cours de ballet.

Je leur explique que Marie s'est mise au régime et qu'elle maigrit à vue d'œil. Je leur raconte l'épisode du restaurant et son malaise pendant la classe de madame Dupré.

— Elle est peut-être anorexique, déclare Sophie à la fin.

— Qu'est-ce que c'est que ça? dis-je.

— C'est quand on se prive de nourriture au point de n'avoir plus que la peau et les os, répond Anne-Marie. Quoi qu'on fasse, on se croit toujours trop grosse, même si c'est le contraire.

— Vous vous souvenez, les filles, comme vous pen-

59

siez que j'étais anorexique quand vous m'avez connue ? dit Sophie.

— Pourquoi ? demande Marjorie.

— Parce que je ne mangeais pas de sucreries. Je ne leur avais pas encore dit que j'étais diabétique.

— J'ai entendu parler d'une fille qui vomissait exprès après chaque repas pour ne pas prendre de poids, dit Claudia.

— Ouache ! C'est fou ! s'écrie Diane.

— Mais ce n'est pas parce qu'on est maigre, qu'on est nécessairement anorexique, dit Christine. Il y a beaucoup de gens qui sont minces de nature.

— Et suivre un régime n'est pas toujours mauvais, ajoute Sophie. Si on le fait bien et qu'on mange des aliments sains ou qu'on coupe seulement les bonbons, c'est parfait. Mais on ne devrait s'imposer un régime strict que si on en a vraiment besoin, et pas avant d'en avoir parlé à un médecin.

— Jessie, es-tu sûre que ton amie exagère ? demande Marjorie.

— Pas mal sûre. Chaque fois que je la vois, on dirait qu'elle a fondu. Il me semble que la perte de poids devrait être plus graduelle.

— C'est juste, dit Christine. Maigrir rapidement, ce n'est jamais bon signe. Pour moi, ton amie a un problème.

— Mais je ne comprends pas, dis-je. En se regardant dans le miroir, elle doit bien voir qu'elle est trop maigre, non ?

Mes amies haussent les épaules. Personne ne semble avoir de réponse.

— Ça me dépasse, dit Christine.

— C'est psychologique, je crois, ajoute Diane.

— Tu veux dire qu'elle est folle ? dis-je, alarmée.

— Non, pas folle, fait Claudia. Je parie que le génie de la famille a des livres là-dessus. Elle étudie la psychologie cette année. (Josée suit des cours universitaires, même si elle n'a que seize ans.)

Nous accompagnons Claudia à la chambre de sa sœur. Elle jette un œil rapide autour, puis entrouvre la porte.

— Parfait, elle n'est pas là.

— Pourquoi ? Elle ne veut pas que tu lises ses bouquins ? demande Anne-Marie.

— Non, non, ce n'est pas ça. Mais si on demandait des explications à Josée, on en aurait pour la nuit. Vous la connaissez. Elle nous décrirait en long et en large le cas de chaque anorexique de la planète.

Claudia tire de l'étagère trois livres de psychologie. (Évidemment, les livres de Josée sont classés par ordre alphabétique, et donc faciles à repérer.) Puis les filles se dépêchent de regagner la chambre de Claudia.

Christine feuillette un des ouvrages, Diane, un autre, et Anne-Marie, le troisième.

— J'ai quelque chose ici ! fait Christine. « Il arrive qu'une jeune fille entreprenne une diète à la suite d'un simple commentaire sur son poids ou sa ligne. »

— C'est justement ce qui s'est passé ! m'écrié-je. Une autre fille lui a dit qu'elle pourrait sauter plus haut si elle perdait quelques kilos.

— Et c'est à ce moment qu'elle s'est mise au régime ? demande Sophie.

— Je pense, oui.

Christine, qui a continué à lire en silence, poursuit :

— Tout se tient. On dit ici que ce qui commence comme un régime normal finit par devenir incontrôlable. La personne — le plus souvent, une adolescente — devient obsédée par sa ligne. Elle ne se voit plus telle qu'elle est véritablement.

— C'est Marie tout craché, dis-je avec excitation. Elle se trouve grosse, alors qu'en réalité elle est maigre comme un clou !

— Dans mon bouquin, on prétend que les anorexiques essaient de dissimuler leur comportement à table, dit Diane. Elles jouent parfois avec leur nourriture, poussent les aliments de côté, les réarrangent dans l'assiette, pour ne pas attirer l'attention sur leur refus de manger.

— C'est exactement ainsi que s'est comportée Marie au restaurant, dis-je. Maintenant, je comprends pourquoi.

— Est-elle irritable, déprimée ? demande Anne-Marie. Mon livre dit que c'est un des symptômes.

— Non, pas vraiment, dois-je admettre.

— C'est bien, dit Sophie. Son problème ne fait peut-être que commencer. Si elle reçoit de l'aide dès maintenant, elle pourra s'en sortir avant que ça ne s'aggrave.

— Que va-t-il se passer si elle n'arrête pas ? demande Marjorie.

— « La maladie peut entraîner faiblesse, fatigue et état dépressif, hypotension, ralentissement du rythme cardiaque et baisse de la température corporelle », lit Anne-Marie.

Elle poursuit sa lecture à voix basse, et devient de plus en plus soucieuse.

— C'est très sérieux, conclut-elle en posant le livre.

— Oh ! la la ! fait Diane. Vous vous imaginez mourir de faim juste pour avoir une silhouette élégante ?

— Non, marmonne Claudia en mordant à belles dents dans une tablette de chocolat. Mais il y a plein de filles qui agissent ainsi.

— Qu'est-ce que je dois faire, d'après vous ? dis-je.

— Peux-tu parler à Marie ? demande Christine.

— J'ai beau lui répéter qu'elle n'est pas grosse, elle ne me croit pas.

— Peux-tu en glisser un mot à un des professeurs de ballet ? suggère Anne-Marie.

Je pousse un long soupir.

— Je ne sais pas. Si madame Noëlle lui conseillait d'abandonner les cours, je me sentirais très mal à l'aise. Marie ne me le pardonnerait jamais. Peut-être qu'elle va arrêter son régime d'elle-même ?

— Peut-être, fait Diane sans conviction.

— Je vais remettre les trois bouquins en place, dit Claudia.

À cet instant, le téléphone sonne. C'est Guillaume Marchand, le beau-père de Christine. Il a besoin d'une gardienne pour ce soir. (Christine doit assister à une partie de basket à l'école de Marc Tardif.)

Sophie s'offre à y aller.

— Si Chantal venait aussi, on pourrait bavarder, dit-elle.

Christine prend un petit air pincé.

— Vous vous êtes bien amusées, en ville ? demande-t-elle.

— Et comment ! fait Diane. Chantal est très amusante. Elle n'arrêtait pas d'imiter les gens qui passaient. Ils ne la voyaient pas, évidemment, mais c'était tordant.

— Tu te souviens de cette femme qui avait une face de

63

poisson ? dit Claudia en riant. Habillée en bleu et vert, en plus !

— Oui ! dit Sophie. Quand elle est passée, Chantal s'est tournée vers moi et elle a fait… (Elle rentre ses joues et roule des yeux exorbités.) Il a fallu que je me retienne à deux mains pour ne pas rire, ajoute-t-elle.

— C'est un peu méchant, non ? remarque Christine.

— Peut-être, admet Diane. Mais les gens ne la voyaient pas.

— Quand même, dit Christine, d'un air presque offensé.

— Pourquoi tu ne viens pas au cinéma avec Diane, Anne-Marie et moi, ce soir ? suggère Claudia à Christine. Chantal sera là.

— Oh ! elle ne pourra pas venir me voir, dit Sophie. Tant pis.

— Pas de cinéma pour moi, fait Christine. Je vais à la partie de basket.

Quelque chose dans sa voix me pousse à la regarder. Mais je n'arrive pas à lire ses pensées. Je me demande ce qu'elle peut bien avoir.

Bon, voilà que, maintenant, je vais me faire du souci pour Marie et pour Christine !

CHAPITRE 8

Vendredi

Voici mon conseil du jour. Ne jamais espérer faire ses devoirs quand on garde. Un peu d'étude, peut-être. Mais jamais de devoirs pressants. Il surviendra toujours quelque chose pour vous mettre des bâtons dans les roues. C'est d'ailleurs ce qui m'est arrivé quand j'ai gardé chez Christine. (Tu as bien du mérite, Christine. La soirée n'a pas été facile.)

Christine ouvre la porte à l'instant même où Sophie s'apprête à sonner.

— Allô! fait-elle avec entrain tout en boutonnant son manteau. Je n'ai pas le temps de parler parce qu'on est déjà en retard.

— Je comprends, dit Sophie. Amusez-vous bien.

— Bonjour, Sophie! Au revoir, Sophie! dit Charles en passant à la course.

Il attrape Christine par le bras et l'entraîne à sa suite.

— Dépêche, Sébastien! crie-t-il avant de sortir.

— Bonne chance! lance Christine à Sophie tandis que son frère la tire vers la voiture.

Sébastien descend en courant, mais s'arrête net en apercevant Sophie. Sébastien et Sophie s'aiment bien tous les deux. Ils sortent même ensemble à l'occasion...

— Hé! je ne savais pas que c'était toi qui gardais ce soir, roucoule-t-il.

— Christine ne te l'avait pas dit? fait Sophie.

Sophie n'est pas vraiment déçue de voir partir Sébastien puisqu'elle s'y attendait. S'il avait été libre, c'est lui qui aurait gardé. Elle est tout de même contente de pouvoir lui dire quelques mots.

Dans l'allée, Charles s'acharne sur le klaxon.

— J'arrive! crie Sébastien. Tu connais mon frère. S'il est deux minutes en retard à un rendez-vous, c'est comme si le monde allait s'effondrer.

— Vas-y, dit Sophie, on bavardera une autre fois.

— J'espère bien.

Il part en courant et se retourne pour lancer:

— Hé! bon courage avec les petits monstres!

Sophie ferme la porte. La mère de Christine s'amène

dans l'entrée, vêtue d'une longue robe de soirée bleue.

— Oh! Sophie! s'exclame-t-elle. Tu m'as fait peur. Je n'avais pas entendu sonner.

— Je n'ai pas sonné. J'ai croisé les autres qui sortaient en coup de vent.

— Charles déteste être en retard, dit madame Marchand en riant.

(Se peut-il que Charles soit plus ponctuel que Christine?)

Elle conduit Sophie à la salle de séjour. Les enfants sont là, avec Guillaume, impeccable dans son smoking. Les Marchand doivent parfois assister à des dîners officiels. J'imagine que ça fait partie des obligations des millionnaires.

— Bonjour, Sophie! dit Karen, qui passe la fin de semaine chez son père.

Ses yeux pétillent. Elle ne se fait pas garder souvent par quelqu'un qui n'est pas de la famille. En plus, elle aime beaucoup Sophie.

— Sophie est là! Sophie est là! s'écrie André en sautant partout.

(Christine dit qu'André et Karen sont souvent survoltés quand ils viennent en visite chez Guillaume.)

David, étalé sur le canapé, lit une bande dessinée.

— Allô, Sophie, dit-il distraitement.

David n'a que quelques mois de plus que Karen, mais ces temps-ci, il aime jouer au grand.

Émilie marche allègrement dans la pièce avec sa poupée dans les bras.

— Angé! Angé! fait-elle en tendant la poupée à Sophie.

— C'est bien! dit Sophie qui n'a pourtant pas la moindre idée de ce que raconte Émilie.

— Nanie va probablement rentrer avant nous, dit madame Marchand. Elle a un tournoi de quilles. Mais si son équipe gagne, elle risque d'être retardée. De toute façon, Christine ou les garçons devraient être de retour pour vingt-trois heures.

Elle donne à Sophie le numéro de téléphone où elle pourra être jointe en cas de besoin, recommande aux enfants d'être sages, puis les embrasse.

— Conduisez-vous bien avec Sophie! leur lance Guillaume en sortant.

Aussitôt la porte refermée, André s'exclame:

— On peut avoir un Coke?

— Je suppose que oui, répond Sophie. Mais juste un verre. Qui d'autre en veut?

Évidemment, tous lèvent la main et suivent Sophie dans la grande cuisine.

— Il n'y en a pas, dit-elle après avoir jeté un œil dans le frigo.

— Dans le garde-manger, l'informe Karen.

Dès que Karen ouvre la porte du garde-manger, David s'écrie:

— Hé! mes legos!

Par terre, Sophie aperçoit une boîte renversée d'où s'échappent un monceau de pièces colorées.

— Je les ai cherchés partout, dit David en s'agenouillant pour les ramasser. Qui les a mis là?

— Angé! Angé! fait Émilie joyeusement.

— J'aurais dû m'en douter, grogne David.

Sophie se lève sur la pointe des pieds pour attraper une bouteille de Coke.

— Qu'est-ce que ça veut dire, «angé»? demande-t-elle.

— Ranger, explique Karen. Nanie essaie de lui apprendre à ranger ses jouets.

— Elle est un peu jeune, non ?

— Nanie pense le contraire, dit Karen.

— En tout cas, elle devrait ranger ses affaires à *elle*, marmonne David.

Sophie sert les Cokes, puis ils retournent tous dans la salle de séjour. Miracle ! les enfants acceptent de regarder la même émission à la télé.

Il n'y a qu'Émilie qui n'est pas intéressée et qui s'amuse à gambader autour de la pièce.

Hélas ! la tranquillité prend fin en même temps que l'émission.

— Où est la télécommande ? demande André.

Tout le monde se met à chercher, sans résultat.

— Mais où peut-elle bien être ? fait Sophie en regardant sous le canapé.

À cet instant, Émilie s'écrie :

— Angé !

— Oh ! oh ! gémit David.

Ils passent la salle de séjour au peigne fin et voici ce qu'ils trouvent : une chaussure d'André dans le coffre à jouets, un bracelet de Karen sous un coussin, une figurine de tortue Ninja appartenant à David derrière des livres, le carnet d'adresses de Christine dans une fente du canapé, et la poupée d'Émilie sous un coin du tapis.

Par contre, aucune trace de la télécommande.

— Je suis sûre qu'on va finir par tomber dessus, dit Sophie. Pour l'instant, on peut changer de canal à la main.

— Non ! s'écrie Karen, très inquiète. Papa dit qu'on ne doit pas toucher à la télé. Il dit qu'on pourrait la briser.

— Il a défendu ça aux enfants, dit David. Sophie et moi, on peut.

— J'ai seulement quelques mois de moins que toi! s'indigne Karen.

— Quelques mois, c'est beaucoup, rétorque David.

— Non, proteste Karen en faisant la moue. Nadine et Annie ont presque un an de plus que moi, et elles ne trouvent pas que je suis bébé.

Pendant qu'ils se chamaillent, Sophie examine la télé. Elle ne pense pas que Guillaume lui en voudra si elle touche aux boutons, mais le problème c'est qu'il y en a tellement qu'elle ne sait pas trop sur lequel appuyer. Elle ne veut pas prendre le risque d'endommager quoi que ce soit.

— Si on voyait d'abord ce qui va suivre à ce canal? suggère-t-elle.

Malheureusement, ce sont les nouvelles. Sophie éteint l'appareil.

— On peut jouer à «Trois fois passera...», propose Karen.

— Pas question! font André et David en chœur.

Finalement, ils optent pour une partie de cache-cache. Sophie et Émilie font équipe pour chercher les autres. (C'est d'ailleurs en cherchant que Sophie découvre un trousseau de clés sur le plancher d'un placard. «Angé!» fait Émilie en la regardant ramasser les clés. Sophie est certaine que quelqu'un sera sûrement content de les ravoir.)

Jouer à ce jeu juste avant d'aller au lit n'était pas une idée formidable. Essayez de coucher les enfants après ça: mission impossible. Émilie ne fait pas trop de difficultés, mais Karen, André et David n'arrivent pas à se calmer. Karen saute sur son lit tandis qu'André et David lui lancent des oreillers.

Le petit jeu se poursuit jusqu'à ce que Sophie décide de confisquer tous les oreillers.

Lorsqu'ils se couchent enfin, elle doit leur lire une histoire pendant une bonne demi-heure avant qu'ils manifestent des signes de fatigue. Quand ils parviennent à s'endormir, il est presque vingt-deux heures.

Sophie est vannée, mais elle veut commencer son devoir de maths. Surprise! Lorsqu'elle descend à la salle de séjour pour prendre son livre, il n'est plus sur la table où elle l'avait laissé!

— Oh non! s'exclame-t-elle en laissant tomber les bras. J'espère qu'Émilie ne l'a pas « angé »!

Elle regarde sous la table et partout dans la pièce. Mais elle doit se rendre à l'évidence: Émilie a encore frappé! Le livre est quelque part, mais où?

Sophie fouille dans tous les coins, même dans le réfrigérateur, au cas où la petite y aurait glissé le livre pendant qu'elle servait les Cokes. Au bout d'une demi-heure de recherches intensives, elle abdique. Désespérée, elle retourne à la salle de séjour et s'affale dans un fauteuil.

Aussitôt, la télé s'allume, le volume au maximum.

Avec un cri, Sophie bondit de son siège, le cœur battant.

Elle soulève le coussin où elle était assise. La télécommande!

Sophie éteint l'appareil. Au même moment, elle aperçoit un coin de son livre dépasser derrière un rideau.

Elle le prend et revient s'asseoir. On sonne à la porte. « Nanie doit avoir oublié ses clés, pense-t-elle. Le trousseau devait être le sien. » Mais ce n'est pas Nanie, c'est Chantal.

— Salut, fait Chantal. On est revenues plus tôt du cinéma et j'ai la permission de rentrer à onze heures, alors je me suis dit que je pourrais te tenir compagnie.

Sophie est contente de la voir et juge que ce serait bête de ne pas la faire entrer. Les maths devront attendre.

Chantal lui raconte le film.

— Claudia et moi, on lui a donné dix sur dix, mais Anne-Marie et Diane, seulement cinq. Elles l'ont trouvé débile, mais c'est justement pour ça que je l'ai aimé.

Chantal et Sophie bavardent depuis quinze minutes quand Christine rentre. Dès qu'elle aperçoit Chantal, son sourire s'efface.

— Je croyais que tu devais aller au cinéma ? dit Christine sans même la saluer.

— Ça s'est terminé plus tôt que prévu, explique Sophie.

— Alors, tu es venu ici, fait Christine d'une voix ennuyée. Chantal, est-ce que tu as des problèmes chez toi ?

— Non, pourquoi ? répond Chantal.

— Parce que tu ne veux jamais y être.

Chantal semble décontenancée et se lève.

— Bon, je ferais mieux de rentrer, dit-elle. Il est presque onze heures.

— Oui, approuve Christine. Tu ferais mieux.

Comme Christine ne semble pas vouloir raccompagner Chantal à la porte, Sophie s'en charge.

— Est-ce que Christine est fâchée ? demande Chantal en enfilant sa veste.

— On dirait, murmure Sophie. Mais je ne sais pas pourquoi.

Chantal partie, Sophie retourne à la salle de séjour.

— Tu vas bien ? demande-t-elle à Christine.

Christine se jette sur le canapé et allume la télé.

— Tout va très bien.

Sophie n'en croit pas un mot.

CHAPITRE 9

La semaine suivante, plusieurs événements retiennent mon attention. Lundi, je reçois une lettre de mon ami Quentin, qui étudie le ballet à Toronto. (En fait, c'est plus qu'un simple ami, si vous voyez ce que je veux dire…)

Il me manque et j'aime bien recevoir de ses nouvelles. Ce qui m'embête un peu, c'est de devoir lui répondre (je déteste écrire des lettres). Enfin, pour une fois, j'ai quelque chose d'intéressant à raconter : les cours de ballet aux enfants. Je lui explique tout et je lui demande son avis sur la méthode d'enseignement de madame Dupré et les commentaires de Raul. (Quentin est Noir, lui aussi, alors je me dis qu'il doit avoir une opinion sur ce que pense Raul de la façon dont sont traitées les minorités.)

Puis je lui parle de Marie. « Je ne veux pas confier mes préoccupations à un professeur, écris-je. Ce serait déloyal envers Marie. Mais je ne voudrais pas qu'elle tombe malade. Je me sentirais responsable de ne pas avoir agi. D'après toi, qu'est-ce que je devrais faire ? »

En cachetant l'enveloppe, je me sens un peu moins

inquiète pour Marie. Je suis persuadée que Quentin aura une bonne idée. Il en a toujours.

L'autre événement de la semaine à souligner est le cours même de madame Dupré. Comme je connais de mieux en mieux le groupe de volontaires, je m'amuse de plus en plus. Seul petit côté triste : David est absent. Peut-être a-t-il décidé d'abandonner.

— Madame Dupré a été trop dure avec lui, dit Raul après la classe.

— Mais il distrayait les autres, fait Marie. On ne peut pas tout avoir, Raul. D'abord, tu dis qu'elle est trop indulgente, ensuite tu l'accuses d'être trop sévère.

— Peut-être, admet Raul, mais j'aimais bien David.

J'admire Marie. Sans jamais s'emporter, elle dit toujours ce qu'elle pense, même si ça va à l'encontre de l'opinion d'un garçon qu'elle estime beaucoup.

Quand je lui demande si elle se sent mieux, elle me répond que ce n'était qu'un virus passager. Pourtant, elle est toujours pâle, et plus maigre que jamais. Je n'ai pas l'occasion de lui parler davantage. Madame Dupré nous fait travailler fort et, après le cours, chacun s'en retourne chez soi.

J'ai découvert que la seule chose qui m'agace dans cette classe du mardi, c'est que ça m'empêche de suivre mon cours régulier ! Je suis étonnée de voir combien il me manque. Je n'ai plus qu'une idée en tête : travailler d'arrache-pied.

Pendant le cours de vendredi, un incident terrible se produit.

Nous sommes en train de faire quelques *pliés*, quand, soudain, Marie s'écroule ! Évanouie !

Toute la classe l'entoure, mais madame Noëlle nous fait reculer.

— Que quelqu'un aille vite chercher la trousse de premiers soins à la réception! dit-elle en s'agenouillant près de Marie et en lui tapotant doucement les joues.

Karine Saint-Onge s'élance et revient aussitôt avec la trousse. Madame Noëlle en sort des sels qu'elle passe sous le nez de Marie. Celle-ci ouvre les yeux et se met à tousser.

Madame Noëlle demande une chaise et ordonne à Marie de s'asseoir, la tête entre les genoux. À cet instant, madame Dupré apparaît à la porte.

— Que se passe-t-il? demande-t-elle.

— Appelez l'ambulance, s'il vous plaît, lui dit notre professeure.

— Non! fait Marie en se redressant, les yeux écarquillés. C'est seulement un virus. Je vais bien. Je vous en prie.

Un autre virus? Tu parles!

Madame Noëlle observe Marie de ses yeux perçants. Elle pose sa main sur son front.

— Pas de fièvre. Vous sentez-vous étourdie, mademoiselle?

Marie secoue la tête.

— Pas du tout, répond-elle.

Madame Noëlle se lève.

— Voulez-vous demander à la réceptionniste d'appeler les parents de Marie pour qu'ils viennent la chercher, s'il vous plaît? dit-elle à madame Dupré qui est toujours à la porte.

— Bien sûr, fait celle-ci.

— Mademoiselle Bernard, je voudrais que vous alliez

75

vous changer et que vous attendiez vos parents dans le hall. Mais ne partez pas sans m'avertir. Je veux dire un mot à votre père ou à votre mère.

— Je l'accompagne, dis-je vivement.

Je dois discuter avec Marie, il n'y a pas une minute à perdre.

— Bonne idée, dit madame Noëlle. Mieux vaut ne pas la laisser seule.

Lentement, Marie se lève et nous sortons du studio. Ce n'est qu'au vestiaire que je me décide à parler.

— Marie, tu dois cesser ton régime, lui dis-je sans détour.

— Qu'est-ce que tu en sais? Tu es trop jeune! rétorque-t-elle.

Oh! jamais elle ne m'a parlé sur ce ton. Mais je me rappelle qu'Anne-Marie a dit que les sautes d'humeur et l'irritabilité étaient des symptômes de l'anorexie. Alors, sans me laisser démonter, je poursuis.

— Tu sais ce que c'est, l'anorexie?

Marie plisse les yeux de colère.

— Oui, je le sais! Et je ne suis pas anorexique!

— Peut-être pas encore, mais tu es bien partie, dis-je en haussant le ton. Tu en as tous les symptômes.

— Je ne savais pas que tu étais médecin, glapit Marie en retirant son maillot.

Elle est encore plus décharnée que la semaine dernière.

— Mes amies et moi avons consulté des bouquins, dis-je.

— Pourquoi?

— Parce que je leur ai dit que ton état m'inquiétait.

Marie, furieuse, pose ses mains sur ses hanches osseuses.

— Tu as raconté à tes amies que j'étais anorexique ? explose-t-elle. Tu as fait ça ? Et puis, ce n'est même pas vrai !

— Marie, je t'aime bien, et tu as besoin d'aide.

Le visage de Marie a viré au rouge. De rage, elle lance son sac de danse contre le mur.

— Mêle-toi de ce qui te regarde ! crie-t-elle en s'avançant vers moi. Je suis assez grande pour m'occuper de mon sort. Et ne parle pas de ça à personne !

Soudain, je remarque que mes mains tremblent. On ne m'a jamais crié par la tête de la sorte. Mes yeux s'emplissent de larmes, mais je les contiens.

C'est alors que madame Dupré entre et demande en voyant notre attitude :

— Y a-t-il quelque chose qui cloche ?

— Non, madame, répond Marie en continuant à se changer.

Madame Dupré me jette un regard interrogateur, mais ne dit rien.

Quand elle sort, Marie se tourne vers moi.

— Désolée, Jessie. Je suis d'humeur massacrante, ces temps-ci, mais je t'assure que tu t'inquiètes pour rien. Excuse-moi de m'être emportée.

— Tu as besoin d'aide, Marie. Je t'en prie.

Elle me tourne le dos et enfile sa veste. À partir de ce moment, elle m'ignore. Dans le hall d'entrée, nous trouvons madame Noëlle en train de discuter avec un homme. Marie lui ressemble tellement, que j'en déduis que c'est son père.

— J'ai suggéré à ton père de consulter un médecin à propos de ce virus, dit madame Noëlle à Marie.

— J'ai seulement besoin de repos, répond-elle.

— Et d'une bonne soupe au poulet, suggère madame Noëlle.

Ah ! si elle savait comme son conseil est précieux !

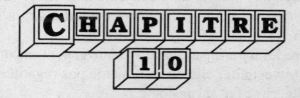

CHAPITRE 10

Le mardi suivant, dès que je mets les pieds dans le studio, un grand sourire illumine mon visage. David est revenu!

Il est là, avec deux de ses copains, riant, comme si rien n'était.

Peut-être qu'il ne se sentait pas bien, mardi dernier. Mais il me semble que quelque chose d'autre a dû se produire. Il avait peut-être pris la décision de ne plus revenir, puis s'est rendu compte que le cours lui manquait trop. Il y a un changement très subtil en lui. D'abord, il ne fait plus le pitre comme avant.

D'ailleurs, tous les enfants ont changé. Ils ne sont plus aussi excités qu'au début. Maintenant, quand madame Dupré entre, elle n'a plus besoin d'éteindre la lumière. Sa présence suffit à rétablir le calme.

Monsieur Tsuji attaque une mélodie enjouée et, sur l'ordre de la professeure, je dirige les exercices de réchauffement.

Parfois, je jette un œil en direction de Marie. Son pantalon me semble de plus en plus ample sur elle, ses yeux de plus en plus grands et ses pommettes de plus en plus saillantes. C'est sûrement l'amaigrissement qui fait ressortir ses traits ainsi. Je me demande si elle est allée chez le médecin comme le lui a conseillé madame Noëlle. Un spécialiste y verrait certainement clair et pourrait la raisonner.

Je ne lui ai pas reparlé depuis l'autre jour. Et aujourd'hui, dans le vestiaire, elle ne m'a même pas regardée. Elle m'évite, ça ne fait aucun doute.

Les étirements terminés, madame Dupré montre quelques petits sauts appelés *échappés,* qu'on peut exécuter à partir de plusieurs positions. Elle demande aux élèves de prendre la deuxième position, de sauter bien droit dans les airs en pointant les pieds, puis de retomber en deuxième position.

Dans la salle, on n'entend plus que le bruit sourd des enfants qui bondissent sur le plancher de bois. Même les vitres semblent trembler.

Ensuite, madame Dupré divise la classe en groupes. Cette fois, Nora et Jeanne sont séparées et David n'est avec aucun de ses amis.

Aujourd'hui, les enfants vont apprendre à exécuter correctement un *pas de chat.* Marie travaille avec le groupe de David. Jusqu'à maintenant, Madame Dupré avait toujours assigné David à Raul. Mais elle observe sans relâche, procède à des ajustements, réfléchit.

Marthe est dans mon groupe. Elle est tellement timide ! Je ne l'ai encore jamais vue parler aux autres. C'est tout juste si elle ose les regarder.

Mais pour danser, elle danse !

Bien que le *pas de chat* soit parmi les premiers sauts qu'apprennent les danseurs en herbe, je trouve madame Dupré un peu ambitieuse de vouloir l'enseigner aux élèves de cette classe. D'un côté, je la comprends : c'est un saut qui ne demande pas trop de puissance, et les enfants aiment bien l'idée de sauter comme un chat.

Cependant, le *pas de chat* demande une certaine expérience pour qu'il soit réussi.

Revenons à Marthe : après son troisième essai seulement, elle frise la perfection. Ses mouvements, sa posture, sa façon de relever le menton, chez elle, tout reste naturel. Et elle saute plus haut que les autres.

Je suis curieuse et, quand elle termine son saut, je lui demande :

— Es-tu sûre que tu n'as jamais suivi de cours ?

— Cinq, répond-elle.

— Pardon ?

— J'ai pris cinq leçons.

— Et pourquoi as-tu arrêté ? Tu es très douée.

Elle sourit, puis détourne le regard et hausse les épaules.

— J'ai arrêté, c'est tout.

— Tu devrais recommencer. Tu as un don.

Marthe baisse la tête, mais elle sourit. C'est la première fois que je la vois sourire.

Je jette un coup d'œil en direction du groupe de Marie. Juste à temps pour apercevoir David sauter. Ses mouvements sont trop amples et désordonnés. Mais il a beaucoup d'énergie et de présence. Quand il atterrit, Marie le replace dans la bonne position.

Chacun des deux a quelque chose à offrir à l'autre : David a besoin des connaissances de Marie, et Marie a besoin du feu de David.

Mais quel changement chez David! Il écoute Marie, il boit chacune de ses paroles. Il a vraiment décidé d'être sérieux.

Le cours passe si vite que, lorsque les premiers parents arrivent, j'ai l'impression qu'ils sont en avance. Pourtant, c'est bien la fin de la classe.

— Beau travail, dit madame Dupré à tout le monde. À la semaine prochaine.

— Vous avez bien fait ça, dis-je à mon groupe.

Les enfants me sourient et se dirigent vers la sortie.

— Surtout toi, dis-je tout bas à l'oreille de Marthe quand les autres sont assez loin.

Sa réaction me prend par surprise. Elle se retourne et me serre très fort, le temps de quelques secondes, puis elle court rejoindre sa mère.

Vous voulez que je vous dise? J'ai une grosse boule dans la gorge, comme si j'allais me mettre à pleurer.

Quelle drôle de sensation! Je suis très heureuse et pourtant, je dois retenir mes larmes. Jusqu'à maintenant, il n'y a que quelques ballets et la fin de certains films qui m'ont laissée dans cet état. C'est la première fois qu'un événement de la vraie vie me fait un tel effet.

Une fois de plus, je croise le regard de la mère de Marthe. Je voudrais lui dire un mot, mais j'ai toujours cette boule dans la gorge. Et je ne sais pas si je pourrais parler. Je regarde au plafond et j'essaie de reprendre contenance. Quand je baisse les yeux, Marthe et sa mère sont déjà parties.

— Bonne classe, hein? dit Suzanne en me rejoignant.

— Oh oui! dis-je en m'éclaircissant la voix.

— Tu viens manger un morceau?

— D'accord. Les autres y vont?

— Je pense. Hé! Marie! Tu viens au resto?

— Je ne peux pas, merci, répond-elle en évitant mon regard. Je dois aller courir.

— Par ce froid? glapit Suzanne.

— On ne le sent pas quand on court.

— Moi, je le sentirais, fait Suzanne en riant. On se retrouve dans le vestiaire, Jessie.

Avant que Marie puisse s'esquiver, je m'empresse de lui demander:

— Tu ne devrais pas te reposer plutôt que de courir?

— Je vais mieux. Ne t'inquiète pas pour moi, veux-tu? Tu me fais penser à ma mère et ça m'énerve.

— Excuse-moi. Mais pourquoi tu ne viens pas avec nous?

— Jessie! Ça suffit, d'accord?

— Très bien.

— Tu arrives, Jessie? lance Danielle qui m'attend à la porte.

— Oui, oui.

Peut-être que Marie a raison. Peut-être que je m'énerve pour rien. Peut-être fait-elle ce qu'il faut pour poursuivre sa carrière, et elle ne veut pas que je m'en mêle. D'ailleurs, ce ne sont pas mes oignons.

En me rendant au vestiaire, c'est ce que je me dis. Mais je n'arrive pas à me convaincre moi-même.

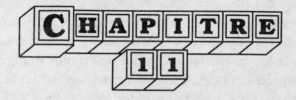

CHAPITRE 11

Mardi, en rentrant de l'école, je trouve une lettre de Quentin. Je l'ouvre en me demandant s'il m'y donnera son avis sur le cas de Marie.

Après quelques lignes sur ce qu'il fait (l'école, le ballet, etc.), il plonge dans le vif du sujet. «RÉGIME! RÉGIME!» a-t-il écrit en majuscules. «Certaines filles de mes cours de ballet n'ont que ce mot à la bouche. Ça me rend fou, mais, en même temps, j'ai pitié d'elles. Elles sont convaincues de subir d'énormes pressions pour avoir la silhouette idéale. Les garçons, eux, n'ont pas besoin d'être aussi uniformes que les filles. Ces dernières se retrouvent souvent devant cet affreux dilemme : suivre un régime draconien ou abandonner. Je ne m'imagine pas devant un tel choix, surtout après avoir consacré la majeure partie de ma vie au ballet. Pourtant, ces filles n'auraient pas à quitter complètement le milieu de la danse. Certaines pourraient devenir professeures et d'autres, danser dans des productions plus «théâtrales», je veux dire moins classiques.»

La lettre de Quentin me rassure un peu. Au moins,

Marie n'est pas la seule à affronter ce problème. « Le poids est parfois un gros problème quand on danse, poursuit Quentin. De nombreuses personnes affirment que les standards requis des ballerines ne sont pas réalistes. Si tu regardes des photos anciennes de danseuses — même de danseuses étoiles — tu verras qu'elles étaient assez grassouillettes, à l'époque. Et je pense que la tendance actuelle veut que les danseuses soient un peu moins maigres que ces dernières années. La transformation est lente, mais elle se remarque quand tu assistes à des ballets. » (J'envie Quentin d'habiter une métropole et de pouvoir voir de grandes productions.) « Peut-être que, si tu parlais de ça à Marie, elle se sentirait mieux dans sa peau. »

Oui, je vais en parler à Marie. Si elle veut bien m'écouter, évidemment !

« J'ai eu une très bonne idée l'autre jour, écrit Quentin. C'est toi qui m'y as fait penser en me parlant de cette affaire de minorités. Oui, c'est plus difficile quand tu fais partie d'une minorité. Ce serait ridicule de le nier. C'est justement pour la même raison que les filles suivent des régimes insensés. Derrière tout ça, il y a le préjugé voulant que les danseuses d'un corps de ballet devraient toutes se ressembler. Les gens avaient (et ont souvent encore) peur d'associer un danseur noir avec une danseuse blanche dans un *pas de deux*. Mais ça change. Il y a maintenant des Noirs dans les corps de ballet et de plus en plus de couples mixtes — surtout dans les ballets modernes. »

Tout ça est très intéressant, mais j'ai hâte de connaître sa bonne idée. J'y arrive enfin.

« Voici donc mon idée : pourquoi ne pas suggérer à madame Dupré d'offrir une bourse à deux ou trois enfants qui semblent particulièrement doués et qui n'ont pas les moyens de suivre des cours ? L'école n'acceptera probablement pas, mais c'est une idée que je lance. »

Quentin termine sa lettre par des réflexions encourageantes sur les vacances du printemps au cours desquelles nous nous verrons peut-être. J'adore ses lettres. Celle-ci est un peu plus sérieuse que les autres, mais c'est à cause du sujet.

Son idée de bourse me plaît beaucoup. Mais est-ce que j'aurai le courage d'en parler ? Ce n'est pas sûr. « Le pire qui puisse arriver, c'est qu'on te réponde non », dit toujours maman. Elle a raison. Mais, parfois, la timidité est plus forte que tout. Je ne suis pas timide avec les jeunes de mon âge, mais, avec les adultes, c'est une autre paire de manches. Je ne me vois pas aborder madame Dupré et lui suggérer que l'école accorde des bourses de plusieurs milliers de dollars. En plus, elle me conseillerait probablement d'en discuter avec madame Noëlle. Juste d'y penser, je rougis ! Je ne crois pas que l'école donnerait des bourses simplement parce qu'une fillette de onze ans l'a proposé.

Est-ce que je me trompe ? Je vais y réfléchir.

Tandis que je replie la lettre de Quentin, le téléphone se met à sonner.

— C'est pour toi, Jessie ! lance tante Cécile de la cuisine.

Je décroche l'appareil dans le salon.

— Allô, fait Christine. Comment vas-tu ?

— Pas mal.

— Es-tu libre pour venir garder ici, samedi ? Tu vas peut-être à cette foire à l'école de Chantal, comme toutes les autres ?

— Oh! oui. Elles m'ont invitée, mais j'ai de l'étude. Je pourrais garder une heure ou deux.

— Parfait. J'ai promis d'assister à une réunion pour organiser la danse du printemps. Je ne serai pas partie longtemps. Peux-tu être ici à quatorze heures?

— Oui.

— Merci. À bientôt.

— À bientôt.

Juste comme je raccroche, tante Cécile entre dans le salon.

— Tu me parais bien songeuse, dit-elle. À quoi penses-tu?

— Tante Cécile, que ferais-tu si une de tes amies ruinait sa santé sans s'en rendre compte?

Tante Cécile s'assoit sur la chaise en face de moi.

— Un problème de drogue? demande-t-elle.

— Non. De régime. De régime excessif.

— Mmmmm, fait tante Cécile, pensive. Je crois que tu devrais en parler à un adulte qui connaît cette personne.

— Mais c'est déloyal, non?

— Pas si la santé de ta copine est en jeu. Personne de son entourage n'a rien remarqué?

— Jusqu'à maintenant, il me semble que non. Elle cache son état en faisant semblant de manger et en portant des vêtements amples.

— Es-tu certaine qu'elle a un problème?

Je réfléchis quelques instants avant de répondre.

— Plutôt, oui.

— En général, ton flair ne te trompe pas, Jessie. Tu devrais en parler à quelqu'un qui pourrait intervenir.

— Merci du conseil. C'est justement ce que je me

disais, mais j'espérais trouver un moyen qui ne blesserait personne.

— Comme on dit parfois, « c'est un mal pour un bien ».

— Comment ça ?

— La meilleure chose que tu puisses faire pour un ami n'est pas toujours la plus facile. Elle peut même t'attirer sa colère.

— Oh ! ça, sûrement ! Elle va être furieuse. C'est certain.

— Un jour, elle comprendra que tu étais une véritable amie, dit tante Cécile.

— J'espère.

Permettez-moi une fois de plus d'avoir certains doutes.

CHAPITRE 12

Mercredi

D'habitude, je dois prendre une grande inspiration avant d'aller garder chez les Cormier. Les enfants-là m'épuisent. Cet après-midi, en plus, les Papadakis et David se sont amenés. Ça fait du monde ! Puis Chantal est arrivée avec ses soeurs Tiffany et Maria. Au moins, elle était là pour me donner un coup de main. On s'est retrouvées en pleine bataille de boules de neige.

La neige ! Ça, c'est la bonne nouvelle de la journée. Claudia doit garder les Cormier avant notre réunion et comme ils ont beaucoup d'énergie, les jeux extérieurs sont un excellent moyen de les tenir occupés (et de les fatiguer un peu).

Lorsque Claudia arrive, ils sont déjà tout habillés et prêts à sortir. La petite Aurore, qui a un an et demi, est tellement excitée qu'elle ne pleure même pas quand sa mère part. (Elle crie « maman ! » et prend un petit air triste, mais c'est déjà mieux que d'habitude.)

Il a neigé depuis le matin. À présent, il tombe quelques flocons et le sol est recouvert de dix centimètres de neige légère, parfaite pour faire des balles.

Benoît (qui a neuf ans) et Mélodie (qui en a sept) se mettent aussitôt à rouler une grosse boule pour faire un bonhomme devant la maison. (Les Cormier habitent dans le quartier de Christine, là où les maisons et les terrains sont immenses.) Soudain, une balle passe tout près de Benoît.

— Une bataille ! crie-t-il joyeusement en se dépêchant de faire une balle pour riposter à l'attaquant.

Léonard et Annie Papadakis arrivent dans la cour en riant, les bras chargés de balles de neige. Sans perdre un instant, Léonard et Benoît commencent à se bombarder mutuellement.

— Hé ! Hé ! attention, les gars ! les prévient Claudia en riant, quand un projectile effleure son épaule.

— Oumf ! fait Mélodie lorsqu'une balle l'atteint en pleine poitrine.

— Prends ça ! dit Annie en visant Léonard.

La balle monte haut et se désagrège avant de retomber. Annie n'a rien d'une championne à ce jeu.

— Les filles contre les garçons! crie Benoît en rejoignant Léonard.

Ils pilonnent les filles, confectionnant leurs balles aussi vite qu'ils les lancent.

Mélodie et Annie savent reconnaître une défaite. Elles se défendent deux bonnes minutes, puis courent se réfugier derrière Claudia.

— C'est pas juste! proteste celle-ci en levant les bras pour se protéger. Je ne suis pas un fort!

— Vous construisez un fort? demande Maria Chrétien, qui a huit ans, en arrivant en courant. Je peux vous aider? Je suis très bonne!

— Excellente idée! répond Claudia.

Elle esquive une balle qui atteint Maria à l'épaule.

— Ça suffit, dit-elle aux garçons. Vous avez gagné. On capitule.

— Hé! faites pas les poules mouillées! s'écrie Benoît.

— Vous pouvez blesser quelqu'un, insiste Claudia. Aidez-nous plutôt à faire le fort.

À ce moment, Chantal arrive, accompagnée de sa sœur de onze ans, Tiffany.

— Hé! c'est le carnaval, ici! lance-t-elle.

— On dirait, répond Claudia. Ça te tente de construire un fort?

— Oui!

Chantal et Tiffany se joignent aux autres qui entassent déjà la neige pour monter les quatre murs. Puis ils creusent une petite porte et des fenêtres.

— Et maintenant, qu'est-ce qu'on fait? demande Mélodie, à la fin.

— Une autre bataille, suggère Léonard. Vous pouvez

rester dans le fort et faire des balles pendant que, Benoît et moi, on vous bombarde.

— Pas question ! dit Maria.

— Oui, c'est idiot, ajoute Annie. Si vous pensez qu'on va vous laisser nous ensevelir sous les balles... Ce n'est pas amusant.

— Il faudrait trouver quelque chose de spécial, dit Claudia. Il n'y aura sûrement plus beaucoup de belles journées de neige comme celle-ci. Si on faisait un village de neige ?

— Un quoi ? demande Annie.

— On va sculpter un village en neige, explique Claudia.

— On pourra faire rouler des camions dedans ? s'informe Léonard.

— Pourquoi pas ? On fait ce qu'on veut.

— Super ! dit Mélodie. On y va.

Les enfants se mettent à l'ouvrage et construisent le village de leurs rêves. Chantal monte une série de boutiques pendant que Claudia sculpte une grande église.

Mélodie et Annie font un ranch, puis Mélodie court à la maison et en revient les bras chargés de chevaux en plastique.

Les garçons ont construit un garage à plusieurs étages et l'ont rempli de petites autos. Maria a créé une maison hantée, flanquée d'une tour ronde et entourée d'une véranda. Même Aurore a fait un gros tas de neige.

— Ce sera le centre de ski, suggère Chantal. Un centre de ski hanté, avec une magnifique cathédrale et un grand espace de stationnement.

— Et un centre équestre, ajoute Annie.

— Que demander de plus ? fait Claudia.

— Je sais! répond Chantal. Des condos de luxe pour les vedettes de cinéma.

— Tu as raison, dit Claudia. Il faut qu'il y ait aussi une piscine et un club chic.

Chantal et Claudia se mettent à empiler la neige pour édifier leurs condos. Au bout d'un moment, elles remarquent que leur tour penche nettement vers la gauche.

— On dirait plutôt la tour de Pise, ricane Chantal.

— C'est normal, il n'y a que des gens aux drôles de penchants qui viennent ici, répond Claudia. Des criminels et des fausses vedettes.

— Il nous faut une prison, alors! déclare Léonard avec excitation.

— Et un poste de police, ajoute Benoît.

Les garçons commencent à modeler deux gros bâtiments carrés.

Chantal regarde les condos penchés.

— On pourrait peut-être les redresser?

C'est alors que Christine apparaît de l'autre côté de la rue.

— Allô! lui lance Claudia.

Christine s'avance.

— Qu'est-ce que vous faites?

— Ça ne se voit pas? dit Chantal gaiement. On construit le village du futur.

— Ah oui? Très joli.

Christine regarde Claudia et Chantal tour à tour.

— As-tu des idées pour notre village? lui demande cette dernière.

— Non, répond Christine.

À ce moment, la sonnette d'alarme se déclenche dans

la tête de Claudia. Christine n'a pas d'idées ? Impossible !
Elle en a toujours — sur tout !

Claudia a senti que quelque chose n'allait pas.

Chantal doit en être arrivée à la même conclusion, car,
lorsque Christine s'en va sans même dire au revoir, elle lui
court après.

Claudia les observe discuter sur le trottoir.

— Peux-tu surveiller Aurore, un instant ? demande-
t-elle à Tiffany.

Elle suit Chantal et Christine, et les rattrape au moment
où Chantal dit :

— Je veux savoir pourquoi tu es si bête avec moi. Et
ne me dis pas le contraire. Tu sais que j'ai raison.

— Bon, puisque tu veux la vérité, dit Christine d'une
voix fâchée, tu sauras, ma chère, que tu ne connaîtrais
même pas le club ni mes amies si ce n'était pas de moi.

— Bon. Et alors ?

— Alors, n'essaie pas de me voler mes amies et de
prendre ma place ! lance Christine, le visage cramoisi.

Chantal reste bouche bée.

— Te voler… Mais je…

— Christine, je pense que tu exagères, intervient Claudia.

— Évidemment ! réplique Christine.

— Qu'est-ce que tu veux dire ? demande Claudia, indi-
gnée.

— Je veux dire que, maintenant que vous êtes toutes les
amies de Chantal, c'est normal que vous preniez sa part.

Claudia reste interloquée.

— Mais je suis toujours ton amie, fait-elle. On est toutes tes amies.

— Ah oui? On ne dirait pas, depuis quelque temps.

Christine se mord la lèvre, puis elle s'éloigne à grands pas.

CHAPITRE 13

Comme vous l'imaginez sans doute, la réunion de ce mercredi se déroule dans une atmosphère très tendue. (Pour ma part, ce n'est que plus tard dans la soirée que j'apprends par Marjorie ce qui est arrivé à Christine, Claudia et Chantal. Marjorie a parlé à Anne-Marie, qui a parlé à Diane, qui a appris l'affaire de la bouche de Sophie, qui, elle, évidemment, la tenait de Claudia.) Mais il ne faut pas être bien maligne pour comprendre que Christine file un mauvais coton. Claudia n'a pas l'air plus heureuse. Avant même la fin de la réunion, elle a englouti tout un sac de croustilles. Signe de tension.

Malgré le silence inhabituel de Christine et la gloutonnerie de Claudia, la réunion se déroule normalement.

— Comment va ton amie au ballet? me demande Diane.

— Pas très bien, elle maigrit à vue d'œil.

— C'est terrible, dit Anne-Marie.

— Quentin m'a écrit et il me dit qu'à son école, c'est fréquent.

Me rappelant soudain son idée de bourse, je demande

aux autres ce qu'elles en pensent.

— C'est génial comme suggestion! s'écrie Sophie.

— Tu crois que l'école accepterait? dis-je. Elle offre déjà des bourses aux élèves plus âgés. Mais il faut passer une audition, ce qui veut dire qu'il faut déjà être entraîné. Les petits ne seraient que des débutants. L'école n'a peut-être pas les moyens de donner plus d'argent.

— Il y a des compagnies qui commanditent des bourses, me dit doucement Christine. (Même déprimée, elle a de bonnes idées!)

— Comment ça fonctionne? demande Marjorie.

— Les compagnies décident de faire un don pour une activité qui apporte quelque chose à la communauté, explique Christine.

— C'est un beau geste de leur part, dis-je.

— Je pourrais en parler à Guillaume et à maman, si tu veux, poursuit Christine. Ils doivent connaître ça.

— Tu ferais ça pour moi? Ce serait très gentil!

— Bien sûr. Je t'en donnerai des nouvelles.

Je quitte la réunion très emballée. Peut-être qu'un ou deux enfants de mon cours pourraient bénéficier de bourses! Puis je me rappelle Marie. Je ne sais toujours pas quoi faire à son sujet. Si elle pouvait abandonner son régime!

Le vendredi suivant, je constate que ce n'est pas le cas. Au vestiaire, je vois bien que Marie est maintenant la plus décharnée de la classe.

Je ne m'en ferais pas autant pour elle si ce n'était qu'une question de maigreur. Mais on dirait qu'elle se décompose. Elle a une mine affreuse et elle paraît très faible.

Elle *est* très faible. Deux fois déjà, elle a quitté la classe avant la fin. Tandis qu'elle se change pour le cours, je remarque qu'elle fait des gestes lents, trop lents. Ce sera facile de lui parler. Je n'ai qu'à attendre que les autres soient sorties. Marie sera la dernière, c'est certain. Alors, j'attends.

— Je peux te parler? dis-je en m'armant de courage pour cette conversation pénible.

— Ne recommence pas, Jessie, explose-t-elle en se penchant pour lacer ses chaussons.

— Je veux juste te dire une petite chose. Si tu ne parles pas de ton problème à madame Noëlle aujourd'hui, c'est moi qui le ferai.

Elle me fusille du regard.

— Et qu'est-ce que tu vas lui raconter?

— Que tu suis un régime au point de dépérir.

— Elle va te rire au nez.

— Je ne pense pas.

— Tu n'as pas le droit de faire ça et je te conseille de la boucler, réplique Marie en sortant du vestiaire.

Je m'assois sur le banc, tout étourdie. J'ai dû faire appel à toute mon énergie pour parler ainsi à Marie. Pourvu qu'elle m'ait prise au sérieux, parce que, si elle ne parle pas à madame Noëlle, je vais être obligée d'agir à sa place pour tenir ma promesse. (À moins que ce ne soit une menace? Non. Une promesse.)

Lorsque mon vertige finit par se dissiper, je me dépêche d'aller au studio.

Et ce qui se produit au cours efface tous les doutes qui pouvaient subsister dans mon esprit. Pendant le travail au centre, Marie trébuche en faisant une *arabesque penchée*. Je l'observe. On aurait dit que sa jambe ne la supportait

101

plus. Évidemment, tout le monde se précipite vers elle. Marie se relève aussitôt et se remet à danser.

Vers la fin du cours, madame Noëlle nous donne une série de pas simples à travailler.

— Maintenant, dit-elle, *jeté, changement, jeté, changement, plié, tour, jeté, changement, échappé* et *tour en l'air.*

Au second *jeté* (un saut d'une jambe sur l'autre), Marie trébuche de nouveau.

Cette fois, elle reste assise par terre, les bras autour des jambes, la tête penchée. Elle n'essaie même pas de se mettre sur pied ou de regarder les autres.

Madame Noëlle s'approche et lui tend la main. Elle a tellement d'autorité qu'il est difficile de lui résister. Marie prend sa main et se lève.

— Je voudrais vous parler après la classe, madame, dit Marie d'une toute petite voix.

Mon cœur fait un bond. Enfin ! Le problème va se régler. Et par Marie elle-même.

— Certainement, répond madame Noëlle. Assoyez-vous ici et reposez vos chevilles.

À la fin du cours, je sors du studio tandis que Marie reste à discuter avec madame Noëlle. Mais je demeure dans le corridor au cas où elle aurait besoin de causer après. Je n'ai pas à attendre bien longtemps. Au bout de deux minutes à peine, Marie sort en courant, la mine défaite. Elle passe sans me regarder.

Elle n'a certainement pas eu le temps de s'expliquer ! Il faut que je sache ce qui s'est passé. J'entre dans le studio.

— Madame Noëlle, dis-je, je voudrais vous parler de Marie.

— Oui ?

— Je m'inquiète beaucoup à son sujet. Est-ce qu'elle vous a confié son problème ?

— Elle a commencé, et puis elle est partie subitement. Vous êtes au courant de quelque chose ?

— C'est son régime. Elle le pousse trop loin et elle se ruine la santé. Vous avez vu ce qui s'est passé aujourd'hui. Ça y est, c'est dit.

— Oui, j'ai remarqué, répond madame Noëlle. Je vais vous dire quelque chose mademoiselle Raymond. J'ai vu déjà ce genre de situation. C'est très déroutant, parce que la santé de la personne se dégrade très lentement. Je redoutais ce qui arrive à Marie, mais j'avais encore des doutes. C'est pourquoi j'ai suggéré à son père de l'emmener voir un médecin.

— Je ne crois pas qu'elle y soit allée.

— Moi non plus. Venez, nous allons essayer de lui parler.

Je suis madame Noëlle au vestiaire. Marie n'y est pas. Les autres filles disent ne pas l'avoir vue. Nous jetons un coup d'œil dans la salle de toilettes. Dans la cabine du fond, quelqu'un sanglote.

Je frappe à la porte.

— Marie ?

La porte s'ouvre et Marie sort. Elle a les yeux bouffis. En apercevant madame Noëlle, elle pousse un gémissement.

— Tu l'as fait ! me reproche-t-elle à mi-voix.

— Oui. Mais madame Noëlle s'en était déjà rendu compte.

Les épaules de Marie s'affaissent et elle semble comprendre qu'elle n'a plus le choix : elle doit parler.

Madame Noëlle s'approche.

— Ma petite Marie, dit-elle gentiment, pourquoi tenez-vous tellement à suivre ce régime?

Une larme coule sur la joue de mon amie. Elle tire sur ses collants.

— Je n'arrive pas à perdre assez de poids, murmure-t-elle en sanglotant. J'essaie, j'essaie, mais ça ne sert à rien. Je ne serai jamais ballerine et c'est la seule chose qui compte pour moi.

Je pose ma main sur son épaule. C'est trop triste de la voir dans cet état.

— Il y a d'autres choses qui doivent compter dans votre vie, mademoiselle, dit madame Noëlle. Pour devenir une grande ballerine, la technique ne suffit pas. Il faut aussi de la passion. Et pour connaître la passion, il faut aimer les autres et s'aimer soi-même.

Marie essuie ses larmes.

— Mais j'adore le ballet! Que va-t-il se passer si je deviens trop grosse pour danser?

— Et que va-t-il se passer si vous devenez trop maigre pour danser?

Marie se met à hoqueter. Je pense qu'elle est prête à admettre qu'elle a un problème. Madame Noëlle passe son bras autour de ses épaules.

— Venez, dit-elle. Vous danserez à nouveau quand vous serez sortie de ce mauvais pas. Pour l'instant, vous devez vous reposer et parler à quelqu'un qui pourra vous aider à comprendre ce qui vous arrive. Qui vient vous chercher aujourd'hui?

— Ma mère.

— Alors, on en discutera avec elle.

Je tends un mouchoir en papier à Marie.

— Oui, séchez vos yeux, dit madame Noëlle. Ce n'est pas aussi désastreux que vous le croyez. C'est une étape qui vous fera grandir. Et avec le temps, vous vous rendrez compte que la vie est faite d'une foule de moments semblables.

Nous sortons de la salle de toilettes.

— Merci pour votre aide, mademoiselle Raymond, dit madame Noëlle en retournant dans le studio avec Marie.

Je suppose qu'elle veut discuter encore un peu avec elle. Ou peut-être veut-elle lui éviter l'embarras d'être remarquée par les autres filles.

Je suis bien contente que ce soit fini. Mais je suis triste pour Marie. Elle a travaillé si fort. J'espère qu'elle pourra danser encore bientôt.

CHAPITRE 14

J'ai l'impression que la plupart des problèmes graves prennent beaucoup de temps à régler. (Le cas de Marie est un de ceux-là.) D'autres se règlent presque tout seuls.

Par exemple, l'idée des bourses semblait irréalisable, et pourtant tout s'est déroulé à merveille.

Quand j'arrive chez les Marchand pour garder, samedi, Christine a le sourire fendu jusqu'aux oreilles.

— Guillaume est à son bureau, me dit-elle avant de partir. Il discute des bourses avec son comptable ! Maman et lui avaient un dîner d'affaires, mais il a annulé et maman est allée seule.

— Oh ! ça commence à être gênant !

— Je le savais. Bon, voici ce qui en est. Quand j'ai parlé à Guillaume du projet de bourses pour les jeunes, il est devenu tout excité et il a dit qu'on n'avait pas besoin de s'embarrasser de compagnies commerciales.

— Comment ça ?

— Parce qu'il voudrait être lui-même le donateur !

— Non !

— Ce n'est pas définitif, ajoute Christine rapidement.
Je ne devrais même pas t'en parler. Alors ne sois pas
déçue si ça ne marche pas.

— Pourquoi ça ne marcherait pas?

— Il faut qu'il discute d'abord avec son comptable.
Guillaume ne fait rien sans le consulter.

— J'espère que son comptable aime le ballet.

— Je ne pense pas que ça ait de l'importance, dit
Christine en prenant sa veste. C'est seulement une question d'argent. Bon, je m'en vais. Karen et André sont chez
les Papadakis. Alors pour l'instant, tu n'as qu'Émilie. À
moins que Chantal ne s'amène. Elle le fait souvent, ces
temps-ci.

Au seul nom de Chantal, les traits de Christine se cris-
pent. C'est peut-être le bon moment pour en avoir le cœur
net.

— Christine… est-ce que tout va… bien?

— Pourquoi? fait-elle en baissant les yeux.

— Tu sais, on aime bien Chantal, mais on t'aime
aussi. Chantal est très gentille, mais toi tu es… tu es toi!
Christine rit.

— Ça, c'est vrai! Merci, Jessie. Je comprends ce que
tu essaies de me dire et… euh… merci.

— Il n'y a pas de quoi.

Christine part pour son rendez-vous et je reste seule
avec Émilie. Sophie m'a mise en garde contre ses «angé»
et je m'arrange pour noter où elle cache les objets. Nous
restons surtout dans la salle de séjour à assembler un
casse-tête.

La mère de Christine est la première à revenir.

— Comment s'est passé votre dîner? dis-je.

— Oh! tu sais comment c'est. (Non, je ne sais pas.) Toujours le même poulet réchauffé et les discours ennuyeux comme la pluie, mais c'était pour une bonne cause : l'hôpital pour enfants.

J'entends alors la porte d'entrée se refermer. Quelques secondes plus tard, Guillaume entre dans la pièce.

— Bonjour, chéri, dit madame Marchand. Alors, qu'est-ce que le comptable en pense ?

— Il n'y voit aucune objection ! répond Guillaume en me regardant, le sourire aux lèvres. Je peux offrir à ton école de ballet deux bourses complètes. Elles seront disponibles dès que vous en aurez besoin et se renouvelleront chaque année.

J'ouvre la bouche, mais aucun son ne sort. C'est trop beau pour être vrai !

— Merci beaucoup ! dis-je enfin. Merci, merci, merci !

— Je t'en prie, répond Guillaume.

Il sort son portefeuille de sa poche et, l'espace d'une seconde, j'ai l'impression qu'il va me tendre une liasse de billets. Mais il me donne sa carte.

— Demande à la responsable de l'école de m'appeler. Voici mon numéro au bureau, et tu connais le numéro ici.

J'aurais voulu l'embrasser, mais je ne le connais pas assez pour ça. Je me contente de sourire bêtement.

— Bon, il me reste un peu de travail à faire, alors excusez-moi, dit Guillaume.

Il sort en sautillant et se met à siffler un air de *Casse-Noisette*.

— Il a l'air très content, dit madame Marchand.

— Il n'est pas le seul, dis-je.

— Nous sommes heureux de rendre service, Jessie. Et merci d'avoir pris soin d'Émilie.

Madame Marchand me ramène chez moi en voiture. Je ne peux m'empêcher de penser aux bourses. Qui les obtiendra? Qui décidera? Que dira madame Noëlle quand je lui apprendrai la nouvelle?

Je suis à la maison depuis à peine une demi-heure, que Christine me téléphone.

— Tu as vraiment rendu Guillaume heureux, me dit-elle. Il n'arrête pas de siffler des airs de ballet.

— En tout cas, c'est très chic de la part de tes parents.

— Hé! quel serait le plaisir d'avoir de l'argent si on ne pouvait pas en donner un peu ici et là?

— Si tu n'avais pas eu cette idée, ce ne serait jamais arrivé. Merci un million de fois, Christine.

— J'ai seulement fait la demande. Oublie ça, et à lundi.

Le lundi, Christine semble avoir retrouvé sa bonne vieille personnalité. (Rien ne la réjouit plus que d'accomplir quelque chose.)

Le mardi, j'arrive tôt au cours. J'ai hâte de raconter à madame Noëlle que Guillaume Marchand veut faire don de deux bourses. En apprenant la nouvelle, elle applaudit comme une petite fille.

— Mais vous lisez dans mes pensées! s'écrie-t-elle. J'ai eu la même idée et j'ai même cherché en vain un commanditaire. J'étais sur le point d'abandonner.

— Maintenant, c'est fait.

— Venez, allons en informer madame Dupré.

Nous tombons sur elle au moment où elle s'apprête à entrer dans le studio.

Enthousiasmée, elle met ses mains sur ses joues et s'exclame:

— C'est fantastique ! Je suis tellement contente !

Je remets la carte de Guillaume à madame Noëlle et elle se dépêche de lui téléphoner. Quand je pénètre dans le studio avec madame Dupré, je cherche Marie des yeux. Je ne suis pas étonnée de son absence.

En voyant madame Dupré, les élèves se taisent.

— J'ai une formidable nouvelle à vous apprendre, dit-elle aux enfants. Nous allons disposer de deux bourses. Mes assistants et moi-même allons choisir deux élèves parmi vous. Ceux qui nous semblent avoir le plus de potentiel recevront les bourses. Le choix sera difficile, je vous assure. Si vous voulez poursuivre les cours, inscrivez votre nom sur cette feuille en partant. Je vais aussi envoyer un mot à vos parents. Vous aurez jusqu'à la semaine prochaine pour vous décider.

Un murmure d'excitation se répand dans la salle. Je me demande qui va s'inscrire.

— Maintenant, après la période de réchauffement, nous allons commencer à travailler un petit spectacle que nous présenterons à la fin des cours, poursuit madame Dupré. Je vous ai préparé une chorégraphie originale. Au travail ! Nous avons beaucoup de pain sur la planche.

Madame Dupré a concocté un beau programme pour les enfants. Comme il s'agit d'une combinaison des pas qu'ils ont appris et d'exercices de réchauffement, ils n'auront aucun mal à les mémoriser. Madame Dupré a intitulé sa chorégraphie « Matin à la ville ». Monsieur Tsuji joue un morceau très enlevant de George Gershwin, un compositeur américain.

Au début de la danse, les enfants sont assis en petits groupes, le corps penché et les mains posées sur les orteils.

Puis, un à un, les groupes se «réveillent» et font des exercices d'étirement différents.

Ils se mettent ensuite à danser. Un groupe fait des *jetés* dans un métro imaginaire, puis des petits *échappés* en gardant les bras levés comme s'ils se tenaient aux poteaux du wagon. Un autre groupe fait des *arabesques* comme pour se saluer mutuellement.

Madame Dupré donne à David un rôle solo. Il doit exécuter une série de *pas de chat* en faisant semblant de traverser une rue passante. Marthe est aussi choisie pour danser seule. À un moment donné, tout le monde doit s'immobiliser, tandis qu'elle fait un *pas de bourrée*, suivi d'un *pas de chat* puis d'une *pirouette* (elle tourne sur une jambe; elle est la seule de la classe à pouvoir le faire).

— Est-ce qu'on va avoir des costumes? demande Yvonne qui a un rôle de brigadier.

— La semaine prochaine, je voudrais que vous apportiez des chapeaux, toutes sortes de chapeaux, dit madame Dupré.

Le temps file. Tandis que moi et les autres assistants aidons à terminer le cours, je vois madame Dupré s'adresser aux parents rassemblés à la porte. Elle leur parle sans doute des bourses et du spectacle.

Quand tout est fini, Marthe court vers sa mère, les yeux brillants. Une fois de plus, la dame me regarde.

Puisque je parle beaucoup ces temps-ci, aussi bien continuer sur ma lancée. Je décide de me présenter.

— Bonjour, dis-je à la mère de Marthe. Je m'appelle Jessie. Je voulais seulement savoir si Marthe allait s'inscrire pour la bourse.

— Tu crois qu'elle devrait? demande la dame avec un petit accent créole.

— Oh oui !

La mère de Marthe serre les lèvres pensivement.

— Je sais que Marthe a du talent, dit-elle enfin. J'ai travaillé très fort pour gagner un peu d'argent et lui permettre de suivre des cours.

— Elle semble avoir très bien appris. Pourquoi a-t-elle arrêté ?

— Une voisine m'a dit que je gaspillais mon argent, qu'il n'y avait pas de place dans les ballets pour les gens de couleur. Je ne voudrais pas que Marthe entretienne des rêves qu'elle ne pourra pas réaliser.

— C'est pour ça que vous me regardiez toujours avec insistance ?

La dame semble embarrassée.

— Excuse-moi si je t'ai gênée. Tu es la seule Noire de cette école. Je me demandais comment tu entrevoyais l'avenir.

— Je suis très optimiste, lui dis-je. Le ballet classique change. Certaines compagnies de danse sont même composées presque entièrement de danseurs de couleur. Je suis sûre que j'ai des chances d'en faire ma carrière. Je ne laisserai personne s'opposer à ce que j'aime. D'ailleurs, j'ai déjà dansé dans plusieurs productions.

— Ah oui ?

— J'ai même interprété un cygne dans le *Lac des cygnes*, dis-je avec fierté.

— Je suis contente de t'avoir connue, dit la dame. Marthe adore ce cours. Elle me parle tout le temps de toi.

— Votre fille est très spéciale, dis-je. Et très douée.

Marthe m'adresse alors son beau sourire qui me réchauffe le cœur plus que n'importe quelle ovation.

113

CHAPITRE 15

La réunion de mercredi est presque aussi chargée que celle de lundi. Nous nous retrouvons vite débordées et nous devons faire appel à Louis ou à Chantal, nos membres associés.

À présent, tout le monde sait qu'il est délicat de parler de Chantal devant Christine. Alors, quand Anne-Marie nous annonce qu'aucune d'entre nous, ni Louis, n'est libre pour garder Charlotte Jasmin vendredi, un silence de mort plane sur le groupe.

— Il faut téléphoner à Chantal, dit finalement Claudia. Tu veux que je l'appelle, Christine?

— Non, non, je vais le faire.

Christine prend l'appareil et compose le numéro.

— Allô, c'est moi, Christine... Je veux m'excuser pour l'autre jour. J'ai eu tort de te parler comme je l'ai fait. Je devais être jalouse...

Je dois dire que Christine a beaucoup de courage de s'excuser ainsi devant tout le monde.

Mais Chantal doit lui avoir pardonné, parce que Christine lui parle de la garde chez les Jasmin. Elle est libre. Christine raccroche, soulagée.

— On a encore un problème, Christine, dit Claudia. On aimerait pouvoir rester amies avec Chantal, mais on ne veut pas te faire de peine.

— J'aime bien Chantal, moi aussi, nous dit Christine. Je voudrais la voir plus souvent, mais avec mon horaire, c'est impossible. Comme vous passiez beaucoup de temps avec elle, j'avais l'impression qu'elle prenait ma place. Je n'aimais pas ça.

— Prendre ta place? s'écrie Diane en riant. Mais tu es irremplaçable!

Un murmure d'approbation traverse la pièce, ce qui doit sûrement faire plaisir à Christine.

— J'ai une idée, dit Anne-Marie. Si on demandait à Chantal d'assister aux réunions, de temps à autre? Elle pourrait même voyager avec toi, Christine. Comme ça, vous vous verriez plus souvent, non?

— Super! dit Christine. J'aurais dû y penser.

— Tu n'es pas la seule à avoir de bonnes idées! rétorque Anne-Marie en faisant mine d'être vexée.

— À propos de bonnes idées, j'ai entendu parler des bourses, dit Sophie. Bravo, Guillaume!

— Voulez-vous assister à un spectacle de ballet, les filles? dis-je. C'est à l'école de danse, pas ce samedi-ci, mais le suivant.

— J'y serai avec mes parents, me dit Christine. Je ne voudrais pas manquer la remise des premières bourses «Guillaume et Élizabeth Marchand».

— C'est le nom des bourses? dis-je.

— Madame Noëlle a insisté.

116

Toutes les membres du CBS veulent venir au spectacle.

— Est-ce qu'on appelle Chantal pour l'inviter ? demande Marjorie.

— Évidemment, répond Christine.

Au dernier cours précédant le spectacle, les enfants connaissent leurs rôles parfaitement. À la fin de la classe, madame Dupré nous donne la liste des jeunes qui se sont inscrits pour les bourses — un peu moins de la moitié de la classe. (Je ne suis pas surprise que les noms de Jeanne et Nora n'y apparaissent pas, mais ça m'étonne de ne pas voir celui d'Yvonne.)

— Choisissez les deux élèves qui vous semblent les plus prometteurs et inscrivez leurs noms sur ces bouts de papier, nous dit madame Dupré.

Nous nous passons la liste et notre choix se fait très rapidement. Il faut croire que nous y avions déjà longuement réfléchi.

Après une répétition épuisante, Danielle suggère que nous allions au restaurant du coin et nous sortons tous ensemble.

— Où est Marie ? demande Suzanne quand nous sommes attablés.

Je n'ai pas l'intention de colporter toutes sortes d'histoires, et je me contente de répondre :

— Elle ne se sent pas bien ces temps-ci. Elle a besoin de repos.

En fait, madame Noëlle m'a appris que Marie était suivie par deux médecins — un généraliste et un psychiatre. Sa famille a eu aussi recours à des conseillers spéciaux.

— Je l'ai vue à l'école, dit Vincent. Il m'a semblé qu'elle avait grossi.

— Parfait, elle doit aller mieux, alors, dis-je en prenant une gorgée de Coke.

C'est la plus belle nouvelle de la journée.

— Le spectacle s'annonce fameux, dit Raul.

— Maintenant que les cours sont terminés, que pensez-vous de madame Dupré ? dis-je.

— Je l'avais mal jugée, admet Raul. Elle est super.

— Oui, ses bizarreries du début avaient un sens, finalement, ajoute Danielle. Vous vous rappelez comme les enfants étaient indisciplinés le premier jour ? Regardez-les, maintenant !

— Ils ne sont plus les mêmes, dis-je.

— Oui, ils se sont métamorphosés, renchérit Suzanne. Et ça fait plaisir de penser qu'on a pu accomplir quelque chose en assistant madame Dupré.

L'après-midi du spectacle, je vais d'un enfant à l'autre, aidant à épingler les chapeaux dans les cheveux ou à maquiller les petits visages excités. Le décor est une simple toile de fond sur laquelle est peinte une ville.

Les enfants deviennent nerveux à mesure que la salle se remplit. Je jette un œil par le rideau et je vois mes amies installées dans les premiers rangs. (Christine et Chantal sont assises l'une à côté de l'autre.)

Derrière elles, j'aperçois Guillaume et la mère de Christine. Quelques minutes plus tard, tante Cécile, Becca et Jaja arrivent. Maman bavarde avec madame Noëlle. Il y a énormément de monde.

Enfin, voici le moment tant attendu. Monsieur Tsuji joue l'air d'ouverture. Les enfants courent sur la scène pour prendre leurs places au sol.

118

Je voudrais bien pouvoir vous dire que le spectacle se déroule à la perfection, mais ce serait mentir. Certains enfants sont debout alors qu'ils devraient être à genoux, d'autres tournent à droite plutôt qu'à gauche. Mais, dans l'ensemble, c'est bon. Je suis très fière des élèves. (Ils sont terriblement mignons avec leurs chapeaux — des casquettes, un képi de chef de gare, un bonnet d'infirmière, un chapeau de cow-boy...)

Les spectateurs semblent s'être bien amusés. À la fin, ils applaudissent à tout rompre. Le sourire fendu jusqu'aux oreilles, les enfants font la révérence.

Madame Dupré s'avance sur la scène avec le groupe d'assistants et monsieur Tsuji. Les applaudissements se poursuivent et nous saluons.

Lorsque les spectateurs se calment enfin, madame Noëlle fait son entrée.

— Je vais maintenant donner les noms des deux récipiendaires des bourses «Guillaume et Élizabeth Marchand», annonce-t-elle tandis que les enfants s'assoient au fond de la scène.

Elle demande aux parents de Christine de bien vouloir se lever et les remercie de leur générosité. Ils sourient et Guillaume répond qu'il est heureux de pouvoir aider les jeunes.

Madame Noëlle se tourne alors vers la classe.

— Il ne nous fallait choisir que deux noms, mais pour moi, vous êtes tous gagnants. Vous avez tous du talent. Je vous invite à revenir au printemps lorsque nous donnerons à nouveau ce cours. Nous serons fiers de vous revoir.

Enfin, elle tire une feuille de papier de sa poche.

— Les récipiendaires sont... Marthe Robert et David Ramirez !

Mes joues me font mal tant je souris. David et Marthe se lèvent. Marthe est tellement contente qu'elle oublie d'être timide. Elle sourit et se pince pour savoir si elle rêve.

Encore plus surpris qu'elle, David est si excité que son naturel revient au galop.

— Ouais ! crie-t-il en bondissant dans les airs.

Madame Dupré les conduit à madame Noëlle qui leur serre la main.

— Je sais que vous allez tous les deux travailler très fort et que vous serez dignes de la confiance que nous mettons en vous.

À la fin, Marthe court vers moi. Elle m'entoure de ses bras et me serre à m'étouffer. J'aperçois sa mère. Elle tient un petit bouquet, et des larmes brillent dans ses yeux.

À l'autre bout de la scène, David est occupé à taper dans les mains de tous ceux qu'il croise. Puis il court vers son père.

— Bon, c'est terminé, dit Danielle en me touchant l'épaule. Mais on pourrait peut-être continuer à se rencontrer au resto le mardi.

— Ce serait super ! dis-je.

Je vais rejoindre mes amies.

— Quel succès ! me dit Christine. J'ai bien aimé.

— Fantastique ! ajoute Chantal.

— Bravo, Jessie ! s'exclame Marjorie.

— Marie n'est pas là ? demande Diane.

Je fais le tour de la salle des yeux mais je ne la vois pas.

— Non. J'aurais aimé qu'elle assiste au spectacle, dis-je. Elle a beaucoup aidé les enfants. Je suis sûre qu'elle aurait été fière d'eux.

— J'ai pris des photos, m'informe Claudia. On pourrait lui envoyer des doubles.

— Ça lui ferait plaisir, dis-je en souriant.

Parfois, je me demande pourquoi je travaille si fort en ballet, pourquoi je laisse la danse prendre tant de place dans ma vie.

Mais, aujourd'hui, je n'ai pas à me questionner. C'est le genre de journée où je n'imagine rien de plus gratifiant que la danse !

Quelques notes sur l'auteure

Pendant son adolescence, ANN M. MARTIN a gardé beaucoup d'enfants, à Princeton, au New Jersey. Maintenant, elle ne garde plus que Mouse, son chat, qui vit avec elle dans son appartement de Manhattan, dans le centre de New York.

Elle a publié plusieurs autres livres dans la collection *Le Club des baby-sitters*.

Elle a été directrice de publication de livres pour enfants, après avoir obtenu son diplôme du Smith College.

Titres de la collection